The Listerine Lunatic
Hits Hoboken
And Other Strange Tales

Special thanks to Jim Ziegener for his technical assistance, editorial advice, and unlimited patience.

And thanks to Guy de Maupassant, the illegitimate son, some say of Flaubert, who gave us the name of our beautiful golden whose picture graces the front cover.

To order additional copies, please contact us.
BookSurge, LLC
www.booksurge.com
1-866-308-6235
orders@booksurge.com

PATRICIA E. FLINN

THE LISTERINE LUNATIC HITS HOBOKEN
AND OTHER STRANGE TALES

2007

The Listerine Lunatic
Hits Hoboken
And Other Strange Tales

TABLE OF CONTENTS

PREVIOUSLY PUBLISHED IN MAGAZINES

The following stories by Patricia Flinn were previously published in literary magazines in the United States and Canada.

"The Night the Burlington Rubber Factory Caught Fire" in *Old Hickory Review*, Jackson, Tennessee.

"Mrs. Brinkoffer and the Lightning Bugs" in *Studia Mystica*, Sacremento, California

"Through a Hoboken Keyhole" (Boobies and Bathtubs) in *Painted Bride Quarterly*, Philadelphia, Pennsylvania; *The Alabama Literary Review*, Troy State University, Troy, Alabama, and *Emory University Literary Review*, Emory University, Atlanta, Georgia

"My Mother's Brain" in *Loss of the Ground Note*, Clothespin Fever Press, Los Angeles, California

"A Responsible Position" in *Wisconsin Review*, Oshkosh, Wisconsin

"The Face on the Wall (Remembering the Dead) in *South Dakota Review*, University of South Dakota, Vermillion, South Dakota

"What God Hath Joined Together, Let No Roof Put Asunder" in *Aldebaran*, Roger Williams University, Bristol, Rhode Island and *The Portable Wall*, Billings, Montana

"The Miracle of the Mouse" in *Nahant Bay*, Swampscott, Maine.

"Occurrence at Suck Creek"in *The Small Pond Magazine*, New Brunswick, Canada

"The Beginning of Love" in *Tyro Magazine*, Saulte Ste., Marie, Ontario, Canada

"Galatea of the Strawberry" in *The Worcester Review*, Worcester, Massachusetts

"The Bedside Companion"(A Matter of Perspective) in *My Legacy*, Artemis, Pennsylvania

"Reflections in a Hoboken Tenement" in *Sign of the Times*, Seattle, Washington, Portland Review, Sonoma Literary Review

"Thanatopsis and 1,000 Points of Light" in *Venture Inward*, The Edgar Cayce Foundation Magazine, Virginia Beach, Virginia

"Old Fashioned Love" in *Crab Creek Review*, Seattle, Washington, Permafrost, University of Alaska, Fairbanks

PREVIOUSLY PUBLISHED IN MAGAZINES

The Woman in the Off-Black Pantyhose"in *Bedtime Stories*, Little River, California

"An Interesting Position" in *Aran Press*, Louisville, Kentucky

"Synge's Ghost" in *Riversedge*, University of Texas-Pan American, Edinburg, Texas

"What Goes Up, Must Come Down. . . Maybe" in *Tandava*, East Detroit, Michigan

"How to Hypnotized the Woman of Your Dreams" in *The South Hill Gazette*, Rochester, Michigan

"The Temporary and the Axolotl "in *Rock Falls Review*, Stamford, NE

"To Be Continued" in *Writers of the Desert Sage*, Sierra Vista, Az.

"Le Feste" in *Sensations*, Secaucus, New Jersey

"An Encounter" in *Sensations* , Secaucus, New Jersey

"Life Sucks" (You Can't Go Home Again) in *Sign of the Times,* Seattle, Washington

"Till Human Voices Wake Us" in *K Magazine*, Ontario , Canada

"Etched in Stone in *Clifton Magazine*, Cincinnati, Ohio

For My Husband, Gene,
My Love And Inspiration,
The Light Of My Life,
The Music Of My Soul,
My Sine Qua Non

And In Memory Of Mick
And Helen, My Loving Parents
Who Were Always In My Corner
And For Jim, My Brother

INTRODUCTION

This collection is remarkable for its range. Divided into five sections, each one distinctive, it takes the reader from the gritty, ultra-realistic streets and tenements of a city to a world of imagination where everything may or may not be of this world.

In "Tales of Hoboken," we meet a girl as child, pre-teen and adolescent and her mother, a memorable character, ever ready to reach for a quote from the Bible or her catechism. But, while mother seems deeply devout, her obsession is sex and guarding her daughter from "perverts" and "rapists" and worst of all, what she terms "lizzies."

Far removed from the world of gritty mops and hallway smells are the imaginative "Tales for Reflection." Here people long for escape and find it by thinking they have become lightning bugs or butterflies (or perhaps by becoming insects) or by finding that a patch of dirt in the backyard has acquired magical therapeutic powers.

"Children's Tales" presents an idyllic picture of happy kids in a happy universe dreaming happy thoughts, until, in the final story, there is a penetrating portrait of a girl molested and her reaction of fear, shame and bafflement.

This story provided a smooth segue to the section titled "Tales on the Darker Side." In these pages characters learn that their pictures of others may differ from the portraits their friends have composed in their minds, and that it may be dangerous to willfully anticipate the death of another, or that a go-go dancer may end up as an angel—or at least a part of one.

Finally "Tales of Relationships" presents accounts of obsessions, eccentricities, and some more or less, normal folk who give off an unusual aura. In short, these absorbing stories offer a vast variety and unusual perspective on people, good, bad, and indifferent, but always intriguing.

Stewart H. Benedict
Author of Curtain Going Up
Former reviewer for Publisher's Weekly

TALES OF HOBOKEN

It is not now as it hath been of yore;
Turn wheresoe'er I may,
By night or day,
The things which I have seen I now see no more.

--William Wordsworth

THROUGH A HOBOKEN KEYHOLE

The thing I remember best about my mother was her fascination for peering through keyholes. Anytime there was the slightest hint of a commotion in the hallway outside our five-room railroad flat on Adams Street in downtown Hoboken, her face would light up like the night sky on the Fourth of July, and she would spring into action, tossing aside her broom or dish rag or whatever else she happened to be holding, and dash to the door. There she would drop to her knees, wedge her head beneath the heavy glass doorknob and with one large and expectant eye, spy to her heart's content on whatever was taking place at that moment on the landing.

"Who's there, Ma?" I would whisper, sometimes crouching down beside her. "What do you see?"

Usually it was Mr. Reilly who lived in the apartment two flights above us with his wife, Rita, whom the neighborhood women referred to as "that long-suffering saint."

We all liked Rita, but not many of us, not even the men, liked Reilly. He was a silent, morose man who worked as a night watchman down in the Maxwell House Coffee plant on Hudson Street. He was forever coming home drunk in the dead of the night, waking everybody up and sending tremors through the house as he staggered and stumbled his long gangly limbs and bone-thin body up the winding, narrow staircase.

For at least two years, I lived in mortal terror of the man. A six-foot-three, two hundred pound Irishman with flaming red hair, beet-red skin, and wild, blood-shot eyes, he was the leading character in all my childhood nightmares. Perpetually tottering, he seemed always on the verge of bloody destruction. In my worst moments I'd see him tumbling down the stairs backwards and crashing through the milky glass pane of our front door like some terrible ogre, his flaming red skull split from end to end.

My mother, on the other hand, seemed to enjoy Reilly. Every time she heard him stumbling along, even in the dead of night when she was already tucked safely in her bed, she'd jump up and rush head-long through the dark, cold rooms until she arrived at the front door, her right eye twitching with anticipation.

Blow by blow as the action unfolded she'd fill me in on all the bloody details: Reilly was down on his hands and knees and crawling; Reilly was being pulled to his feet by two burly cops; poor saintly Rita was bending over Reilly, weeping and wailing as she wiped the blood from his long pointy nose.

From time to time my mother would get so excited watching the continuing adventures of the Reilly family that she'd even clean out the dusty keyhole with a Q-tip dipped in rubbing alcohol just to make sure she didn't miss anything.

But despite the endless fascination my mother held for Reilly, he was not the only person in the building who captured her attention and devotion.

There was also Mary the Mop Lady who lived in the apartment below us and who wandered the halls on occasions mumbling to herself as she searched high and low among the rickety rails of the banisters for her dead husband, Harold, who had died one night scrubbing down the linoleum on the third floor landing.

After his death, which Mary never quite believed in--she claimed he had simply gotten lost in the building somewhere--Mary took over his duties as janitor. In return for her labors of hauling out the garbage from the back cellar and mopping up the hallway floors once a week, she was given a three-room flat on the first floor at half rent.

We'd see her every day as we went up and down the stairs since she kept her door always open a crack. My mother claimed this was Mary's way of letting Harold know he was still welcome, but other people in the building thought differently.

"She does it to let out the stink," they'd say, joking that they had to hold their noses every time they went by her door.

And it was true. There was a terrible stink to Mary's flat. It came from all the mops and dirty rags and old pails she used for cleaning the halls. She kept them lined up against the wall in her bedroom where she'd sit for hours mumbling to herself in the gloomy dark.

Since we all felt sorry for Mary, however, and knew that she was a bit off her rocker, no one ever complained. Nevertheless, it wasn't easy. Moldy mops are a terrible thing to keep on smelling every day. But despite all this, my mother always got excited when Mary came up to our landing to scrub down the floor.

"She's here," my mother would exclaim, rubbing her hands together and kneeling down to watch the show begin. "And this time she looks bad, real bad."

I would sit at the dining room table glancing at the back of my mother's head, as I did my long division and dreamed of Sister Ellen, my English composition teacher, whom I was madly in love with at the time.

As far as I was concerned, she was the most beautiful, exciting woman in the world. Not only did she have exactly the kind of eyes I wanted--sapphire blue flecked with hints of purple--she also had the kind of voice I wanted: soft and low and lilting like notes from a toy xylophone.

It was like no other voice I had ever heard. Certainly nothing like my mother's, which some people described as being similar to a gasoline explosion, and certainly nothing like any of the voices of the people I knew who lived within our red-brick tenement. But since my mother got angry every time I mentioned Sister Ellen, fearing that I would one day grow up and turn into what she called a "lizzie," I rarely talked about her.

"What's Mary doing now, Ma?" I'd say from time to time, just to let her know I wasn't thinking about Sister Ellen. "Is she rambling on about Harold and Lithuania again?"

"Oh, you want to see her," my mother would exclaim. "The poor thing looks like she's about to drop. She doesn't know what the hell she's doing. She doesn't even know enough to rinse out the rags. No wonder this place is crawling with cockroaches.

Sometimes my mother would insist I take a peek to see for myself what she was talking about, but the sight of Mary down on her hands and knees among the filthy soap bubbles did not work the same magic on me as it did on my mother. In fact, if you want to know the truth, it made me kind of sad. Especially when I saw how the hem of Mary's dirty yellow slip used to hang down from her house dress and trail in all that filthy water and how her stockings, which she tried to hold up with big round garters, would slip and sag beneath her fat, knobby knees.

But on top of all that, I knew how important that keyhole was to my mother, and how she really savored the moments she spent at it. The last thing I wanted to do was to steal those moments or hog them in any way.

In fact, most of the time I was very generous with my mother's keyhole. That is, until the Two Women arrived. Only then did I acquire my mother's fine taste for peeking.

They moved into the five-room flat directly above us--Edna, a pleasant-face buxom woman in her early forties who, we soon learned, wore see-through blouses and long flowing kimonos that opened to the waist, and Dorothy, a tall, blonde lady in her early twenties who, it was rumored, sang and danced in exotic nightclubs all over New York City and was once engaged to a man on death row.

On the day of their arrival, however, my mother and I knew nothing about our new neighbors, but after listening to all the excitement taking place outside our door, as the women came trudging up and down the stairs with box after box of belongings, my mother's curiosity was driven beyond its limits. By nine a.m.. she was already at the keyhole, providing me with one of her finest play-by-plays ever.

By noon I learned that our new neighbors were two women who spoke a foreign language, wore long funny dresses, went in for lots of weird jewelry, had pointy fingernails, drank lots of white wine, and owned lots of unusual things like feathers and fur pillows and bright orange and purple paintings and big statues of fat, naked women with gigantic boobies, and large round bellies.

"Talk about shit!" my mother said, her mouth pressed against the doorjamb. "You wanna see this crap! Come on, take a look."

I didn't need much persuasion, especially since it wasn't everyday I got a chance to see naked boobies. My own hadn't begun to appear yet, and so naturally I was more than curious to see what I was in for.

I knelt down, pressed my right eye up to the keyhole and stared. At first all I saw was part of my eyelash, but after blinking a few times I focused in on the two women. They were standing a few feet from my door, facing one another, their hands resting atop each other's shoulders. Then all at once they both leaned forward and kissed. A long, lingering kiss, smack on the lips. Just like that.

I was so flabbergasted, I almost fell over.

"What's the matter?" my mother screamed in my ear. "What's happening? Why are you so pale all of a sudden?"

I couldn't say a word. I simply hung onto the keyhole as if it were a life preserver.

"Answer me," my mother roared. "What's going on out there? What do you see?"

Never before in my life had I seen two women kiss like that. I felt like I was going Down in an Up elevator at breakneck speed.

"Move over!" my mother shouted, pushing me aside. "If you're not going to tell me, I'll see for myself."

It was an eternity before she removed her eye from the keyhole, but when she did her face was ashen.

"Did they stop?" I asked, after a long moment, wondering if it were safe to steal another peek.

"Never you mind," my mother said, grabbing my arm and dragging me to my feet. "Get out of here. Go to the bathroom. Go pee. Do something."

From that moment on the keyhole, Edna, and Dorothy became my obsession. Every time I heard their door slam shut and their feet tapping down the stairs, I longed to throw myself on my two knees and press my face to the door. But since my mother's startling and terribly unjust pronouncement that keyhole-peeking was now suddenly off limits, there was no way for me to satisfy my curiosity.

Thus, I was forced to live only for those rare and exquisite moments when I encountered both women in the flesh.

"Bonjour, Mademoiselle," they would say, smiling at me as we would pass on the narrow stairway. "Comment allez-vous?"

Most times I was too shy and tongue-tied to say a word. Compared to all the fat housewives in the building who spent their lives hanging out their windows screaming after their children, Edna and Dorothy were like creatures from another planet. Especially Dorothy who within only a few short weeks had captured by heart by becoming the talk of the building, the scandal of the whole neighborhood.

To my mind she was even more exciting than Sister Ellen who wore a black veil all the time and whose hair I had never once even seen. Dorothy's hair, on the contrary, was like satin. Long and flowing and brightly gleaming, it shone like the sun on a lovely lake or a soft wet flower.

Night after night I would lie in my bed, picturing her in the room above me smoking cigarette after cigarette as she tiptoed around in her open kimono kissing Edna and crying a little over her old dead fiance who to my mind was the spitting image of Jimmy Cagney.

Why someone as fascinating as Dorothy could inspire so much gossip among the neighborhood women was something I just couldn't figure out, but there was no question that she was on everyone's lips. Even Mr. Reilly and Mary's stinky old mops took second place to what people had to say about poor old Dorothy.

"If only she wasn't that obvious," Mrs. McCarthy, who lived on the top floor, said to my mother in the laundry room one day. "If only she didn't flaunt her aberration so much. I mean, you think those kind of people would at least know how to use a little discretion."

"What kind of people," I asked, staring up at my mother defiantly. "What's she talking about?"

"None of your business," my mother said, giving me a vicious shove. "Now go over there and play."

I went no farther than earshot would allow, figuring that if I couldn't peek at my friends at least I could eavesdrop on my enemies.

"Oh, I tell you, it's terrible what this world is coming to," Mrs. McCarthy continued. "And to think they actually go around naked and wash one another's backs in the bathtub!"

"No!" my mother said, grabbing hold of her throat. "You can't be serious?"

"That's what I heard," Mrs. McCarthy insisted, nodding her head. "One of the neighbors across the street said she saw them from the window. Their shades weren't even down. Can you imagine?"

"That's unbelievable!" my mother exclaimed.

"Yes, and what's more, they do it all the time too. Right here in this very house under our very noses!"

The thought of Dorothy and Edna being so maliciously maligned while they sat naked and un-suspecting in their bathtub was simply too much for me. I burst into tears.

"What's the matter?" my mother screamed, running toward me in a frenzy. "What's happened now?"

All I could do was wail, my face swimming in misery and snot.

"Stop it!" my mother said, yanking me by the hair. "Stop it, you hear?"

"But it's not fair," I screamed. "It's just not fair."

"What's not fair?" my mother asked, eying me suspiciously. "What are you talking about?"

"Dorothy and Edna," I sobbed. "Everybody's always picking on them."

Mrs. McCarthy glared down at me.

"It's not polite to listen in on grown-up people's conversations," she said. "And what's more, children should be seen and not heard."

I began to wail even louder until my mother shut me up by clouting me on the ear with a right hook that left me reeling. By the time my head cleared, I knew it was all-out war, and what's more, I knew I was firmly on the side of Dorothy and Edna. Even if it were true that they were taking baths together and looking at one another's boobies, I didn't think it was right for other people to go around snooping on them and then talking about them behind their backs.

I began plotting my strategy. My imagination knew no bounds. Like Superman, it soared through the air faster than a speeding bullet, more powerful than a locomotive.

I saw myself crawling through their bathroom window as they sat together naked in the tub scrubbing one another's backs.

"Beware of windows and keyholes," I warned. "Your lives are in danger."

Other times I imagined myself flying straight through the ceiling like a mighty bird and burrowing myself in the warm sleeve of one of Dorothy's silky kimonos where I would lie in wait for her enemies like a deadly vulture ready to spring.

In bed at night as I lay listening to their soft laughter rise and fall in gentle ripples above my head, I pictured myself in the bathtub with them, splashing among the warm bubbles and then rushing to their rescue with one of Mary's mops as Mr. Reilly came crashing through their front door, his red lips frothing at the sight of their wet naked bodies.

For weeks I racked my brain, wondering how best to declare my love and allegiance. Then one morning out of the blue I came upon the answer. It was the simplest, most natural thing in the world. I would write them a long, passionate letter explaining everything that had ever been said about them, and how much I loved them. Then I would quietly slip it beneath their door and wait for their message.

All that afternoon through my geography, spelling and science classes, I wrote and rewrote, telling them in the kindest way I knew that, although lots of people thought them bad, I would always remain their true and faithful friend no matter what. And although I tried not to mention anything about bathtubs and boobies, I did manage to say something about how important it was for them to keep their shades down "whenever they did funny things together." Finally, after six drafts and lots of crossing- outs, my letter was complete.

I was about to put it into the nice blue envelope I had brought along when suddenly I heard Sister Katherine Eucharia, my Earth Science teacher, call my name.

"Laura O'Neill, bring whatever you are writing immediately to my desk."

At first I couldn't believe my ears.

"I must be dreaming," I thought, remaining glued to my chair. "This can't be happening."

But I wasn't dreaming, and before I knew it Sister Katherine was charging down the aisle at me like a raging bull, her long black veils flying behind her like the wings of a rabid bat.

She snatched the letter from my hands, pulled me up from the seat, and slapped me soundly across the face.

"Next time you obey when I talk to you, young lady, understand?"

I was so stunned I couldn't even cry.

***

The rest is history. By the time Sister Katherine, Sister George, Sister Veronica, Sister Mary Louise, Sister Grace Edwards, Sister Claire, Sister Thomas, the principal, and my mother got through reading my letter, my fate was sealed. Justice came quickly and unmercifully. For almost a week, I couldn't sit down without crying out in holy terror, and although I was permitted food, I might as well have been dining in the State penitentiary, bread and water being all that was allowed me until I confessed my terrible sins and begged for God's sweet mercy.

As luck would have it, I remained the topic of hot conversation throughout the school until the day Felix Fitzpatrick snuck up onto the roof and threw a brick at Sister Louise's head while she monitored her class of fifth grade girls skipping rope in the courtyard at recess.

After that, my reputation as the school's leading misfit faded considerably.

Slowly the weeks rolled on and by the time spring arrived, turning the only two trees on Adams Street from dirt brown to dull green, things were back to normal again.

The nuns stopped telling me what an awful child I was; Mr. Reilly broke two ribs by falling into one of Mary's metal pails; and Rita, Mr. Reilly's saintly wife, suffered a miscarriage after trying to drag her husband by the necktie up three flights of stairs.

As for Dorothy and Edna, well, I really don't know if they went on kissing and taking baths together since my mother wouldn't let me anywhere near them. All I know for sure is that one day I came home from school and saw them driving away in a big moving van.

Where they went is anybody's guess, but for years I prayed like hell that they would remember to keep their shades down and to stay clear of keyholes.+++++

THE LISTERINE LUNATIC HITS HOBOKEN

Two weeks after Nikki Coler's husband, Andrew, slipped out the back door of their house and quietly vanished from her life, the Listerine Lunatic struck again, this time in broad daylight only one block away from Nikki's Hudson Street brownstone.

The whole neighborhood, naturally, was in a state of shock. Not since Sammy the Slicer had there been such panic along the busy waterfront streets of Hoboken, New Jersey. All day and into the night police cars cruised up and down the quiet lanes looking for the man who for months had been tying dozens of women to their beds and dousing their naked bodies with Listerine Mouthwash. All across town women huddled for safety in their kitchens and pine-paneled basements, afraid to leave their homes, even so much as to retrieve their mail. Some slept with hammers beneath their pillows, others refused to sleep at all, fearful that in the dead of the night they too might become victims.

Nikki, quite understandably, was terrified. Never before had she realized how vulnerable she was--a young woman living alone in a big house without a man to protect her. At first she considered buying a large dog, but decided against it when she remembered she was allergic to anything with a tail and four legs. Still, the thought of being pinned to her bed as some madman hovered above her, pouring mouthwash into her belly button, left her weak and delirious. She dreamed continually of men in woolen ski masks stealing through her window wielding giant toothbrushes and reams of dental floss. Every time her phone or doorbell rang she broke into a sweat, imaging herself at last face to face with the Listerine Lunatic. And, like most women in the neighborhood, her fears only increased as word began to spread that the Lunatic was not only an accomplished assaulter but a master of disguise. One by one, his tearful victims told in grim detail how he had tricked his way into their homes and then viciously assaulted them, sometimes washing out their mouths with water pics, other times threatening to gag them with cottonballs and tongue depressors. Afterwards, he would stand up on his victim's bed and break into a song, usually something from Billy Joel, his favorite recording artist."

"It was hideous," one woman said. "I mean, the man was completely tone deaf. Which was ironic because he told me he was a D.J. In fact, that was the only reason I let him into my house. I thought he'd make me famous. Then before I knew what was happening, he was coming at me with that awful Listerine bottle. As long as I live, I know I'll always remember that terrible smell."

"I thought he was a Jehovah Witness," said another woman. "I mean he looked so innocent."

"To me he looked just like my brother-in-law," said a third victim. "I mean, after a while all guys in ties and dark suits begin to look alike anyway, right?"

The Listerine Lunatic struck at all hours of the day and night, sometimes surprising his victims by breaking through a window or slipping past a sliding door. Other times he would arrive calmly on their doorsteps, posing as the meter reader or the Culligan Water Man. Because his methods were so erratic and unpredictable, and because no one had a really clear idea of what he looked like—one woman said he resembled Ed Koch, another said he was a dead ringer for George W. Bush--every male who bought more than one bottle of Listerine at the A&P, Home Druggist, or the Shop-Rite Save-A-Lot Pharmacy was immediately suspect. And, for women like poor frightened Nikki, pushing their grocery carts through the lonely aisles of Mott's Delicious Red Apple Juice and Lemon Pledge Furniture Polish, every male was potentially dangerous, including Walter the Chimney Sweep, whose services she was forced to elicit one day after nearly choking to death from smoke and fumes pouring into her living room from her cozy but clogged family hearth.

She saw his ad in the local paper and left a brief message on his answering machine. Walter, a large, rather handsome man, arrived on her doorstep the next morning, smiling and nodding politely as Nikki reluctantly cracked open the door and stared at him over the double lock pull chain.

"Mornin', Ma'm," he said, tipping his black leather cap. "I'm Walter from Walter's Chimney Sweep. I spoke to you on the phone."

"Do you have an I.D.?" Nikki asked, keeping a watchful eye on the toe of his thick black boot for fear that he would try to wedge it between the crack in the door.

"What kind of an I.D.?" he asked, scratch-ing his head.

"An I.D. to let me know you're a real chimney sweep. I have to know that before I let you in."

Although he looked nothing like Ed Koch or George W. Bush--he was tall and muscular with dark wavy hair and soft blue eyes--Nikki was suspicious. For one thing he smelled funny. More like coal dust than Listerine to be precise, but Nikki wasn't taking any chances. She knew the Listerine Lunatic was pretty clever.

"Oh, I'm insured, Ma'm, if that's what you mean. If I fall off your roof or anything like that, I'm covered by the company. You got nothing to worry about."

"But I need to see some I.D.," Nikki insisted. "Don't you carry a little card or anything?"

"Little card? Why, no, but I. . . I have my driver's license if that's what you mean?"

He reached into the back pocket of his long blue overalls.

"I think I may also have my Social Security number. 145-44--"

"No, no, I must see something that proves you're who you say you are. Have you no certificate of verification?"

"Veri--veriferation?"

"Proof!" Nikki said. "You know, like the kind the FBI carry. A little badge or something that proves you're a chimney sweeper?"

Sadly, he shook his head.

"No, I'm sorry. I've got no badge on me for that. I just do my job, that's all. I never needed a badge for blowing soot away."

"Good heavens," Nikki swore, "don't you have something, anything to prove to me that you are a real chimney sweeper?"

"Oh, yeah, sure I do, " he said, after a moment, his face brightening. "I got my brooms and sponges and I got my truck over there. Take a look. It says right there in black and white letters—Walter's Chimney Sweep.

"That's not proof," Nikki snapped, growing impatient now. "Anybody can paint anything on a truck. And besides, you may have stolen that truck for all I know."

"I beg your pardon," he said, taking a step backwards. "Lady, I am no crook, and I certainly take exception to you thinking I am one. And besides, anyone with good eyes can see that that truck ain't worth a dime. The transmission's broke, the breaks are gone, the clutch is shot. Why would I want to steal it? Or paint it?"

"Under the circumstances I'm afraid I cannot let you in here," Nikki said, beginning to shut the door. "Perhaps you can come back at another time when you . . ."

"Look, Ma'm, if for some reason you don't want me to come inside your house, I understand, but if you got a problem with your chimney you'd be silly not to let me have a look at it from up top the roof. I mean, considering that I'm already here and all. I could just run a ladder up and . . . "

"Ladder?" Nikki asked, "What kind of ladder?"

"Why, a ladder's ladder. You know, the kind you climb on. I could look down your chimney with my flashlight here. If we're lucky maybe I could see something. You know, like a squirrel's nest or something. Sometimes things like squirrels nests or dead birds or poisoned rats get stuck inside those flue liners. If that's the case I should be able to just pull it out from the top without stepping one foot inside your house. Clear up your problem in a jiffy."

Nikki considered her options. If she could just be certain that this man was not the Listerine Lunatic, then her problem would be solved. She would be able to use her fireplace again without choking to death on smoke and ash, and she wouldn't have to worry about dealing with another male until something else went wrong inside her house. If it turned out, he was the Listerine Lunatic, she could call the police and have him nabbed. In any case, she would have to observe him very carefully.

"Well. . . O.K.," Nikki said, trying her best to appear casual. "If you think you can handle it, you can go on up to my roof. I'll just make sure to bring Killer down from the attic so he doesn't hear you."

"Killer?"

"My Doberman-Pinscher and German-Shepherd-Pit-Bull mix."

"Oh! Well, thanks, Ma'm, I appreciate that."

He tipped his hat. Nikki slammed the door and locked it. From the window she watched as the man walked back to his truck, his heavy boots crunching against the thick chunks of gravel in her driveway. There was something about him that couldn't be trusted. All that smiling and hat-tipping and calling her Ma'm stuff. It made her uncomfortable. No normal person did that anymore, she thought. She watched him remove his ladder from the top of the truck and balance it carefully upon his broad shoulders as he cut across her driveway and headed for the rear of the house. Heart-pounding, she dashed through the hallway, heading for the kitchen window which she felt provided the best view. Outside, just beyond the thin glass, she watched as the man tucked something that looked like a small bottle into his thick leather tool belt. Nikki wondered if she had done the right thing, after all. Chimney sweepers don't carry bottles. They carry brooms and brushes. In mounting terror she watched as the man gripped the ladder and began to climb, first one foot and then the other, rising and falling before her eyes like death blows. Her ceiling groaned from the sudden weight of his body as he jumped off the ladder and began walking across the roof toward the chimney. Suddenly, in a loud clear voice he began to sing, "She's got a way about her."

Nikki ran across the room toward the telephone as a thin rain of black soot and ash fell in a soft clatter past the window.

"Hello, hello, operator. Get me the police. This is an emergency. The Listerine Lunatic is up on my roof. He's armed and dangerous."

Something flew past her window. A brick, maybe.

"Operator, hurry. Please hurry."

There was heavy pounding, like sledge hammers breaking through sheer rock.

"Operator? Hello! Hello!"

Moments later the ladder began to creak again.

"Operator! Please. This is an emergency."

"Ma'm," the chimney sweep called from behind the door. "Are you there? Can I talk to you?"

Nikki froze.

"Officer Walkowski," a man's voice said in her ear. "Go ahead, please."

"It's . . . it's him," Nikki whispered. "He's . . .here."

"You'll have to speak up, Lady," Officer Walkowski said. "I can't hear you."

"I . . . I said . . ."

"Ma'm?" the man called again. "Can you hear me?"

"He's here," Nikki whispered into the phone.

"Who, Lady? Who's there?"

"The Listerine Lunatic. He's outside my door singing Billy Joel songs."

"What's the name, please?"

"Nikki. Nikki Coler."

"Where you calling from, Ms. Coler? What's the location?"

"193 Hudson Street. . . ."

"Ma'm?" the chimney sweep said. "Hello! Hello, Ma'm!"

"He's . . . he's trying to get inside . . . . "

"Try and hold him there, Ms. Coler. We'll be over as soon as we can."

Nikki hung up the phone, wondering what to do next. If she ignored the man, he might take off. If she opened the door, he might assault her before the police arrived.

She decided to stall for time by talking to him through the locked window.

"Just a minute," she called, searching for something to defend herself with, just in case he broke through the window. She picked up one of the old andirons lying in her fireplace and held it in front of her chest like a shield.

"Yes? What . . . what were you saying?"

"Do you think you could open the door, Ma'm? I got to talk to you a minute."

"Well, go ahead, talk. Talk to me through the window."

"Through the window?"

"Yes," she said, tapping the end of the andiron against the glass. "I can hear you."

She saw the man's face loom up against the pane. His eyes reminded her of the eyes of fish staring out of small green aquariums in Five and Ten Cent stores.

"But I . . . I can't see you, Ma'm. Your curtains are in the way. Everything looks kind of cloudy."

"Oh, that's all right," she said sweetly. "I can see you just fine."

"Whatever you say, Ma'm," the man shrugged. "Anyway, I just wanted to let you know I was right. You got a nest of squirrels in that flue of yours big enough to choke a hog. The buggers are down pretty deep.

Looks to me like the only way we're goin' to get them is to go through your chimney wall from inside the house. That's why I need to take a look at your fireplace."

"My . . . my fireplace?"

"Yes, Ma'm. That's where your problem is."

"No . . .I'm . . . I'm afraid that's not possible," Nikki said. "You . . . you see, I'm expecting company any minute now and I . . . I don't want my rugs to get all messy."

"Oh, I'll be careful. I promise."

"No. I . . . I'd be too nervous."

"Well, O.K. if that's how you feel, but since there's nothing else I can do out here, I guess I'll be leaving."

"No," Nikki cried, ramming her head against the glass. "Don't leave. Please. I--I want you to meet my friends. They're. . . they're very nice people."

"Your friends?" the man said, bending down again and blinking as he peered into the curtained window. "Why would you want me to meet your friends?"

"Because they just love chimney sweepers. They have for years. They're always talking about what an interesting occupation chimney sweeping is and how Charles Dickens wrote about it in his novels. You can have a nice long chat with them."

"Oh, I'm afraid I can't, Ma'm. I got a few other jobs to do before the day is over."

High-pitched whirling sirens suddenly cut through the air.

"Boy, those things sure are loud," the man said, turning to walk back to his truck. "Must be a fire nearby."

Tires screeching, lights flashing, four patrol cars, coming from four directions, careened to a halt in front of Nikki's house. All at once their doors flew open and half a dozen policemen swarmed across the front yard surrounding the chimney sweep, their guns drawn, their hands steady.

"Police! Stay where you are. Hands Up."

Walter's hands flew up into the sky.

Nikki burst through the front door.

"You got him," she screamed. "You got him."

"Stay back, lady!" someone ordered.

"It's him. It's the Listerine Lunatic."

"Walt?" one of the cops asked, coming closer and peering into the chimney sweep's soot-covered face.

"Walter Klinkman from Nam? 34th Airborne Division? Company 63?"

"Charlie! Charlie Dwyer! Why, I'll be."

"Hey, Charlie, you know this fellow?" the sergeant asked.

"Sure, I know him," Charlie laughed We were in Viet Nam together. We were best of buddies."

"Those were the days," Walter said, patting his old friend on the back. "

"So, what goes here?" Charlie asked, turning toward Nikki. "Is this the man you thought was the Listerine Lunatic?"

"Why, yes, Nikki said. "I. . . I think this is the man you have been searching for."

"And what makes you think that, Lady?" one of the cops asked. "You got any evidence against this man?"

"Of course I do," said Nikki. "I know it's him. He's got a bottle of Listerine in his pants and he was singing Billy Joel's song, "She got a way about . . . ."

Suddenly Nikki realized how crazy she sounded. What real proof did she have?"

"I love that song," Walter said, grinning at the cops. I sing it all the time."

"Are you carrying any Listerine bottles," the Sergeant asked.

"Hell, no, said Walter, shaking his head. "All I got in my pants are my bottle of spring water and my hand rags."

He pulled them from around his belt and handed them to the cops.

"You certainly have the right to come down the station and swear out a complaint if you feel this man committed a crime against you," the cop named Charlie said to Nikki, "but if you have nothing to back up your accusation, we'll have to let him go and then he could sue you for false arrest. Do you understand?"

"Yes," Nikki said, " I guess I do but. . . ."

"Ah, why don't we just forget this whole mess," Walter said, turning toward Nikki. "I don't know what your problem is, but I'd like to put this behind us. I mean, I'm tired. I just want to git out of here and have a beer with my old pal."

"I . . .I guess you're right," Nikki said, shrugging her shoulders. I'm so sorry. You see, I was scared hearing all those stories about the Listerine Lunatic."

"We understand," one of the officers said. "Lots of women are jittery nowadays."

***

That night Nikki couldn't sleep. The thought of how she had embarrassed herself before all those policemen kept her wide awake. Hour after hour she imagined them back in the station house, laughing at her and calling her names like "dumb broad" and "crazy dame," and all those other demeaning terms men used against women.

And she thought, too, of all the harm she had done to that poor fellow named Walter. How she had mistrusted him simply because he liked to sing and didn't go around carrying papers to prove his identification.

Perhaps she was a bit nutty, neurotic and overly suspicious of people at times. She promised herself that in the future she would try to be more trusting and relaxed among men. Eventually she fell into such a pleasant deep sleep that she failed to hear the truck that was slowly pulling to a halt in front of her brownstone, or the dull thud of the ladder that dropped heavily against the side of her house.

In fact, it wasn't until she actually looked up and saw a large male coming out of her fireplace with two family-sized bottles of Listerine Plus did she even consider the possibility that something was amiss. But even then she wasn't totally sure. It might have been, after all, just another one of her nutty and neurotic feminine delusions. +++++

THE NIGHT THE BURLINGTON RUBBER
FACTORY CAUGHT FIRE

I was a little kid at the time. About six, I would say, and in the first grade of Our Lady of Grace Grammar School when the Burlington Rubber Factory on Observer Highway caught fire and burned to the ground.

I know it was the first grade because I remember bargaining with God that if He insisted on killing off my father, who was one of the fireman battling the blaze that bitterly cold night, by making him fall through a smoldering roof or burning floor, He would at least spare Sister Ellen, my religion and drawing teacher, whom I was passionately in love with at the time, from a fate I considered worse than death.

It wasn't that I didn't love my father or that I wished him harm. It was just that I worshipped Sister Ellen more.

Not only did she have exactly the kind of eyes I wanted—sapphire blue flecked with hints of purple—she also had the kind of voice I wanted: soft and low and lilting like notes from a toy xylophone.

It was like no other voice I had ever heard before in my life. Certainly nothing like my mother's, which my father once described as being similar to a gasoline explosion, and certainly nothing like any of voices of the people I knew who lived within the railroad flats of the four-story red- brick tenement on Fourth and Adams Street where I was born and raised. People like Mary the Mop Lady who washed down the hall floors every Wednesday afternoon with her smelly rags and filthy buckets of greasy water in exchange for a week of free rent, and people like Crumb-Bum Frankie who worked for the Salvation Army and got drunk every night, sometimes falling backwards down the staircase and ramming his head against the narrow posts of the wobbly wooden banister.

No, Sister Ellen belonged to an entirely different world than any of these people, and so the mere thought of her and the way her long white hands beneath the wide cuffs of her black sleeves might someday touch the top of my head in silent gratitude, was enough to make me glad that I had a father to lose in the first place.

My mother, however, was an entirely different story. The thought of killing her off for the love of Sister Ellen was absolutely horrifying to me. Not that I loved my mother more than my father. It was just that I couldn't imagine myself surviving without her. She was, after all, as she was forever reminding me, the only one who had taken care of me when I had the whooping cough, the German measles, the Hong Kong Flu, the chicken pox, and the worst case of gingivitis you can ever imagine.

"You'd be dead if it weren't for me," she used to tell me as she stood over my bed rubbing vaseline onto the rectal thermometer she was constantly plunging into me. "Face the facts. Your father is never here. He's always out gallivanting with his cronies who knows where."

Gallivanting. It was my mother's favorite expression. Where she got it from I'll never know since it was not the kind of word normally found in her rather sparse vocabulary, but it definitely worked its magic on me.

From my sick bed I was able to see with perfect clarity my father riding merrily and carefree through the streets of downtown Hoboken on a beautiful white horse through crowds of naked women who waved and blew kisses at him while my poor mother slaved and sweated in our tiny kitchen pouring me endless cups of beef broth and Lipton's tea.

Thus, there was little doubt in my mind, despite all the attention I might receive from Sister Ellen, how absolutely essential it was for me to keep my mother healthy and alive.

"Please God," I used to pray every night before going to bed. "Whatever you do, remember this: if you got to take somebody, please let it not be her."

Which is why I guess I was so upset and confused when I woke on the night of the Burlington Rubber Factory fire and discovered my mother down on her hands and knees, wailing hysterically before the little Infant of Prague statue she kept on the bureau in my bedroom.

"Oh, dear God, dear God" she roared, clutching her face and hair, "Sweet Mary Mother of Jesus and all the angels, have pity upon me."

"Mama, Mama," I began to howl, seized with a terror I had never known before. "Mama, Mama."

I was so frightened, I couldn't speak, other than to utter nonsensically the words Mama! Mama! over and over again as I stared wildly into my mother's blotched and teary face.

"He's going to be killed," she screamed. "I know it. He'll never walk through that door again. Never. God help him."

"Who?" I cried, my knees knocking beneath the bed sheets. "Who, Mama? Who?"

"Your poor father. Daddy."

"Daddy?" I asked, baffled. Why he wasn't even there. Why was she talking about him. It was she who was dying, right?

"Louie. My poor, poor Louie. My darling, darling husband."

Now I was totally confused. Never in my life had I heard my mother refer to my father as her "Darling, darling husband." Most of the time she called him either "Shitface" or "You dirty bastard." Something was definitely going on and I had no idea what it was.

"Please, Mama," I began to whisper, "Please, oh please."

"Oh, it's terrible, terrible," she cried, swaying back and forth on the cold floor. "To burn to death is terrible. It's a horrible way to die."

Burn to death? I had no idea what she was talking about. Who was going to burn to death? My father? Why? Where was he? Vaguely, I remembered his leaning down to kiss me good-bye that night before going out the door to work in his blue and gold fireman's uniform.

"They'll never find his body. He'll be nothing but teeth and ashes. That's all we'll have left of him. Teeth and ashes."

Terrorized by the sudden picture of my father as a huge molar lost within a ball of dust, I began to howl again.

My mother, sensing the effect her words were having upon me and realizing for perhaps the first time in her life, the power of language, rose triumphantly to the occasion and became even more eloquent.

"And, God help us, they'll probably find a few of his toes and fingernails too. They say they're one of the last things to go on a burning corpse, you know."

Outside the window, high above the wail of screeching fire trucks and roaring ambulances, which I was only now beginning to hear, flashes of bright red and angry orange were criss-crossing the sky like firecrackers exploding on the Fourth of July.

"Oh, if only I could be there with him," she said, shaking her head sadly. "If only I could see him go."

"Oh, Mommy, Mommy," I cried, holding on to her against the cold blackness of the shadowy room. "Let's go. Let's go find Daddy. Please. Please. I want to find Daddy. Can't we go? Can't we? "

Quickly she turned and looked at me, a faint smile lighting her eyes.

"Do you really think we should? I mean, it's terribly late and you've school in the morning."

How my mother could think of school at a time like that was beyond me, but I must confess that as the two of us headed out the door dressed hastily in our long wool coats, hats and fur-lined boots, I did begin to wonder about Sister Ellen and whether she was sound asleep in her warm, cozy bed, dreaming about the Immaculate Conception, or kneeling in some dark lonely chapel praying for all the little children in China.

***

The Burlington Rubber Factory was clear across town, almost ten blocks away from Fourth and Adams Street, and it was a windy, bitter night, but as we dashed along the icy pavements, our arms locked firmly together like trusty conspirators, we hardly noticed the cold. Both of us were too caught up in our own fantasies of what lay in wait beyond the distant buildings where thick, billowy clouds of jet black smoke rose menacingly into the glowing red sky.

"I'm sure the priest will be there to give him the last rites," she said, wiping my nose with the tip of her grey woolen mitten. "It'll probably be Father Donnelly or Father Burke. Father Fitzgerald is much too old to be out on a night like this, God help him. Why, the wind alone would kill the old bugger and blow him away."

"Do you think that Sister Ellen will be there too?" I asked, excitedly. "I'd love to see her again."

"Sister Ellen who?" my mother asked suspiciously. "Who is she?"

"My religion and drawing teacher," I said, skipping along now at the joyful prospect that the love of my life might suddenly materialize from out the dark, smoky night like a beautiful angel from heaven.

"God, no," my mother said, shaking her head emphatically. "Nuns aren't allowed out at night. It's much too dangerous."

"Dangerous?" I asked, "Why would it be dangerous?"

"Because they might be raped, God help them. Men are forever raping nuns on dark nights, didn't you know that?"

"No," I said, my eyes welling with tears at the thought of some wicked, hairy old man leaping out from behind the bushes and pouncing upon my poor Sister Ellen.

Unlike most of my first grade classmates at Our Lady Of Grace, I knew perfectly well what the word "rape" meant. In fact, it was one of the first words my mother had ever taught me.

"It's something that horrible, old men do to nice ladies like you and me," she had said. "And once it happens to you, forget it. Your life is ruined. No decent man will want to marry you after that."

The thought of Sister Ellen being so grievously wronged was enough to make me forget all about my poor father who may have been at that very moment, for all I knew, disappearing beneath a tongue of flame.

"I won't let them," I shouted, my throat thick with the terrible acrid taste of burning, melting rubber. "I won't let anyone rape Sister Ellen. I love her. I love her."

"Hush!" my mother snapped, fiercely jerking back my hand. "Be still. You don't want people to think you're queer, do you? You're not supposed to love a nun. Nuns are women."

We were fast approaching the scene of the fire. Police cars, fire trucks and ambulances sailed past us, their flashing, whirling red lights casting long blood shadows far into the smoky darkness.

"But I do love her," I said, shouting at the top of my lungs. "I love her because she's good and kind and happy and pretty and . . . . "

My mother wasn't listening. She was much too intent on fighting her way through crowds of onlookers who stood by, gaping, as firemen in long black helmets, raincoats and boots dashed to and fro, hauling hose lines and scrambling up shiny metal ladders.

"Oh, this is terrible, terrible," she began to cry again, as she dragged me along. "I don't see him anywhere. Surely, he must be dead by now."

After a while, I stopped paying attention to her. I was too busy wondering about Sister Ellen and where she might be at that moment. In fact, it wasn't until my mother suddenly let go of my hand and grabbed hold of her chest, that I even thought about what she was saying.

"This will kill me too. I know it," she sobbed. "You wait and see. I'll be gone within a week of your poor father's funeral."

My mind began to swirl. Never was I so desperate. Sister Ellen was going to be raped. My mother was going to die, and my poor father was going to turn into teeth and ashes. I closed my eyes and began to pray.

"Please, God, please. I'll do anything. I promise. Anything. Just protect them. Protect them all."

And then I remembered that it wasn't enough just to pray and promise to be good. If I wanted something from God, I had to give Him something too. Something I really liked. And so I began to think about my father. Of the three--he, my mother and Sister Ellen--he was the one I saw the least of. He was the one who went gallivanting through the neighborhood on horses with naked women. He was the one who wasn't there when I had the whooping cough and the German measles and the Hong Kong Flu and so on.

He was the one I could live the most without.

"Do you understand?" I shouted to God above the wail of an approaching siren. "If you got to take somebody, take him. Just leave my mother and Sister Ellen alone, O.K.?"

"What?" my mother asked, hearing me mumble. "What did you say?"

"Nothing," I told her, tears streaming down my face. "I was just talking to God, that's all."

And then, before I knew what was happening to me, someone was grabbing hold of my waist and hoisting me high into the air.

Looking down, all I could see was the sharp peak and wide, sloping brim of a fireman's helmet.

"Charlie!" I heard my mother shout with surprise. "Good heavens, I didn't know you were working tonight. Tell me, have you seen him? Is he dead or alive or what?"

"Helen, Helen," said Charlie, "calm down. He's around here somewhere."

And again before I knew what hit me, I was back on the ground tangled within the rough wet folds of my Uncle Charlie's smoke-drenched raincoat.

"Hello, sweetheart," he said, stooping over to plant a cold wet kiss on my frozen left cheek. "What's cooking? Are you being a good little girl for Mommy?"

Throwing my arms around his neck, I burst into tears.

"No," I confessed. "I'm bad. Very bad. I told God that he could take Daddy so that Mommy wouldn't have to die and poor Sister Ellen wouldn't have to get raped."

"What?" he cried, rising to his feet. "Where on earth did you ever get that notion?"

"From my religion book from school," I said, staring up at him through a screen of tears. "It says on page ten that whenever you ask God for something you've got to remember that He is going to ask for something back."

"Oh, really?" said Uncle Charlie. "Well, ain't that something now? I didn't know that at all."

"Yes," I said, nodding my head. "It's a fact. You've got to be willing to compromise when you talk to God."

"I see," he said, glancing over at my mother. "Well, I'll be sure to keep that in mind. But in the meantime now, what do you say we try and find your Daddy?"

"O.K." I shrugged, grabbing hold of his hand. "As long as nothing bad happens."

***

Of all the fireman I saw that night, my father was the only one who was smoking a cigarette when we finally spotted him strolling casually across the small narrow walkway that bridged the burning North and South sections of the once massive Burlington Rubber Factory.

"Well, will you get a load of that," Uncle Charlie said, nudging my mother and pointing to my father. "I bet the crazy, son-of-a-gun didn't even have to use a match."

"Jesus, Mary and Joseph!" I heard my mother whisper as I closed my eyes and began to pray. "I never would have guessed. The dirty bastard is alive after all!"

LE FESTE

The girl pressed her pale forehead against the dusty window screen and gazed down into the street where the workmen were building the bandstand. Another September had come to Hoboken and another Feste was beginning under her window. All day she had found herself trembling with pleasure, longing for nightfall when Le Feste would begin. After lunch she had to grip the edge of the table and concentrate on holding her body very still to control her excitement. Although she was only thirteen, she could still remember last summer's Feste and the summer's before that : the brightly colored lights and bulbs like Christmas decorations spraying crimson and orange rays over the gray brick buildings, the people laughing, singing, dancing, eating thick, forbidden sausages long after midnight, the smells of hot bread and tomato sauce and red burgundy, the sounds of zeppoles frying in the hot, sputtering oil.

Last year she was a child, her mother insisted, and too young to visit Le Feste alone. She had to watch everything from the safety of her window, but she soon grew restless and longed to race into the crowded streets and mingle with the dark-eyed, black-haired boys and girls she saw walking together arm-in-arm. Now only one year older, she could go to the Feste herself and wander up and down the noisy sidewalks doing anything she liked until 10 p.m. when she had to be back home.

As she gazed down at the workmen hammering and sawing, she thought of the five dollars she had been saving since July. It was tucked safely inside her underwear drawer waiting to be spent on anything she chose. She could buy helium balloons, the kind that floated way above the five-story tenement houses, if you let go of their strings. She had seen many of these same balloons sail aimlessly past her window during last year's Feste. One came close to her and she tried to reach it but couldn't and almost fell out the window. Her mother had yelled and insisted she come inside and stop her foolishness.

She also thought of spending the money on her mother by buying her a silver bracelet with a small pennant that said "Le Feste de Moffeta" She had seen these bracelets worn to school by her classmates who had been to Le Feste last September. They were so small and delicate and feminine that she knew her mother would like one. Besides, a bracelet would remind her all year of the excitement of the day when she bought it.

Lord knows, she didn't have excitement much of the time. In fact, things were usually pretty dull around Adams Street. The five tiny rooms she lived in with her mother and grandmother ran like railroad cars back-to-back. Her bedroom didn't even have a door. People had to walk straight through it to get from the living room to the kitchen. The room she was in now overlooked the corner of Fourth and Adams. All along Adams and up to Jefferson the houses were alike, gray and red brick tenements with front stoops and black iron fire-escapes.

Only the Spot Tavern directly across from her house lent energy to the neighborhood. Here naughty women would gather at night to laugh and drink with men. These women, her grandmother said, were naughty because they wore heavy make-up and danced in the hot smoky backroom on Saturday night instead of being home with their children or falling asleep, like her own mother, in front of the T.V.

The girl would stay up past midnight on Saturday just to catch a glimpse of them leaving the tavern in the moonlight. Now because Le Feste had arrived, the women would leave the smoky backroom long before midnight and go outside to dance by the bandstand until the early morning, swaying their hips and clacking their heels along the cobblestones to the beat of loud, pulsating sound. When the music stopped momentarily, fat ladies in sequin dresses and long, gaudy earrings would sing songs in high pitch screeches, songs in Italian she couldn't follow but somehow understood.

To think that the bandstand would be finally built that night. Green poles and colored paper hangings would fill the streets and loudspeakers would send static along the gutters and up through the wooden frame tenement houses keeping everyone awake. For three days her world would come alive.

Soon her mother and grandmother would return from shopping and she would help them unpack the groceries and stack the cans of

Del Monte's vegetables and fruits into the little cabinet alongside the kitchen sink. Then she would go into the refrigerator and get a cold can of Schaeffer beer for the grandmother. Nanny, as the girl called her, liked to have a drop of beer before supper. Every evening she would waddle with her newspaper and reading glasses into the tiny living room with the brown kerosene stove and plop herself down into the overstuffed armchair in the corner where the upright lamp with the dirty yellow shade stood. Then the girl would fetch the beer and Nanny would smile and say, "Thank you, darling, you're a real dear. What would Nanny do without you?"

She didn't particularly like her grandmother even though her grandmother was kind and many times gave her nickels and quarters out of the little oil cloth pouch she kept inside her handbag. She believed her grandmother spied on her from the front window when she was out playing tops and fly ball with the other kids on the block.

"Bridget shouldn't be mingling with those gutter- snipes, Helen," she would say to the mother. "She'll never grow up to be a lady. Mind you, the child needs careful watching."

Although Bridget no longer played tops or fly ball, she resented her grandmother's meddling. Many times Bridget would be reading in the parlor while the T.V. was on and while her mother was mashing potatoes in the kitchen for supper. The grandmother would wander over and peek across the girl's shoulders to see what she was reading.

"You don't want to be letting trash into your head, Bridget. Books just make people foolish. Why not watch the T.V., child; at least that can't do you any harm."

Bridget would only grow silent and then after five minutes leave the room. That was why, when she came away from the sooty screen which left a black dust stain on her forehead, she began to worry. Suppose the grandmother tried to talk her mother out of letting her go to Le Feste. She would have to wait another whole year before September returned. That would be awful, almost unbearable, and Bridget shuddered to think of those long, dark months--January, February, March--she would have to endure when days seemed never to end. She would be quick, subtle, and would think of an easy way of leaving before her grandmother had the chance to betray her. Bridget thought and thought and was still thinking long after her grandmother and mother came home, put away the groceries and were relaxing in the living room after supper.

"Gertie was telling me about that Rita O'Brien girl, Helen," the grandmother said to the girl's mother.

The mother was barely listening. She was watching the last five minutes of her favorite re-run, "Fantasy Island."

"She's in trouble again, Gertie told me. Only two years after her first trouble. Why, everyone is saying what a disgrace she is to that lovely family."

"Huh," the mother grunted.

"I'll tell you later," said the grandmother, flipping through the classified pages of The Jersey Journal.

Outside the window where the girl had watched half the day, night was descending on the small neighborhood and lights were beginning to shoot across the sky. The girl who hadn't said a thing since supper, walked over to her mother's chair and spoke very rapidly.

"I'm leaving now, Mama. Le Feste has already begun. I'll bring you home a surprise. Wait and see."

The girl kissed her mother swiftly and dashed to the front door. Just then her grandmother spoke.

"Bridget, are you going somewhere?"

Bridget froze and felt the blood rush from her head.

"Yes, Nanny," she said, swinging around and feeling the room go round too, although she tried to smile and look at ease. "Mama said I could and I'm going to surprise her with a present from Le Feste."

The grandmother rustled her papers and leaned forward heavily in her chair.

"Bridget, don't you think it's a little dangerous going out alone so late at night?"

Bridget felt herself on the edge of tears. She hated to be challenged by her grandmother who seemed to take delight in her confusion and fear but, fortunately, her mother was not listening. She was staring into the blue light of the small T.V. screen.

"No, Nanny, it's perfectly safe outside, and besides I won't be far from the house. You can even watch me from the window, if you like. Don't worry."

"It's not you, Bridget, I'm worried about but those perverts who pick up young girls and do horrible things to them. Those are the people I worry about."

During her grandmother's speech Bridget had managed to reach the door and unlock it. She was ready to leap out into the hallway whenever she saw her chance.

"Besides," the grandmother continued, "those young Italian boys who belong to the Moffeta club are nothing but troublemakers. Why I wouldn't let my daughter near them. After all, look what happened to Rita O'Brien."

Bridget looked quickly to her mother who still, apparently, hadn't heard a word. The child took a deep breath and cried out, "See you soon, Nanny."

She flew from the door and down the musty stairwell which smelled of moldy mops and stagnant water. Outside in the street under the bright, dripping lights and colors, Bridget felt the miracle she had waited for take root within her. She felt washed, pure, renewed, ready to begin. All around her was life. The life she had longed for but could only watch from her window. Now she could walk among the crowd, be jostled by tall, dark-eyed men, hear music throb through her brain and eat and drink strange, spicy foods and red wines. She was no longer a child. Nearby, men in dark suits and women in gaily-colored dresses were holding one another closely and swaying to slow scintillating music. Young men in tight pants and half-opened silk shirts walked up and down in pairs, smoking and grinning shyly. Over by Fiore's Cheese Shop, Bridget saw a young Montague kissing a slender, long-haired girl with bare arms. He was rubbing his hand along her hips. Bridget stared, fascinated, then quickly hurried away, ashamed to be seen by anyone who might turn and catch her watching. Before long, however, it was difficult to walk through the perpetual rushing waves of people. They filled every available inch of space and moved forward with tiny mincing steps. Still, Bridget was enthralled to be swept up in the great mass of flowing bodies and voices and, although the five dollar bill in her hand burned to be traded for the shining silver bracelet, Bridget clung to the belly of the crowd.

At the intersection of Fifth and Adams, she reluctantly freed herself from the arms of the throng and turned up Jefferson Street toward the gambling stands and fruit-seller booths. She saw a small, wizened old man in a peaked cap and white apron standing behind a makeshift counter selling blood-red apples and thick clustered grapes. She was hot and thirsty and hungered for a piece of cold fruit to cool her throat. The man looked like a character from one of her adventure stories, and she wanted to talk to him and hear his foreign accent. As she was about to buy a bunch of seedless grapes, she spied a young man close by gazing and smiling at her. She felt her face flush and her hands begin to shake. He was tall and thin but looked strong and muscular. Was he going to talk to her, she wondered? She became so excited she forgot what she had purchased and looked quickly at the old fruit vendor. She was confused and befuddled and stood waiting for him to take charge. The fruit seller, who had been observing the contact between the two youths, knew what both of them were thinking. He was a cunning man and wise to the ways of the young. Deftly, he took Bridget's money and asked her if she wanted anything else. Bridget hesitated, believing the young man would approach and address her. She fumbled some oranges and then chose two red apples. Again, she looked into the face of the young man who stood near her. She smiled and coyly lowered her eyes the way she saw women do in the late-night movies. When she had the grapes and the two apples in a bag, she held her hand out waiting for her change. The old man shook his head with a disdainful look.

"No, no, I'ma sorry, miss, you owa me. I don't owa you."

"But I gave you five dollars," Bridget protested, panicking.

"No, no,--you crazy girl or something?"

Bridget stood speechless, trembling like a little girl. Deeply embarrassed to see the young man observing her, she turned away and continued to plead with the old man.

"But I gave you five dollars only a moment ago. Don't you remember?"

The old man shook his head adamantly. His eyes shut like doors slamming in Bridget's face. She felt tears welling up and a thick lump forming in her throat. She was shaking more violently and fearing she would become sick right there in front of everyone. She thought of the presents she had promised her mother . . . the silver bracelet. What would her mother say when she returned empty-handed? What would her grandmother say? She wiped her eyes and turned; the young man was still staring at her.

Oh, God, go away, she thought. Please go away.

But the young man did not go away. In fact, he took a step closer, curious yet hesitant, as if the earth might give way beneath him.

Bridget stared at him, her face burning with shame, her heart racing like a marble down a long flight of stairs.

The young man took another step. And then another until the space between them closed to almost nothing. Until their bodies touched beneath the flickering shadows of the multi-colored night.

Within his eyes, large and frightened like her own, Bridget could see herself, a tiny figure floating in a pool of blue.

Her grandmother and mother were both asleep and snoring in front of the television set when Bridget returned home later that night. Although it was very late, long past any of their bedtimes, she thought it best not to wake them. In the morning, they would all feel much better. Then she would tell them about her adventures and give them their presents—a silver bracelet for Mama; a pearl brooch for Nana.

She would not tell them about the young man, though.

Nor the fruit seller.

Nor any of the other things she had learned from her long night at Le Feste. No.

Not a word.

Not for now at least. +++++

AN ENCOUNTER

I was seven and a half when I first met Miss Casey on that park bench in Hoboken, not far from the intersection of Willow and Clinton streets. She was sitting upright, staring straight ahead past the children's playground in the direction of the bronze fireman and the pigeons. Some pigeons were parading back and forth atop the fireman's gargantuan helmet; others were huddled and cooing within the deep folds and crevices of his long raincoat and tall, thick boots.

Seven foot high and surrounded by a forbidding picket rail fence, the fireman was an awesome sight. He stood dead center in the park, fixed in a fierce, eternal pose of a fearless rescuer: head high and determined, legs straight, eyes blazing, arms clutching the limp body of the small child he had just carried from a burning building. Some people said he was Hoboken's only genuine monument; others argued he was a health menace and a threat to neighborhood children who'd climb through the fence, scale his immense torso, and swing from his ears. Whatever, he was certainly more than a statue; he was the delight and fantasy of every passing kid who imagined himself up there: the town hero, intrepid savior of the hopeless and helpless.

To the pigeons, though, the fireman was just another statue. One of their favorites, in fact.

Every six months or so, workmen would come and clean him up, making sure to polish the gold-plated plaque beneath his left boot which read, "In honor of Those Brave Men Who Gave Their Lives to Save Others." For a while, he'd sparkle like a night star, but after a few days of relentless pigeon bombing attacks, he'd look more like a fire hydrant than fire hero.

On the day I encountered Miss Casey, the bronze fireman was at his worst. And I suspect now so was Miss Casey. She looked like some grotesque human pipe-cleaner with cotton candy for hair and billiard balls for eyes. She was so thin every bone and edge of her seemed to slice the air like a razor blade. Yet she barely moved.

When I first laid eyes on her, she was so still I thought she was fake—some hideous manikin dragged out of a moldy basement for public airing. I had been in the park for over two hours with my mother and I had absolutely nothing to do except sit beside her on the bench and watch the perverts go by. That was my mother's favorite expression: "watching the perverts go by." My mother truly believed everyone who frequented a park—with the exception of herself and her few lady friends—was perverted, deranged, and highly dangerous to young children. She was constantly on the watch for old men in raincoats lurking behind garbage bins and trees who might assault me. She refused to ever allow me into the little girls' room by myself and she adamantly insisted that I never be out of her sight for more than two minutes. She even forbade me to drink from the park's water fountain, convinced as she was that perverts used it as a urinal when no one was looking. Thinking back now, I realize my mother had her troubles, but at the impressionable age of seven and a half, I accepted the idea that she knew what she was talking about.

At night when other kids were hearing tales of Red Riding Hood and Snow White and the Seven Dwarfs, my mother was reading headlines to me from the Daily News like "Attractive Blonde Slashed in Alley," and "Mother of Nine Raped in St. Patrick's Cathedral." She was convinced these lessons were good for my vocabulary and that they might teach me a few things about the world. Although I felt infinitely superior to my classmates who knew little about perversion and the powers of lust and evil, I was still a sheltered and over-protected little girl. Rarely was I allowed to venture far outside the range of my mother's sonic radar.

On the day I first saw Miss Casey, however, I was unusually restless. It was a hot summer afternoon and most of the other kids in the park my age were roller-skating, playing two-hand touch, climbing trees, and eating ice cream cones. I, however, was stuck on the park bench between my mother and her two friends Mrs. Mueller and Mrs. Dugan. For two hours they had been talking nonstop about their good-for-nothing husbands and their snotty, ungrateful children. I was bored silly listening to them and I longed to dig a deep hole in the dirt, climb in and wiggle my way clear across town to Washington Street where I could buy a chocolate ice cream soda and some Oreo cookies. Since I didn't relish the idea of encountering any sewer rats or perverts, who my mother insisted, lived beneath the city sidewalks, I decided instead to become a pigeon and see what it was like to fly. I wandered over to the empty bench right beside the one my mother and her friends were on, and climbed atop it. I flexed my legs, stretched out my arms, and leaped high into the air. I discovered that being a pigeon was a whole lot of fun, so I kept up the game: climbing, flexing, stretching and leaping. After a while I got bored again and decided to experiment with a few variations. Pretty soon I was sailing across benches some distance away from my mother's range of vision on my way toward the bench where Miss Casey sat staring into space. I landed atop her balding, wispy cotton skull before she knew what hit her. Bouncing off the bench, I fell into a heap at Miss Casey's feet, and burst into tears.

"Good heavens, child," she cried, bending down and lifting me off the ground, "Are you hurt? Where did you come from?"

She reached out her hand and stroked me gently on the head. The hand itself, so bony and sharp, felt like a caliper, but the gentleness of her touch and her soft reassuring voice worked a kind of magic upon me. Almost instantly I stopped crying and removed my fist from my mouth. The two of us sat there staring into one another's eyes. Hers were bulging and yellow and lake-large. They reminded me of my cat's eyes—Foo-Foo's eyes—strangely penetrating yet detached, just the way Foo's eyes looked the day she was killed when she was run over by a milk truck.

"So you're not hurt then, little girl?" she inquired, glancing down at my legs which were spotted with dirt. "No nasty scrapes or bruises, no cuts or unpleasant scratches? You must be made of cotton."

I giggled.

"What's your name, sweetheart?" she asked. "You're as pretty as a picture. Do you know that?"

"I shook my head and told her my name was Mickey-Lou. Then I asked her hers.

"Oh, you may call me Miss Casey," she said.

I stood straight to get a better view of her. She was the oddest person I ever saw. She was so thin her shoulders stuck out like angel wings.

"Now tell me, Miss Mickey Lou," she asked. "Just where did you come from? Did a stork drop you full grown onto my bench."

I blushed, shook my head, then wiggled closer, making sure to keep my voice very low in case any perverts were listening.

"Mommy and Daddy had me one night after they had sex," I said.

She gave a little start, then roared laughing.

"Where on earth did you learn that?" she cried.

I told her about my mother's fondness for the Daily News.

"Good lord, child, you are a treasure," she laughed, grabbing my shoulders and rocking me back and forth. "I haven't laughed this much in some time."

I had been staring at her head which looked like the skull of a new born baby in a bassinet: bald with just a few wisps here and there of white, pinkish fluff that any soft breeze might suddenly carry away.

"I'm a sight for sore eyes, aren't I?" she asked, observing my stare." If you must know, I have been very sick."

"Do you think you'll die?" I asked, remembering poor Foo-Foo.

She shrugged and didn't respond for a moment. Then she pointed toward the bronze fireman.

"See those pigeons over there?"

I followed her finger and nodded.

"Why don't we bet that they will all die before I do? Do you think that's a good bet?"

"How much do you want to bet?" I asked cautiously.

"Oh, I don't know," she said. "A dime?"

"What makes you think those pigeons are going to die?" I asked. "Did someone poison them?"

"I should hope not," she laughed.

"Well, why then do you think they are going to die?" I persisted.

"Because everything on this earth dies, sweetheart. Death is a part of life. A very real part. It's all a matter of time even for pigeons."

"Think you'll go to heaven?" I asked, taking another peek at the pigeons who I imagined were suddenly keeling over like plugged Indians in a shooting gallery.

"Sure," she said. "Don't you?"

"No," I said sadly. "I don't think so."

"And why is that?" Miss Casey asked.

"Because sometimes I'm very bad," I said. "Sometimes I say bad words like 'shit' and 'asshole' out loud like my Mommy and Daddy do, and once when Sister Lucille, my teacher, heard me she made me wash my mouth out with soap, and then she told me I was going to go to hell if I said those bad words again."

"My, that Sister Lucille is a pretty tough cookie," Miss Casey replied. "I'm glad she's not my teacher."

"I'm glad too," I said, taking hold of her hand, "because you're a nice lady and I like you a whole lot even though you have funny hair and I just met you."

Her eyes suddenly got very wet.

"Oh," she said. "If only I had a little girl like you."

"Don't you have any kids?" I inquired, glancing around as if they were about to materialize from beneath the bench.

"No, I'm not married. I never was, but I do wish I had a little girl like you," Miss Casey said.

"Oh, you don't have to get married to have a kid," I reassured her." Mommy told me you can get a baby just by kissing a boy."

"Oh, did she now?" Miss Casey laughed. "Well, your mother is quite a character then, isn't she?"

"Yep," I said. "My mother knows all about babies and sex. That's how come she had me."

"Well, your mother is a very lucky woman," Miss Casey said, patting my cheek.

"Are you really going to die?" I whispered, as I climbed onto her lap and made myself more comfortable.

"Yes," she whispered back. "But promise you won't tell anyone except those pigeons and that fireman over there."

"I promise," I said, crossing my heart and giving her a kiss.

She rocked me back and forth in her arms while I listened to the low cooing of the pigeons and the distant shouts of children playing. It felt so good and peaceful there in her warm lap I never wanted to leave again. I shut my eyes and began drifting off to sleep when suddenly I heard my mother's voice crash through my head like a window pane. shattering into little pieces.

"Mickey-Lou! What in God's name are you doing?"

Startled, Miss Casey jumped to her feet, and I toppled to the hard pavement.

"Who are you?" my mother asked, taking a menacing step toward Miss Casey. "What are you doing with my daughter?"

Behind my mother stood Mrs. Mueller and Mrs. Dugan, big as bulldozers and more powerful than locomotives.

Miss Casey reeled backwards to escape the forces bearing down upon her.

"Please," she said. "Let me explain. Just let me catch my breath for a moment."

"I take my eyes off you for only a few minutes, and what happens?" my mother asked, now turning toward me. "Didn't I warn you not to talk to strangers?"

"But, mommy," I cried, snot beginning to run down my nose, "Miss Casey is not a stranger. She's a very nice lady who says she wishes she had a daughter like me."

"Oh, yeah," my mother said, glancing over at Miss Casey, "Well, let her get her own daughter then. But you're my daughter now and I'm taking you home before you get into any more trouble talking to strangers and park perverts."

"Please," Miss Casey said, shaking her head. "Please don't upset the child."

"I should call the cops," my mother said to Mrs. Mueller and Mrs. Dugan who stood there nodding their thick broad skulls in silent agreement. "I should report all this."

"All what, mommy?" I asked, looking back at Miss Casey and trying not to cry as I waved her a quick goodbye. "I didn't do anything bad and neither did Miss Casey. We were only talking about having babies and dying and going to heaven and all."

"Shut up," my mother said, pulling me away by the arm. "You could have been kidnapped."

The entire park—men, women, dogs, kids, pigeons-seemed to be bearing down upon us from every direction. My mother was so mad every vein in her face and neck was popping out like jack in the boxes. I thought she would explode there before me and go flying off into the air like a ruptured balloon. Overwhelmed, I burst into such a wail it sent shivers up my own spine.

"Stop that," my mother shouted, clouting me on the behind with such force my eyelids instantly shut like window shades slamming down against the sunlight.

"That's what you get from wandering away from me," she said.

In my confusion, I failed to see Miss Casey slip quietly away, lingering perhaps for only a moment in the long shadows cast by the bronze fireman before losing herself within the maze of winding streets and tall tenements.

I never saw her again after that day, but whenever I am passing through the park , I always think of her, and what she might have to say about all the pigeons who didn't die and still live there atop the bronze fireman.+++++

TALES FOR REFLECTION

Our birth is but a sleep and a forgetting:
The soul that rises with us, our life's star,
Hath had elsewhere its setting,
And cometh from afar.

--William Wordsworth

MRS. BRINKHOFFER AND THE LIGHTNING BUGS

Mrs. Brinkhoffer began raising her children with the best of intentions, but one day, as was the case with most things in her life, she simply lost interest. Whether Dottie, her daughter, wore her mittens on wet windy days, whether Ralphie, her ten-year-old, had clean socks for school was of little concern to her. Most of the time she did not even notice her offspring, or her husband, Teddy, who worked for T.T.& T, a company that manufactured umbrella spokes. Oh, she knew that they were there, of course, and she spoke and smiled at them whenever the opportunity arose, but in her heart Mrs. Brinkhoffer knew that if they were suddenly to disappear and be heard from no more, it wouldn't have mattered to her in the least. In fact, it was something she expected. One moment people were there and the next they weren't. Why all the fuss? It wasn't that Mrs. Brinkhoffer was a cruel woman or an unhappy one. When she found her children in her arms, she kissed and hugged them as all mothers do. When they were away from her, she simply forgot about them. It was that simple.

For all intents and purposes she was a loving wife. She never cheated on her husband or refused him comfort on those evenings when cold draughts blew into their dark bedroom. When Mr. Brinkhoffer complained of gas or a decline in umbrella sales, Mrs. Brinkhoffer was the first to succor him. She would rub his head, tickle his chin, and say some words--any at all, it didn't matter. Before long Mr. Brinkhoffer would be himself again: absent.

To Mrs. Brinkhoffer it was all very natural. People were like little birds. They flew this way and that way, self-important and noisy, dropping their dirt in mid-air and making a mess of trees. If you paid little attention, they would eventually go away. So, when Mr. Brinkhoffer arrived home, tired and grumpy from the umbrella factory, complaining about all the sunny days they were having and all that lay ahead, or when little Dottie cried because her teacher had called her a moron for coloring a rabbit green in her crayon book, Mrs. Brinkhoffer stared out her window and thought of lightning bugs.

***

Once upon a time she had trapped and locked them in mayonnaise jars. She liked the way they'd light up, fling themselves in protest against the thick glass, and then go out again. Since she was a very little girl lightning bugs had intrigued her. In high school she wrote a paper about them which she entitled "On and Off," but the teacher, an amateur entomologist, criticized it as "frivolous" and gave it a "D."

***

That was a long time ago, way before Mrs. Brinkhoffer realized that she too went on and off like a lightning bug. In those days before her discovery she thought like everyone else. She believed her days had three distinct parts: a beginning, a middle, and an end. She thought each day, traveling in a straight line, cut through the previous one like an eraser wiping away old sentences on a dirty blackboard. She pictured her life as a series of moments moving forward toward some unswerving destination, each precious second bumping, pushing, rolling against the next and merging into something like a large beach ball which had to be bounced and kicked up some steep hill, before true happiness could arrive. In those days she wasn't quite sure she knew what true happiness was, but like everyone else she believed it was worth having. She assumed it had something to do with marriage, children, a belief in tomorrow and confidence in one's self. In her dreams she saw herself growing larger and larger like the beach ball, bouncing higher and higher toward happiness until she exploded.

For years it never occurred to Mrs. Brinkhoffer that there was any other way of looking at things. Like most people she scoffed at the notion that life held innumerable possibilities and passions, and that there might be countless Mrs. Brinkhoffers in other worlds all flashing on and off like whimsical blue dots on an immense wheel of fortune. Frankly, such thoughts never entered her head, and they would have given her a headache if they had. Mrs. Brinkhoffer in those days, you see, was like everyone else. She was content simply to accept the fact that she was here—one woman with one body, one husband, one family and one future, all bouncing through time on way to a happy, blissfully unaware oblivion.

Then one day something unexpected occurred. Mrs. Brinkhoffer was hanging laundry on the line in her back yard, dreaming of pork chops and liverwurst sandwiches when suddenly she began going on and off like a faulty electric light bulb. Mrs. Brinkhoffer gave a little squeal of surprise. Naturally, she had no idea what was happening. One moment she was there, glowing like a full moon and the next she was gone again. An odd sensation, something between a tickle and blow to the chin passed through her. Mrs. Brinkhoffer giggled, then gasped. For a brief second she thought she heard the grass singing and growing in circles and loops beneath her feet. She felt light-headed, giddy, strangely bewitched. Am I dreaming she asked herself? Am I here or not? Although her questions seemed vaguely familiar, like an old song reminiscent of by-gone days, Mrs. Brinkhoffer was still confused. What would happen if she went out and didn't come on again? She clutched her clothespins, shut her eyes, and called for Teddy, who was at that moment opening and closing an umbrella fifteen miles away.

More than likely Teddy and the children would have noticed if Mrs. Brinkhoffer didn't come back on again but that is hard to say. After all, no one can really be sure about anything, or anyone, as Mrs. Brinkhoffer was in fact to discover.

By the time her husband and children arrived home that evening, Mrs. Brinkhoffer was still going on and off. She stood shivering in the doorway like a small child waiting to be comforted, but Teddy only walked passed her and asked what was for supper and Dottie and Ralphie wanted to know if they could go play outside in the drainage ditch. Mrs. Brinkhoffer was crushed. It was as if someone close to her had forgotten her birthday or failed to say God bless after she had sneezed. Although she made a nice beef stew for dinner, read the children a lovely bedtime story, and didn't mention a word about her day to Teddy, Mrs. Brinkhoffer was crestfallen. Why hadn't her family noticed anything? Didn't anyone care? Didn't anyone love her? All through supper Mrs. Brinkhoffer watched little Dottie and little Ralphie tease and throw spaghetti at one another, as she blinked on and off in front of them. Teddy, as always, talked on and on about the umbrella business, the rising cost of raincoats, and the coming hurricane season, but didn't say a word about his wife changing into a neon sign right before his eyes. Later that evening after the dishes had been washed and the children put to bed Mrs. Brinkhoffer began to think about love. She lay on her bed flickering on and off beside her husband. She wondered if love too went on and off like a lightning bug, and if it was really there when it didn't appear to be.

**

All through the night Mrs. Brinkhoffer thought and thought. And all through the next day and the next. She knew there was something extraordinary happening to her, but she couldn't imagine what it might be. Then, one afternoon while she was slicing pea pods, Mrs. Brinkhoffer went off for a very long time. When she returned, she was no longer the same. Friends said later she began to act peculiar. She seemed no longer to care in the least who noticed her and who didn't. No one seemed to guess that she was no longer even there to care. When her friends called on the telephone, she held a towel across the mouthpiece and told them they had the wrong number; one day she unscrewed the family mailbox and dropped it in the town dump. On another occasion she searched through the house and threw out anything that carried her name: credit cards, bills, licenses even her library card. One morning she sat on the living room floor and shreded her pictures in the family photo album with a rusty pair of garden shears.

At night when everyone was asleep Mrs. Brinkhoffer began slipping out to the backyard to do her burying. She buried everything she could carry: rugs, Venetian blinds, slipcovers, quilts, dinner napkins, window shades, plastic mats, tablecloths, etc., etc., etc. One evening she struggled with the old armchair in the living room that used to be her favorite, but she had trouble fitting it through the doorway. She finally dragged it down the basement and hacked off the legs with Teddy's old Boy Scout ax.

Eventually people began to ask questions. Teddy received a phone call from a roofing company which had apparently been contacted by a Mrs. Brinkhoffer to remove all the ceilings and walls inside the family residence. The roofing contractor wanted to know if the caller had been serious. Teddy told the man there had been some mistake, and hung up. Shortly thereafter a plumber called. He told Teddy that he was on his way to disconnect all the pipes and toilets, as the lady of the house had instructed. Could Teddy, perhaps, give him directions on how to get there? Baffled, Teddy searched for Mrs. Brinkhoffer but couldn't find her anywhere. Eventually he stumbled upon her in the backyard sitting beneath the clothing line. When Teddy asked what the hell she was doing Mrs. Brinkhoffer smiled and told him she was waiting. Waiting for what Teddy asked?

That night they slept apart. Mrs. Brinkhoffer, going on and off in steady pulses, curled up beneath the clothes line while Teddy slept in the king-sized bed. His dreams were fierce. A large cow was beneath his bedroom window chewing off pieces of the house and ripping up all the azalea bushes. Teddy warned, shook his head, swore, threatened to shoot the damn thing, but the cow kept on chewing: determined but at the same time indifferent.

Next morning Mrs. Brinkhoffer moved all her clothing and belongings to the backyard while Teddy and the children got ready for their new day. Shortly thereafter Teddy's mother came for a visit and the kids went off for a long stay in Aunt Lucille's house. Then, somewhere about that time--given a few weeks here or there, it was hard to tell under the circumstances—all the light bulbs in the house mysteriously disappeared. Teddy and his mother had just come in from grocery shopping and the house was pitch black. For a while the two of them groped in the dark looking for light switches and extra bulbs, but they couldn't find a thing in all that darkness. In fact they had to call out each other's names to be sure they wouldn't bump into one another. Even the flash lights were missing. The only light they had was the moon's which shone weakly through the uncurtained windows. Teddy and his mother moaned and groaned and stubbed their toes all night long.

Outside, however, under the clothing line, Mrs. Brinkhoffer sat unconcerned. Waiting. +++++

HOW MUCH LAND DOES A DOG REALLY NEED?

It was a pitiful time for Marge Alwell. Her dog, Lou-Lou, a bow-legged black Lab with Peter Lorre eyes and a snout the color of wet coal ash had gone sick and was fading fast. All day the dog lay panting and groaning beneath the kitchen table, rolling its watery eyes and pale tongue in helpless bewilderment. All night Lou-Lou lay wasted and half-crazed at the foot of Marge's bed, growling and nipping at presences only she could see.

No one knew what was wrong. Not Marge. Not George, her husband, not even Dr. Greyfleck, the town vet. One minute Lou-Lou had been fine. A perfectly normal dog: scratching her fleas, chewing her tail, lying in wait for the postman. The next minute everything had changed. A grotesque and terrible weariness had come upon her, and poor Lou-Lou, as if struck dead center by some mighty, mysterious force, suddenly collapsed: grey, shrunken and immeasurably old.

"She's a goner, that's for sure," Grayfleck declared on the afternoon Marge arrived in his office with Lou-Lou in her arms. "All I can do now is give her a shot. Put the old gal out of her misery."

Marge, one eye on her dog and one eye on the door, reached for Lou-Lou's red doggie collar, which Greyfleck had casually discarded on the edge of the examining table. Its looping emptiness resembled a forlorn hangman's noose.

"If you don't know what's wrong with her, how can you be so sure she's a goner?" Marge asked.

Grayfleck eyed her suspiciously.

"I've seen cases like this before, Mrs. Alwell. "It's known as the Doomed Dog Syndrome. Believe me, there just isn't any hope."

Lou-Lou, as if stuck by an invisible hammer, fell back against the table.

"Well, I refuse to accept that," Marge snapped. "As my grandmother used to say, while there's life there's hope."

She swept Lou-Lou off the table, and headed for the door.

"Suit yourself," Dr. Greyfleck called after her. "You got nothing to lose, I suppose."

All the way home Marge watched helplessly through the rear-view mirror as Lou-Lou heaved and vomited across the vinyl back seat of the blue-white Rabbit.

That evening Lou-Lou shook and howled until the pilot light in the gas stove went out. Shortly thereafter Marge discovered her climbing onto the stone fireplace hearth toward the open flames which had been burning a fierce orange and blue since sundown. Before Marge could scream, however, Lou-Lou's legs gave out and she fell headlong into the ash bucket, spewing the floor with gray soot. George, a psychiatric social worker, who knew little about dogs and even less about people, swore Lou-Lou was trying to kill herself, but Marge insisted suicide was unheard of among dogs.

"She'd never do a thing like that" Marge said. "Black Labs are above despair. Her ancestry just wouldn't allow it.

"What do we know about her ancestry?" George argued. "We found Lou-Lou in the pound, remember?"

Marge stiffened.

"Pound or no pound. Lou-Lou is a first class dog. I tell you she is above despair."

"Oh yeah? What was she doing in our fireplace then? Toasting marshmallows?"

"No doubt she was seeking warmth and light," Marge said with dignified calm. "A perfectly understand- able thing to do when one is troubled."

"Yeah, if you're a Buddhist monk. Why the hell couldn't she have settled for a candle?"

"She's undergoing a crisis. George. She needs us."

"O.K., O.K., so she needs us. Let's just make sure she doesn't burn the house down in the process. O.K.? A sick animal I can take. Joan of Arc, forget."

Two days later a cluster of hard angry lumps surfaced like brooding bullets on Lou-Lou's soft pink underbelly.

Marge wept. That night she slept on the floor next to Lou-Lou who was huddled in the pink comforter she used to chew as a puppy.

"I'm here," Marge cried, gently stroking Lou-Lou's lumpy belly. "I'm right here with you."

Lou-Lou trembled under her hand.

Outside, beneath a pale brooding moon, clumps of earth rose and fell in mournful cadences. Marge closed her eyes and dreamed of Lou-Lou as a puppy. She was jet black and sleek and her eyes resembled flying saucers. All through the dream she chased a white-tailed rabbit along a purple-stained meadow and somersaulted in the tall grass.

When Marge woke up she found herself thinking of Lassie and a poem Emily Dickinson had once written. "Hope is the Thing With Feathers/ That Perches in the Soul and Sings the Tune/ Without the Words and Never Stops At All."

"You know that poem, now don't you?" she asked Lou-Lou who was curled in a painful knot beside her. "And, no doubt, you remember Lassie, right? That big Collie dog that always barked and came on T.V. right after the Walt Disney Show?"

Lou-Lou kept her bloodshot eyes on the screen door across the room, whimpering like a small mouse caught in a steel rat trap.

"Well, I want you to remember all the things that happened to Lassie. O.K.? All the terrible things that she survived: the avalanches, the dog-nappings, the train wrecks."

Lou-Lou didn't respond.

"That animal went through hell, real hell, but she made it. Do you hear me, Lou-Lou? She made it. And all those other dogs like Rin-tin-tin, and Arf-Arf Sandy who were always running around barking and wagging their tails in the sunlight--they all made it too."

In the back yard a hundred feet or so away under a weeping willow tree a grey squirrel sat atop the wet grass, waiting patiently.

Over the next two weeks, hour after hour, Lou-Lou lay on her pink comforter, her mouth slobbering, her eyes wide and remote.

Marge, sustained by her own irreducible, internal energies, rarely left her side. George, touched yet furious, drank endless cups of coffee and read everything he could find on death and dying and animal fixation.

One morning, seemingly out of the blue, as George sat drinking his coffee and arguing the benefits of canine euthanasia, Lou-Lou attempted to stand. Before she could maneuver her tottering legs into a supporting position, however, she pitched forward, and collapsed in a heap beside the frost-free refrigerator. Marge rushed to help her, but paused when she saw Lou-Lou begin to crawl toward the screen door. In healthier times it took no effort for Lou-Lou to open this door, which led to the back yard where she would lie the whole afternoon in the warm sunlight that splashed across the grass and patio. Now, however, it took every ounce of Lou-Lou's strength just to make it across the room. George and Marge watched in awe as she clawed, pawed, and weaved her way over the bright red tiles like a punch-drunk fighter staggering to his corner.

When Lou-Lou finally arrived in front of the door, Marge rushed to open it. Lou-Lou slithered past Marge's feet, worming her way down the two back steps. Then without so much as a word or glance in Marge's or George's direction, Lou-Lou began crawling to the center of the yard where the grass and daffodils were the thickest.

By early the next afternoon Lou-Lou was flopping happily up and down on her back in the dirt, yelping like a bitch in heat and kicking the air like a crazed up-side-down cyclist.

By the following evening Lou-Lou was joyfully somersaulting from one end of the yard to the other. After each leap she'd flop onto her back and wiggle her spine into the earth.

All next day and the days following Lou-Lou continued this strange ritual. Rolling, pitching, burrowing, catapulting, yelping into the pebbly dirt, and baying at the scarred, white-faced moon. Late at night under a star-bright sky Lou-Lou slept peacefully, curled into a ball beneath the shadows of the willow tree.

Meanwhile inside the Alwell house, life had taken an unusual turn. George kept insisting that Lou-Lou had finally gone crazy and was frantically trying to bury herself alive. Marge, however, maintained that Lou-Lou knew exactly what she was doing and that it was absolutely essential that no one disturb her.

Mrs. Ormsby, George and Marge's next door neighbor who saw the world from her kitchen window through a pair of high beam binoculars, held the opinion that Lou-Lou must have been slipped some terrible drug by some nasty neighborhood hoodlums.

"The poor creature's been jerking and tumbling like a holy roller on holiday," Mrs. Ormsby said, squinting at Lou-Lou from across the yard. "If you ask me, she's higher than a kite on a cloudless Sunday."

The fact was no one could adequately explain Lou-Lou's sudden and extraordinary behavior. Not Marge, who was wild with hope; not George, who was suspicious and bewildered; and certainly not any of the neighbors, who had heard Lou-Lou's daily chorus of ungodly yappings and yelpings and had come to see for themselves what might be going on.

"My dog has been very sick," Marge told them from across the back fence.

"Sick? Her?" the neighbors asked, incredulously." "Are you sure?"

"Dr. Greyfleck told me himself there was no hope."

"Well, maybe, but she sure doesn't look so sick now," one of the ladies said.

"Could be she's getting better," offered another.

"What do you suppose she's doing?" a man with bifocals asked.

"I dunno," said Marge. "My husband and I are still trying to figure that out. But whatever it is, it appears to be working for her."

"Looks to me like she's trying to get under the ground." said a lady in a pink kerchief. "Could be some- thing's buried there. Maybe an old bone or something?"

"I think she trying to talk. Or maybe show us something," suggested another lady.

It sure is strange," the man with the bifocals agreed. "Strange and curious."

One by one, Lou-Lou's lumps began to vanish. Even the gray around her muzzle disappeared. Slowly, she began to gain weight. Before everyone's eyes she grew stronger, sleeker, more confident. One neighbor remarked that Lou-Lou no longer even looked like a dog.

Her face seems almost human, wouldn't you say?" the neighbor declared. "Very peaceful-like, especially around the mouth and eyes. In fact, it almost looks like she's laughing at something."

"All I know is that she's getting better," Marge cried. "I can't say how it's happening or why it's happening, but I can tell you she's getting better."

"All she did was roll around in the dirt," George said. "How could she possibly be getting better?"

That was the question almost all the neighbors wanted to know, for word had begun to spread through the quiet tree-lined community that there was something extraordinary happening to the Alwell family dog in the Alwell back yard and that their half acre of red-brown clay-like dirt might possess unusual, even magical powers.

When people saw Lou-Lou's amazing transformation, some of them speculated that the dirt probably contained special proteins and nutrients and thus was responsible for not only curing Lou-Lou of cancer but for giving her almost superhuman health and vitality. Other people of a more religious bent said that the dirt wasn't really dirt at all but a blessing from God and meant to be shared by all. More than a handful--called crazies by the majority--believed that the dirt was really stardust from out of space dropped by a spying UFO in some midnight rendezvous across the heavens.

In a sense, then, it was only natural that people, so caught up by these extraordinary tales and speculations, wanted to see for themselves what was going on. Every day more and more curious faces appeared at the back fence to get a glimpse of Lou-Lou and her fantastic acrobatics. Some of these people brought along their garden chairs, their children, their lunch baskets, their newspapers, their knitting. Others merely stood and watched, hanging across the three-rail fence for hours on end. Occasionally, a few of the more daring would crawl under the fence to sneak a roll in the dirt; others reached in to grab pocketfuls to take home.

After awhile all the local newspapers and radio stations came to investigate. Cynical reporters and photographers, forever underfoot, peeked through windows and waited for hours on the front steps; one day the Mayor himself arrived, and that night his picture and Lou-Lou's appeared on the evening news.

As word traveled outside the area, scientists and environmentalists began pouring in to study the phenomenon of what eventually became known to the locals as "Lou-Lou and the Magic Dirt." Teams of investigators set up elaborate, sophisticated equipment in the back yard, taking dirt samples, air samples, and Lou-Lou samples to dissect and evaluate under super-sensitive microscopes. At the same time, curious vets from all over the country pleaded for permission to examine Lou-Lou and find out for themselves the true state of her health.

What amazed the town more than anything, however, was the day a bus from Chicago pulled up in front of the house and its passengers, all on crutches or in wheelchairs, begged with tears in their eyes to be allowed into the back yard "to touch the sacred dog and roll beside her in the holy dirt."

Marge, overcome with surprise and sympathy, opened her heart and the gate almost immediately and waved everyone inside. As the crowd roared and the cameras clicked and flashed, dozens of people dove head first from wheelchairs, stretchers and crutches onto the earth, tumbling and rolling their bruised and battered bodies through the tall green grass and lovely flower beds.

George, flattered and inspired by the attention and presence of T.V. cameras, radio crews, and talk show hosts, went among the people shaking hands and giving out autographs. As the crowds grew larger, singing and dancing merrily among the cripples, several jealous neighbors began to complain. The police were called, a few people were arrested at random, and a 24-hour special protection squad was set up to maintain order and public safety. Marge and George were given strict orders to remain indoors and keep Lou-Lou out of sight until all the excitement had died down, two things Marge absolutely refused to do, even though one of the officers had insisted there were threats that Lou-Lou might be kidnapped and held for ransom.

"It's our back yard," she said, "and no one has the right to tell us what we can or cannot do in it. And besides all that, Lou-Lou is good for people. She makes them happy."

"Well, that may be true in one sense," George said, "but you have to admit the police might have a point. You can't allow everyone to run all over our property."

"And why not?" asked Marge. "What harm could it do if it helps people?"

"But we have to be practical, Marge. We have to use discretion. We can't let everyone in. We have to separate the wheat from the riff raff, as they say."

"And how do you intend to do that, if I may ask?"

"Well," said George. "I was thinking it mightn't be such a bad idea when things die down a little if we started charging a little admission fee. Nothing too high. Just something to meet our expenses."

"You want to charge people for simply rolling across our dirt? How could you even imagine such a thing?"

"Why not? It's our property and it's helping them isn't it?"

"In a sense, yes, but I still don't know if their getting better has anything to do with our dirt. It may be all in their own minds."

"What difference does that make? Do doctors ask those questions?"

"George, I refuse to even consider such a thing. Besides that dirt doesn't really belong to us anyway. It belongs to the earth."

"Yeah? Who pays the taxes on it then? The earth? Like hell! I do."

"Screw taxes. I never believed in them anyway."

"O.K. screw them but just remember I pay them and I own that land. I have a right to say who and what comes onto it."

"George, nobody, not you, not me, not anyone alive owns the earth or for that matter anything else. If people want to come and roll in our dirt, I say let them."

"Then they'll have to roll in your half because they're not getting on mine. You hear me, Margaret? They're not setting one foot on mine."

***

Meanwhile, thousands of miles away in Rome, the Pope was about to be informed by his advisors that somewhere in America a dog with strange miraculous powers had begun to heal the sick and raise the dead.

"What position should the Holy Father take on this?" one cardinal asked.

"He's got to come down on it hard," another answered. "The church can't allow people to believe that dogs can perform miracles. It's bad enough that they think statues can cry."

"Now just wait a minute, Anthony," the first cardinal objected. "The Holy Father can take a stand against people idolizing statues and magic medals because we have commandments that cover that. But don't forget this time we're dealing with a dog. And you know how most people feel about dogs."

"He's right, Anthony," another cardinal agreed. "We've got to consider this from a public relations point of view."

They compromised by persuading the Pope to send a delegate to the Alwells' back yard.

The pope's representative, along with agents from the CIA, the Security Council and the Pentagon, converged on the small town of Meyersville at approximately the same time, only to discover that half of the Alwell back yard was missing.

At Marge's signal, people had poured through the police barriers in droves. Some carried spoons and children's sand pails. Others lugged shovels and garbage cans. One lady carried a pooper scooper and a huge pocketbook. A young man whose leg was missing just below the knee arrived pushing a red wheelbarrow.

As George and the police watched in horror, Marge's sea of suffering humanity, their mouths stuffed with dark brown earth, their heads blazing with hope, swam across Marge's half of the back yard like starving piranhas.

Within two hours the entire left side of the Alwell backyard was en route to China.+++++

WHAT GOES UP, MUST COME DOWN . . . MAYBE

One day when Rita Foley and her friend Robin were driving around downtown looking for a nice place to have lunch-- preferably some fettuccini and mushrooms--they got to talking about the Astral Plane.

"I hear it's a very interesting place to visit," Robin said, staring out the window and stifling a yawn. "Have you ever been there?"

"No," Rita replied. "Nowadays I rarely go anywhere. Everything's too expensive."

"Yeah, but not the Astral Plane," Robin said. "From what I hear you can travel there round trip and it won't cost you a dime."

"Really?" Rita said, peering over the steering wheel at her friend. "That's wonderful. But I wonder why. Do you have any idea?"

"Well," Robin replied, "for one thing you don't really need your body to get there. I mean, it's not like traveling to Cincinnati or Seattle. You don't get on a plane or anything. And you don't have to worry about things like luggage or hotel accommodations. You just have to sit down in a quiet spot and sort of think about being there and presto--there you are."

"Just like that?" Rita exclaimed, "It's that simple?"

"Well, that's what I heard, " Robin nodded. "But I suppose there are people who sometimes prefer to get a little help."

"Help?"

"Yeah, you know, advice from people who have been there themselves. Or maybe information from things like books and tapes showing you how to get back and forth so you don't get lost or anything."

"Gee, that's interesting," Rita said slowing down for a red light. "I wouldn't mind looking at some of those things myself. I mean, I'm curious to know what the place is like. What it has to offer, if you know what I mean."

"Supposedly it's got something for everybody. Sort of like the ideal vacation spot in never-never land if you can picture that."

"Wow, that must be fantastic."

"Oh, it is. I'm sure."

"But I wonder what people do once they're there? I mean, since they don't have bodies or anything?"

"Oh, they just sort of float around, drifting here and there."

"But do they feel anything? I mean, are they awake or what?"

"Oh, they're awake, all right, and they feel really good. Sort of like flying, as I understand it."

"Flying?"

"Yeah, or getting stoned."

"Oh!"

"But others say it's like coming."

"Coming?" Rita exclaimed. You mean, coming as in coming?"

"That's right," Robin smiled. "Some people have even compared it to that."

"Wow," Rita said, gripping the steering wheel. "Then it must be wild."

"Oh, I'll say. Why else would anyone go there?"

The two women drove in silence for a while until they came to Dante's Inferno, an Italian restaurant specializing in home-grown mushrooms and garden fresh salads.

"God, if only I could picture the place a little better," Rita said, pulling over into an empty parking space. "Sometimes I have no imagination for that sort of thing."

"Oh, we'll be inside in another minute or so," Robin said. "You'll see it then."

"Oh, I don't mean the restaurant," Rita said. "I'm talking about the Astral Plane."

"Oh, that," Robin shrugged, "Well, we can go there too if you like. I mean, after we have something to eat. Right now I'm starving."

"Really?" Rita said. "You mean, we can go to the Astral Plane right this afternoon?"

"Sure, why not?" said Robin. "We've already gone shopping. We've nothing else to do."

***

By nightfall, they were ready. After purchasing a tape entitled "All Aboard: Your Round Trip Ticket To the Astral Plane" for $12.99 (Money

Back Guaranteed) from Allegro's Stationery and Office Supplies on Main Street, the two women returned to their apartment and began their preparations. Robin, who quickly took charge of the operation, insisted that they lock all the doors and windows and shut off all the lights before doing anything else.

"How come?" Rita asked. "What's the point of it?"

"The point is that while we're on the Astral Plane, our bodies will be right here on earth, alone and defenseless. We've got to protect them. Make sure they are safe. I mean, after all, you wouldn't want to come back and find out you were robbed or raped, would you?"

"God no," Rita shuddered. "That would be awful."

"And you certainly wouldn't want to miss any important telephone calls either, right?"

"Right," said Rita.

"Or television specials. Don't forget this is Friday night and we'll be gone during Prime Time."

"That's right," Rita nodded. "I had forgotten all about that. How stupid of me."

"So let's turn on the VCR and the answering machine, O.K.?"

"O.K.," Rita agreed, hurrying off to complete the task.

When she returned a few minutes later, Robin was kneeling in the middle of the bedroom floor, fooling around with the knobs of her portable stereo-cassette player.

"I guess we're almost ready," she said, glancing up at Rita.

"I guess," said Rita, squatting down next to her friend on the floor.

"Do you have any questions you want to ask me?"

"No," said Rita. "Not at the moment, but I'm sure I'll think of something once we're on the Astral Plane."

"We might not be together," Robin replied. "Sometimes people get separated."

"How? I thought you said everybody just floats around."

"Yeah, but from what I've heard it's a pretty big place. There are all kinds of levels and everything. I mean, we could get lost."

"Well, if that happens," Rita said. "I guess I'll just have to ask somebody else. It's no big deal."

"O.K., that's good," said Robin, beginning to make herself comfortable. "I guess we should get started then."

"O.K.," said Rita, rubbing her hands together excitedly. "I'm ready."

Robin cleared her throat.

"According to the little slip of paper that came with the tape there is absolutely nothing to worry about. All we have to do is sit back, relax and listen to the instructions while we joyfully explore the Astral Plane."

"Excuse me," Rita said, interrupting, "What instructions?"

"The instructions on the tape. What else?"

"But how can we listen to the instructions on the tape if we're on the Astral Plane?" Rita asked. "Won't the tape be here while we're up there?"

"I--I don't know," Robin said, slightly annoyed. "I guess we'll be able to hear it somehow."

"But how?" Rita asked. "We won't have any ears, remember? Our bodies will be down here."

"Look," Robin shrugged, "according to this little slip of paper, we'll be able to hear everything. O.K.?"

"You really think so?" asked Rita, looking somewhat skeptical. "I mean, I can't really see how you can hear without ears."

"Things are different on the Astral Plane," Robin said. "They got another whole set of rules up there."

"Really?"

"That's what I've heard. On the Astral Plane all you got to do is think something and--bingo--you got it."

"Honest? No questions asked?"

"None whatsoever."

"Well then," Rita said, "I guess we've got nothing to worry about, right?

"Right," Robin agreed, smiling.

"Well, O.K.," replied Rita. "In that case I guess we should get started again."

"O.K.," Robin said, reaching over to turn on the tape recorder. "Here goes."

There was a small click, then a long moment of silence. Both women waited expectantly, eyes closed.

"Greetings and Welcome," resounded a deep male voice.

Agnes, Robin's five-year old Siamese, scooted beneath the sofa bed, her tail thick as a skunk's.

"You are about to begin an incredible journey," the voice continued. "A voyage into the realm of the Astral, the Eternal, the Infinite. You will leave behind your fears, your doubts, your lower emotions and vibrations. All those things that belong to the frail human ego. You will lift out of your body and rise higher and higher toward that which is Real, that which is Truth, that which is Self. Now take a long, slow breath, hold, and follow my voice."

Rita and Robin inhaled loudly.

"Mentally count from eight to zero and then let go. Begin. Eight. . . seven. . . six. . . . "

Both women were holding and counting.

"Five. . . four. . . three. . . "

Rita was beginning to feel a bit dizzy; Robin was swaying slightly.

"Two. . . one. . . zero . . . "

Together, they exhaled in a loud burst and quickly sucked in more air."

"Good," the voice said. "Now that we're completely relaxed, we're about to ascend. To astrally project with our full and complete consciousness. To lift and separate ourselves from the container of our bodies."

Oh, boy, Rita thought. Here goes. Here goes.

"We are lifting," the voice continued, "higher and higher. Faster and faster. Surround yourself with the light, with the shield of protection so that no harm may come to you."

"Jesus!" Robin suddenly exclaimed. "Can you believe it? I think I'm getting my period."

"Higher. Faster. Into the tunnel. Into the light. Into the incredible, the unbelievable, the absolutely unforgettable Plane of the Astral."

Rita felt a sharp, sudden jolt, as if a small goat had come along and butted her. For one brief moment she felt as if she were being hurled head first into outer space. When she opened her eyes, she discovered to her amazement that she was standing on something that looked like a dirty penny or the surface of the moon surrounded by a thick impenetrable fog.

"Greetings and welcome," someone was saying, "Welcome to a whole new universe."

"Robin? she whispered, glancing around nervously. "Robin? Are you there? Can you hear me?"

69

"Shit," her friend shouted, from what seemed an immense distance. "Shit! Shit! Shit!"

"Robin," Rita began to cry, "Robin! Where are you?"

"This is awful," Robin was saying. "This is terrible."

"Robin," Rita continued to shout, "Robin!"

Strange white shapes began to swim round her eyes, hovering just beyond her head like dust clouds.

"Robin! Robin!"

"It's just no use," her friend was saying, "I can't concentrate. I've got to go to the bathroom."

"Robin! Hey, Robin!"

"We'll have to do it some other time."

Slowly, the fog around Rita's head began to lift, separate, and clear. Gradually, things began to take shape, come into focus. She saw Robin and someone who looked like herself kneeling on the floor of their bedroom, light-years away. From the corner of the room a deep, male voice was speaking:

"To return to the Earth all one need do is. . . "

She watched as Robin rose to her feet and began to walk toward the tape recorder.

"Sorry," Robin was saying as she clicked off the machine, "but it's no big deal, right? I mean, we can always do it again sometime, can't we?"+++++

THE WOMAN IN THE WALL

It was a beautiful day in early spring when Wanda Whitlock became stuck in her bedroom wall while practicing a series of seemingly harmless experiments from a little handbook entitled "Miracles of Mind Control."

A curious, but somewhat skeptical woman, Wanda had apparently been attempting to prove whether there was any validity to the claim that mind is a more powerful force than matter by mentally trying to project her consciousness and thus herself into and out of the wall.

Mid-way through the experiment, however, when Wanda was passing through the very center of the structure, something apparently went wrong, and, to her horror, she found herself trapped inside a thick slab of plaster that was pressed between an old oak beam and a sturdy four by four.

At first Wanda thought her imprisonment was just a temporary lapse of confidence on her part, a momentary lack of faith in her own powers of imagination and concentration, but as her arms and legs became more and more encased in the shell of plaster, she began to realize the seriousness of her situation.

This is awful, she had said to herself. Why, I feel like I have been buried alive.

And buried alive she was. Utterly unable to move or speak, trapped in total darkness, her face jammed up rudely against a wedge of rough wood, Wanda was sealed inside the plaster as securely as a candle wick lodged in a tub of wax.

If only Walter would come home, she thought, trying her best not to panic. He'd get me out of this mess. I know he would.

But since Walter was not expected home until later that evening, Wanda found it extremely difficult not to panic, despite the dire warnings in the opening chapter of her book.

Under no conditions should the mind ever resort to terror, the instructions had specified. Extreme care should be taken at all times to guard against any and all types of negative and debilitating reactions, such as fear, hysteria, acute anxiety, dementia praecox, temporary insanity, delirium tremens, etc., etc.

But since Wanda hadn't bothered to read the entire chapter, she was clearly at a loss on how not to panic under such terrible circumstances. Everything in her nature told her to panic. Her very being cried out for panic, especially when she considered that she might not be entirely alone inside the wall. Every so often she would hear strange little noises--scratchings, scurryings, hungry gnawings above her head, beneath her feet. Once or twice she even thought she felt something wet and furry brush past her leg.

I have to control myself or I'll go crazy, she thought. Maybe I should try some yoga or deep breathing. Perhaps that will calm me.

She knew from her other experiments in mind control that yoga and deep breathing were always recommended as ways of relaxing the body and calming the emotions during periods of stress, but as far as she could see, in her particular situation, yoga and deep breathing seemed out of the question. For one thing, she could barely breathe, let alone breathe deeply, and for another thing how on earth was she to do yoga when she couldn't even lift her finger?

I have to think of something, she told herself. I just can't stay locked inside of here forever.

She closed her eyes and tried to think.

I know, she said, after a few moments. I'll do what the first chapter in my Creative Visualization book recommended. I'll think positive thoughts and try to imagine a pleasant outcome to the problem.

She closed her eyes again and this time began to picture herself passing through the wall as smoothly as a oiled snake easing itself from beneath a clump of rock.

Yes, she said, thinking as many positive thoughts as she could muster, pretty soon I'll be standing right smack in the middle of my kitchen. Lovely warm sunlight will be streaming in softly from my big bay window. I'll sit down, make myself a nice cup of tea and--

She paused, her spine suddenly turning to ice. Did she or did she not shut off the gas burner from beneath the boiling tea kettle?

She couldn't remember. Good God, here she was stuck inside a wall with her kitchen possibly on fire and she couldn't remember.

Think, she told herself frantically, think.

She had fed the cat, she had emptied the garbage bin, she had watered the plants in the garden room, she had swept the porch, the patio, but she couldn't remember if she had ever returned to the kitchen to shut off the tea kettle.

Jesus, she said, sinking deeper into the plaster. This is horrible. Any minute now this house could go on fire and I could burn to death in here. I've got to remember.

But there was simply no memory inside her head. No picture of what had occurred in those few minutes just before she had entered the wall. Had she shut off the damn stove or not? Her mind was as foggy as the bottom of a dirty milk glass.

No wonder I'm stuck inside this place, she moaned. My mind is a dud! A complete failure. Why, it can't even remember a simple thing like whether or not I shut off a lousy stinking stove. Why, I must have been a fool to think it would stay focused long enough for me to get in and out of a goddamn wall.

She sighed. It was the same old story, over and over again. No matter how hard she tried or how many times she worked at her exercises, her mind was as unreliable as a horse in heat, galloping off for a romp in the woods.

Even now, in fact, when it was absolutely essential for her to concentrate, her thoughts were crashing like noisy billiard balls in the raw pocket of her brain. If only she could control them somehow.

Maybe I should try meditating, she thought, fighting for calm. Maybe that would help.

Slowly, painfully she began counting backwards from 1,000.
999, 998, 997.

By the time she reached 832, however, she thought she heard something that sounded like her front door shutting.

That's funny, she said to herself. Could that possibly be Walter?

She longed to cry out, but her mouth was sealed tightly with the plaster.

Heavy footsteps began passing back and forth in the hallway outside her wall.

That must be Walter, she thought. It has to be Walter. I knew he would save me. I knew everything would work out just fine. Now the house will be safe, I'll be rescued and everything will--

73

"Looks like the coast is clear, Lou," said a man's voice from the other side of Wanda's wall. "What do you think?"

"Looks pretty good to me, Joe," Lou replied. "No dogs, no neighbors, nobody home. Maybe we finally struck it lucky for a change."

Wanda could hardly believe her ears. Was it possible? Were there really two men in her house or was it just her mind playing tricks again?

"Think the family's on vacation or something?" Lou asked.

"Who knows?" said Joe. "Nowadays people can be anywhere."

I'm not imagining it, Wanda thought. There are two men in my house. But where on earth did they come from and what do they want?"

"Well, where should we start?" Lou asked. "The bedroom, the living room, the den?"

"Let's start here," Joe said. I'll check out the stereo.

and the T.V. You go through all the drawers. You might run across a couple of credit cards."

"Good idea," replied Lou.

Credit cards? Wanda thought. What in heaven's name would those men want with credit cards?

"Hey, Joe, what do you think of this camera."

"What kind is it?"

'Cannon."

"Grab it," Joe said.

Wanda tried to stay calm. She tried to think positive thoughts.

Well, at least now maybe the house won't burn down, she told herself. After all, even if the kettle is on, I'm sure one of those men will have enough sense to shut it off.

"Hey, this T.V. is a lot heavier than I thought. You wanna gimme a hand here, Lou?"

"You think that thing works?" Lou asked. "It looks kinda old."

"I donno," said Joe. "What do you say we try it and see."

"O.K." Lou replied. "Maybe there's something interesting on now. "

They clicked on the set. A woman's soft voice came drifting through the wall toward Wanda.

"Hey, what do you know?" Joe said. That's Marcia on All My Children. I like that show."

"Me too," said Lou. But I haven't seen it for a while. Do you know what's been happening?"

"Yeah," Joe replied. "The last time I tuned in, Marcia there found out that she was pregnant by this guy named Tony, and so she got this abortion, and then she met this dude named Maurice who--"

This is incredible, Wanda thought. Why, it sounds like those two men are about to watch television.

"Pretty good picture, wouldn't you say?" asked Joe.

"Not bad," said Lou. "Could use a little more blue though."

"Yeah, I agree," Joe replied. "Marcia's eyes are usually a little darker than that."

"Hey, you feel like a beer, by any chance?" Lou asked as he plopped down on the sofa.

Wanda could hear the springs squeal.

"Yeah, that would be very nice," Joe said, dragging something heavy across the floor. "You relax. I'll check out the fridge. Maybe there's a few cold ones in there."

"Great," said Lou. "And if you don't mind, see if there's something we can eat. I'm starving."

"Righto."

Joe's footsteps disappeared down the hall.

Walter is going to be very angry about this, Wanda thought. Very angry indeed.

"Oh, Maurice," said a woman's voice from across the room. "Who would have ever dreamed it would be like this?"

"Darling," Maurice replied, his French accent as heavy as the darkness surrounding Wanda. "You don't know how long I've waited for this moment. You're everything I've ever wanted. You're beautiful, you're lovely, you're. . "

"Hey, Joe," Lou called out, "Hurry up, you're missing all the good stuff. This dame Marcia's about to have all her clothes ripped off."

Moments later Wanda heard footsteps racing back into the room.

"God, what a doll!" Lou sighed. "What knockers!"

Wanda heard two sharp pops.

"A couple of buds and some nice cold chicken coming right up. That should tide us over for a while, right?"

"Great," laughed Lou. "It looks delicious."

Walter's chicken, Wanda thought. Those two men are eating Walter's chicken.

"I looked all over for the salt, but I couldn't find any," Joe said. "I hope this is O.K.?"

"It's fine," said Lou. "I never use salt anyway. I got high blood pressure, remember?"

"No fooling? I didn't know that," Joe said. "You look healthy to me."

"Thanks," said Lou. "I feel pretty good, knock wood."

Wanda heard three short knocks.

I can't believe this, she said. Those men are actually sitting out there eating my husband's chicken.

"God, talk about a good-looking woman," Joe said, choking on a swig of beer. "That Marcia is a real knock out, huh?"

"I sure as hell wouldn't throw her out of my bed," Lou agreed. "No siree. She can lay her head down on my pillow anytime she likes."

Wanda's mind began darting back and forth like some small, frightened animal startled from its sleep.

If she didn't stop those men from eating that chicken, there would be nothing left of Walter's supper.

"Boy, oh, boy," she heard Joe say. "This is finger-licking good, isn't it?"

"The best," replied Lou. "My compliments to the chef, wherever he may be."

One of the men began sucking on a bone.

"Geez, wouldn't you just love a nice hot plate of french fries now?" Joe asked.

"Yeah," said Lou. "Why, I'd give my--"

"Hey," Wanda heard Joe shout. "What the hell is going on? What happened to Marcia?"

"I donno," Lou said, his mouth full. "The damn picture got all cloudy all of a sudden."

"Try shaking the box," Joe said. "Maybe a wire or something got loose."

Wanda heard several loud thumps.

"Must be a bum set after all," Lou said, pounding it with both his fists.

There was a sharp crack, like a light bulb exploding.

"Jesus, pull the plug," Joe said. "Pull the plug! This damn thing is smoking like hell."

Something burst, then began to sizzle.

"Christ, what a mess!" Joe said. "Look at this thing."

"The rug's all burned."

"Talk about a piece of shit."

"Good thing we didn't decide to lug it out to the truck, right?"

"Yeah, but now we won't know what happens to Marcia."

"We still got time," Lou said. "Maybe we could hit another house before the show ends and watch it there."

"Hey, that's a real good idea," said Joe. "Now you're using your head. Before we split, though, let's grab the beer and the rest of the chicken. And, oh, yeah, we might as well take along the camera, the stereo and the V.C.R. too. I mean, just as long as we had to go to so much trouble and all."

Wanda listened as the men began moving back and forth in the living room. Moments later the front door slammed and the house grew silent again.

Jesus, she thought, talk about rudeness. I sure am glad they're gone. Wait till I tell Walter about this.

She sighed. Poor Walter. He'd have to eat an omelet now, and he hated omelets. But there was nothing else left in the house.

If I could just get out of this damn wall, she thought. If I could just concentrate. Then maybe I could get to the butcher's and buy Walter a nice steak or maybe a nice piece of pot roast. Walter loves pot roast.

To calm herself, she began meditating again, this time counting backwards from 2,000. 1,999, 1,998, 1,997--

***

Wanda meditated all afternoon, but she was still stuck inside the wall when Walter arrived home later that evening.

Oh, God, she thought, hearing his key turn in the door. I can't believe it! He's here. He's finally here!

She heard the door click shut.

"Honey? I'm home."

She listened as Walter walked down the hallway toward the living room.

Walter! she longed to cry out. In here. I'm in here. But her voice was as silent as a tomb.

"Honey? Where are you? Are you there?

Walter's footsteps suddenly stopped dead.

"Holy Christ! What the hell--"

All at once she heard him running across the room. Something crashed to the floor.

"Hello! Operator? Get me the police. That's right. The police. This is an emergency."

She could hear Walter's labored breathing. He seemed very upset.

Relax, darling, she tried to tell him. Everything's going to be all right now. Just take a nice deep breath and relax.

"Hello! Police? This is Walter Whitlock. 209 Colinwood Lane. I'm calling to report a robbery. Yeah, that's right, my house."

Close your eyes and count to ten, dear. One—two--

"No, of course I wasn't here. I just got in. But you wanna see this place. There's stuff all over. I think they might have even broken my television set."

Three—four--

"And my camera and stereo. They're gone."

Five--six--

"And, oh, yeah, my wife. She's gone too. I looked all over, but I don't know where she is."

Seven—eight--

"Well, yeah, it's true she does take off from time to time, but not usually at this hour."

Nine--

"Well, maybe, but I really don't know why anyone would want to kidnap her. I mean, we're not wealthy people or anything like that."

Ten!

"Yeah, well, O.K., thanks, Officer. I'll be waiting for the squad car."

Walter slammed down the phone. He began walking back and forth across the room.

"Of all the damn, rotten times--"

Oh, the poor man, Wanda thought. He's still upset. I guess I'm still not doing those exercises correctly.

She heard Walter pick up the phone again. He was still breathing pretty heavily.

"Hello," Wanda heard him say. "Lucille? This is Walt. Look, there's been a problem. I don't think I can make it tonight. My house has just been robbed."

Lucille? Wanda thought. Who was Lucille?

"No, I ain't pulling your leg. Really, I'm serious. There's stuff all over the place and my wife is missing."

I'm not missing, Walter. I'm here. Right here.

"No, I have no idea where she could be. Yes, of course, I'd rather be with you, sweetheart, but what can I do? Right now I got the cops coming. I gotta stick around. But look, I'll see you tomorrow, O.K.? We'll meet at the--"

Wanda's heart began to beat, softly at first, then harder and louder, like tiny fists pounding against a plaster moon.

To calm herself, she began counting again, this time starting with zero and making her way upward.+++++

THE ANGEL IN THE NIGHTIE

One night shortly after Marcia arrived home from work, she entered her bedroom, kicked off her shoes, and discovered to her acute amazement an enormous angel standing in her clothes closet wearing her prettiest see-thru nightie.

The angel's gossamer wings, soft and lovely as a butterfly's, rose gracefully from out the tiny armholes of the gown, trembling and fluttering like flower petals in the first burst of spring warmth.

I must be hallucinating, Marcia thought, taking a step backwards and stumbling over her fallen shoes. I can't possibly be seeing what I'm seeing.

The angel, whose fine feathered pinions were the most beautiful part of its anatomy, was almost ten feet tall and entirely too stout for the delicate nightie. Great chunks of its glowing flesh hung out shamefully in numerous places where the flimsy garment had torn in the process of being fitted over the gargantuan head and torso.

Dangling precariously from the angel's extremely large toes--almost the size of full-length sausages--were Marcia's favorite pair of high heels, the black velvet ones she had bought in Rio the summer before.

Atop the angel's head was Marcia's auburn wig, dangerously askew and shaggy as a sheepdog.

Marcia closed her eyes and tried to think. There was no reason in the world why an angel should be standing in her clothes closet, wearing her nightie, her high heels and her auburn wig. It just didn't make sense, especially since Marcia didn't even believe in angels. She had to be hallucinating.

After taking a deep breath, she reopened her eyes. The angel was still there, staring and blinking at her like the North Star, its wings glowing and dipping among the coat hangers.

Even if I am hallucinating, Marcia continued, why would I ever imagine an angel who looked like that?

Except for the wings which were utterly spell- binding, it was a perfectly absurd angel. It was so bulky and hairy it looked more like a gorilla than a celestial being.

Vaguely, Marcia recalled her catechism teacher, Sister Grace Catherine, a grey-faced woman in a long black gown smeared with chalk stains, telling her class that angels were as transparent and sexless as the inside of light bulbs.

But the angel standing in front of Marcia now--if that's what it was- looked more like a light pole than a light bulb. And it was far from sexless. Except for the fact that it was wearing Marcia's nightie, wig and heels, it looked unmistakably like a man, a very big and bizarre man, but clearly a man. Beneath the thin gauze of the nightie lay all the evidence of maleness: chunky thighs, fleshy hips, overhanging beer belly. Marcia paused.

Were there such things as transvestite angels?

While she puzzled over this question, the angel, meanwhile, was doing his best to escape by attempting to slip through the closet's rear wall. Never before in the eons of his existence had he felt so humiliated. To be caught red-handed in a human female's bedroom closet was simply horrendous. In fact, not since the days of his first fall had he ever felt so low. The only thing left, as far as he was concerned, was to get away as quickly as possible and hope for mercy. However, when he attempted to pass through the plywood wall, only his wings fit. The rest of him was left behind, stuck and wiggling like some half-squashed bug on a patch of flypaper.

Teary-eyed, he pulled himself back together, and considered the situation. If he was losing his power--and that was only to be expected under the circumstances--he had to act quickly. He took a deep breath and began flapping his wings up and down, back and forth like some half-crazed buzzard trapped in a mud hole, but for all his efforts he managed to raise himself only a few inches before falling against a shelf of shoes and coat hangers.

The loud crash, however, succeeded in bringing Marcia back to her senses. She looked down at the floor and saw the angel--his left wing jammed awkwardly between her orange raincoat and her low-cut burgundy dress--entangled in a mess of broken heels and twisted soles.

Marcia took a step forward and touched the top of the angel's head, which, save for a few thin hairs, was almost bald now that the wig was gone. It felt hard as a cue ball. Then she reached out and placed two fingers lightly upon the angel's right wing which was hanging limply in mid-air like a long-abandoned cocoon or the cast-off web of a fallen spider.

The shock went through her like a bolt of lightening. Without warning she began to spin round and round like a terrible tornado in a pink swirling sky.

By the time the angel had untangled himself, working his way free from the shoes and coat hangers, Marcia was already mid-way through the ceiling, and half-way onto the roof, but it wasn't until she was back in the bedroom lying safely at a distance from the angel that she finally stopped spinning.

"If I didn't know better," she said, looking at him from across the bed, "I'd think you were real."

The angel, his heart half-broken with grief, dropped his head in sorrow. Would trouble never end for him? It seemed to follow him about the universe like some dark shadow or spiteful gremlin come to wreck havoc on his dusty soul. In his worse moments he swore the gods were out to get him, to clip his wings and root him like a tree trunk into a pile of senseless dirt. Probably they were watching him now, grinning like fools and basking in contempt.

Except for the bed sheet he had managed to wrap around his waist after shedding the nightgown, he was stark naked. Shyly, he glanced at the woman in the bed whose eyes were running up and down his great wide wings.

In spite of my strangeness, I think she finds me fascinating, he mused, glancing at her again. She was so small and fine, so very delicate like the lovely rainbows he had seen over the Grand Canyon. It's no wonder her clothes are so pretty, he thought, shamefully avoiding her gaze at his memory of her red satin slip and silk lacy petticoat. She's more beautiful than a burning star.

Oh, what a boor he had been, wings or no wings. To sin against such a creature was unspeakable. He deserved to be ice-picked, or plucked until he screamed for mercy.

Still, compared to what other angels had done in their time, he supposed his offense hadn't been that bad. Pilfering a few slips and dresses here and there was, after all, relatively harmless, and besides he always saw to it that he left behind more than he took anyway.

As everyone who was in the business knew, being an angel was no easy task and those who were willing to do it deserved some compensation. But not once had he ever used the full extent of his powers unfairly upon an unsuspecting female. Besides the sheer immorality of the act, there was the utter impracticality of it. Human women, as everybody knew--exquisite as they were--were simply too fragile to tolerate the full affections of a passionate angel. Although that was one of the real tragedies of the universe, as he saw it, it was also something that couldn't be ignored except at the risk of disaster. Thus, he had been forced to content himself over the years with touching, smelling and, sometimes, pocketing the trappings of these women: their most intimate and secret apparel where the tantalizing afterglow of their perfume and the warm radiance of their earthiness lingered like moon-dust atop a light beam.

Not everyone shared his feelings, however. After his first mission, when he returned home with a bagful of bras and corsets, he had been demoted two full steps and assigned nothing but graveyard duty for three whole centuries. Although everyone had believed he had learned his lesson, he alone seemed to remember that old habits die hard.

And now, here he was again, with most of his power quickly fading, and his poor self a fraction of what it had been--fat, old and bald-- sitting, bare-ass and half-dead, at the foot of some nice lady's bed, waiting for his wings to fall off and his heart to turn to stone.

He took another peek at the woman who was still staring fixedly at his wings. She appeared to be in something of a trance, not uncommon, he supposed, after her strange journey upward. He wished he could say or do something that might comfort her, but he didn't want to make things any worse. There was simply no way of ever telling how a human would react once an angel shot off his mouth.

For now he'd let her believe what she was thinking anyway--that he wasn't an angel at all, but only some weird figment of her imagination come from out the blue to tease and confuse her.

He glanced around the room. Except for the torn nightie, the broken shoe rack, the smashed hangers, and the hole in the roof there was little evidence of his presence. Certainly nothing like the time he left behind a dozen of his feathers at that YWCA in downtown Boston.

If all went well, perhaps, by morning, after a good night's sleep, she would have forgotten, or thought she had imagined everything. Which is how things usually worked on earth anyway.

Tucking the blanket carefully beneath her chin, the angel rose quietly from Marcia's bed and walked toward the window in the nearby dining room. Perhaps once he hit the air his wings would start working again. If they didn't, well, the drop down was certainly not as bad as others he had already experienced.

He flexed his legs to get some circulation going, touched his toes twice, then hoisted himself up onto the window sill. However, by the time he had begun flapping his wings for take-off, Marcia was standing in the doorway, screaming. She was quite hysterical, in fact, running up and down and pulling out her hair like a crazy woman. The angel, badly shaken by her behavior, forgot where he was, lost his balance and fell backwards, striking his head against the china closet and sending it toppling to the floor.

Screaming "No, no, no!" at the top of her lungs, Marcia--her face grey as ash, her eyes the color of lead—flew over the mess of shattered plates and cups, and flung herself before the window, her arms outstretched like a crucified Madonna.

"You. . . You," she wailed, gazing down at the quivering prostrate angel whose wings were now crumbled beneath him. "You cannot do this. No! I won't let you. It's sick. Sick."

Directly above her head through the new hole in the roof giant stars sharp as lions' teeth smiled down at her.

"All those hours, all that money to all those shrinks," she muttered on and on, "And not once, not once was there any mention of an angel committing suicide."

Startled, the angel sat upright. Was he hearing correctly or had his ears begun to fail him too? Did this woman actually say something about suicide? Did she think that just because he had stood on her window sill he was going to try and kill himself? What about his wings? Had she forgotten them? Didn't she know it was impossible for an angel to kill himself?

He sat there thinking, perched among the jagged edges of glass. To her he wasn't really an angel. Well, in that case, what was he then? Did she really see him only as part of herself? Was that why she had become so upset? The thought made him dizzy. Its implications were staggering.

Even if this strange woman did believe him to be only a part of herself, it was clear that she had cared enough about him to try and save him from disaster. Obviously that was why she had run toward the window and now stood blocking it with her outstretched arms. She was afraid he'd try a second time. Afraid of what it might mean to them both.

Overwhelmed by the magnitude of this thought, the angel found himself speechless. Never before had such a marvelous thing happened to him. Never before had a human creature actually interfered in his fate. For centuries it had always been the other way around--with him in charge of saving people. No wonder the pressure had been a bit too much at times. But now here he was, sitting in a sea of broken glass at the feet of this remarkable woman, overwhelmed by emotions he had never felt before, awestruck by the mysteries of creation. It was enough to make him want to fly to paradise and back nine eternities without stopping. Enough to make him start believing in miracles again.

Lifting himself slowly off the floor, he dusted off his rumpled wings, raised his ancient eyes skyward and headed straight for Marcia's open arms. +++++

THE MIRACLE OF THE MOUSE

Thelma Peckingwood's life took a drastic change on the day she met God in the laundry room. She had been down in the basement of her four-story tenement separating the whites from the pastels when out of nowhere she heard someone call her name.

"Thelma," the voice said. "Thelma Peckingwood?"

Startled, she leaped almost two feet into the air, convinced that some creep had come wandering in off the street to attack her. When she glanced around, however, no one was there.

"I guess I imagined it," she shrugged, tossing a pair of yellow socks into one of the dryers.

Seconds later, however, she heard the voice again.

"Thelma," it called, "Thelma Peckingwood. Are you listening? Can you hear me?"

"Who--who's there?" she cried, grabbing hold of her king-size green and white bedspread and pressing it up against her chest like a shield.

"What . . . . what do you want?"

"I want to tell you something very important, Thelma," the voice continued. "Something that you must know."

"Who--who are you?" Thelma asked again, gazing around the damp, shadowy cellar with large frightened eyes. "How do you know my name?"

"Oh, I know a lot about you, Thelma," the voice said. "I'm God and I know everything."

"God?" Thelma shuddered, her brain spinning as fast as the fine washables in the nearby Maytags. "God who?"

"God! You know, the maker and . . . "

"Look, Mister," Thelma interrupted, her whole body trembling like the last leaf on a wind-blown autumn tree, "I don't know where you came from or what you want, or where you are for that matter, but you better leave me alone because my husband is right down the hall."

"Now, now, Thelma," the voice said, "Don't fib. We both know Leo is at work. He called you a little while ago to complain about the baloney sandwich you made him this morning, remember? He said the bread was moldy."

"How--how did you know that?" Thelma gasped, taking several steps backwards until she was wedged between the trash bin and the soap dispenser.

"I already told you," the voice said patiently. "I'm God. God knows everything, remember?"

Thelma began to open her mouth but to her amazement nothing came out.

"Look, relax," the voice continued. "No one's going to hurt you and this will only take a minute. Nowadays I learned to dispense with the theatrics. There will be no angels. No trumpets, no burning bushes, nothing of that sort. I'm just here to pass along some simple information. Something I thought you should know."

Thelma froze, her brain tumbling in wild disarray like her cotton panties and Maidenform bras in the sudsy water of a nearby washer.

"From this day forward, doubt the truth of all human existence. The secret to one of life's greatest mysteries."

"Me?" Thelma gasped, her eyes widening like those of cat cornered by a monstrous German Shepherd. Without warning all the washers and dryers came to an abrupt halt.

"Yes, Thelma, that's right. You. You are about to learn that reality--what you call your world--is nothing more than a bundle of infinitely malleable energy controlled and manipulated by your ever-changing thoughts.

Thelma was about to reply when she felt something press against her left foot. When she looked down, she saw a small white mouse perched atop the lattice of her white laces, nibbling happily at her long blue and green sock.

"Thelma, the universe has blessed you. Bear in mind the great responsibility that this knowledge brings, and always remember that you are the maker and creator of your world. Your thoughts, be they great or small, are the stuff that holds you together--the magic from which reality is made!"

With that, all the washers and dryers suddenly kicked on again and the voice of God disappeared into the slosh of spinning water and whirling hot air.

"Wait!" Thelma cried, shaking her left foot wildly. "Don't go. I—I don't understand. Do you hear me? I don't understand."

But despite all of Thelma's cries, the voice of God did not reply.

Alone in the damp cellar with a small white mouse atop her foot, Thelma Peckingwood was like someone whose brain had been wired and then short-circuited. At first all she could do was scream and shake her leg like someone whose foot was on fire. Then she threw herself down on the floor and began to roll back and forth like some pathetic dog with a giant flea in its ear. Finally, after a brief period of hysterics in which she tore out great clumps of her hair and swore bloody roses, she attempted to knock the creature free by slamming her leg against one of the nearby washers. Exhausted and hopelessly unsuccessful, she sat back to catch her breath, when, to her utter amazement, she caught sight of the small white mouse turning into a beautiful red rose right before her very eyes. Her first reaction naturally, as she stared down at the soft satiny petals, was that she was hallucinating. But just as her hand was about to touch the long, prickly stem of the flower, the blood-red rose turned back into the snow-white mouse.

"This can't be happening," she insisted, her whole body shaking. "It's much too crazy, too bewildering!" Almost immediately the mouse became a huge question mark, three times the size of Thelma's foot. Thelma's whole body quaked as the voice of God once again rang through the laundry room.

"Thelma? Thelma Peckingwood? Can you hear me? It's me again. God."

"Please, " Thelma cried, her eyes hollow as the inside of a Halloween pumpkin. "Help me. I--I can't take this anymore. I don't know what's happening and I'm--I'm going crazy."

"I know," God said rather apologetically. "But don't feel bad because it's all my fault. You see, I forgot to tell you about Moses."

"Moses?" Thelma cried. "Moses who?"

"Moses, the mouse," God said. "I completely forgot to mention him."

"What about him?" Thelma asked, watching in horror as the huge question mark on her toe began to metamorphose first into a long whitetail and then into the body and head of Moses the mouse.

"I forgot to tell you that Moses is a gift," God said, his voice light as a raindrop. "He's my way of showing you as clearly as I can the truth of what we were discussing just a short time ago."

"Please," Thelma cried, grabbing hold of her head. "I'm going crazy. I can't take this anymore. I don't know what you're talking about."

"I know," God said, obviously amused. "Not many people do, but that's no reason to get upset. Not until I tell you about Moses. You see, it's very important that you know this stuff."

"I don't want to know anything," Thelma said. "Just leave me alone."

"Moses is part of you, Thelma. Understand? Whatever you think, Moses becomes. It's as simple as that. You think a rose, he becomes a rose. You think a mouse, he's a mouse. You ask a question, he becomes—"

Thelma's head shot up straight as a rocket.

"A--a question mark?" she gasped.

"That's right," God replied. "Looks like you're finally catching on."

"But--but that's incredible," Thelma cried. "It's--it's impossible."

"Nonsense," God said. "Nothing is impossible once you think it."

Thelma looked down at Moses who was wiggling happily on her toe. Hesitating only slightly, she closed her eyes and began to think very hard. Within seconds Moses metamorphosed into a beautiful rainbow whose bright colors lit up the entire laundry room.

"Why, it's--it's a miracle," Thelma cried, gazing down at the glorious colors shining from her left foot. " My thoughts have created a miracle!"

"Well, from your point of view I suppose it is a miracle," God said. "But from where I'm coming from, well, it's really just a perfectly explainable law of the universe. And it doesn't just affect mice. It affects everything."

"Everything?" Thelma exclaimed. "Everything in the world? Not just Moses?"

Instantly, Moses reappeared, his nose twitching like a bunny rabbit's.

"That's right," God said. "Moses is really just a prop. A metaphor, if you will, to explain the principle."

Thelma's brain reeled. From that moment on she became a changed woman, a creature transfigured. By the incredible cosmic power of her own brain she would create miracles in her life and reshape the universe. The future would be hers. She would have fame, fortune, untold happiness. She would transform Leo, her husband, into the handsome lover with the green eyes, cleft chin and wavy black hair she had always secretly desired. They would dance under the moonlight and run naked through the wet grass of their paradisiacal French mansion set high atop the sea-kissed cliffs of romantic Etretat in Normandy. Every night they would swoon for hours in each other's arms, pulsing with pleasure, their hearts aflame with wild, uncontrollable passion. Her double chins and flabby thighs would vanish, and before Leo's unbelieving, grateful eyes, she would become the envy of Venus herself. Such were her thoughts as she said good-bye to God late that afternoon and climbed the stairs to her apartment with Moses atop her toe. But no sooner did Thelma open the door and step into her apartment when Leo, home earlier than usual from work and spying the mouse atop his wife's foot, let loose with a terrified scream, and lunged for her instep

"Stop!" Thelma cried, taken completely by surprise. "What are you doing?"

"There's--there's a mouse on your foot," Leo screamed, grabbing hold of the poor creature and wringing its sweet, little white neck. "A dirty, filthy varmint!"

Thelma was so shocked she forgot all about the wondrous powers lurking within her cosmic brain. Instead, she began to hammer the top of her husband's bald head with the bottom of her laundry basket.

"Leave Moses alone," she cried. "Do you hear me? Let him alone."

"Moses?" Leo cried, completely flabbergasted. "Moses who?"

"Moses the Mouse!" Thelma wailed, picking up the poor creature and stroking it gently. "Proof that I am the maker and creator of my own reality!"

"Have you gone crazy?" Leo cried, grabbing his wife by the shoulders and shaking her. "What the hell's the matter with you?"

"Nothing's the matter with me," she said, shrugging off Leo's big hands. "But poor Moses is half-dead. I must concentrate."

"Concentrate?" Leo asked. "Concentrate on what?"

"On my thoughts," Thelma replied. "I must think Moses well again."

Leo watched in mounting terror as his wife held the half-dead mouse in the palm of her left hand.

"Rise!" she wailed over and over. "Rise and heal thyself."

Ironically, it was at the very moment when Leo decided to sneak away and call for help from the local psychiatric hospital that the power of Thelma's thought finally managed to awaken Moses from his stupor and transform him into the lovely bunch of yellow daffodils that she sat holding when Leo reentered the room.

"Where--where's the mouse?" Leo asked, looking quite perplexed as he gazed all around. "Where did he go?"

"Here!" Thelma replied, smiling down happily at the pretty, glowing daffodils. "It's quite a miracle, isn't it?

While Leo sat holding his wife's hand, waiting anxiously for the doctors to arrive, Thelma told him all about her day: how she first heard the voice of God in the laundry room and how she slowly came to realize that the miracle of the mouse was living proof that thought affects reality. In fact, so caught up was Thelma in her story that she was rather surprised when Leo quietly got up to open the door to the three large men in white coats who very softly tiptoed into the room and surrounded her.

"Nice flowers, lady," she heard one of the men say.

"Why, thank you," Thelma replied, smiling proudly as she cradled her daffodils. "I made them myself, you know." +++++

EVERYTHING THAT ENDS MUST BEGIN

Jennifer Grogan sat motionless before her type- writer, her fingers resting gently upon the cold keys.

Since five o'clock that morning she had been waiting patiently for Flannery O'Connor to come down and help her. Now, three hours later, she was still waiting, with no sign of Miss O'Connor anywhere in sight.

Jennifer wondered what she had done wrong. As far as she was concerned, she had followed all the instructions to the letter just as her books had advised.

She had relaxed her body from the top of her head to the tips of her toes by inhaling and exhaling and counting backwards from one thousand; she had closed her eyes and pictured herself floating peacefully upon a fluffy white cloud; and she had opened her heart and mind to the universe by releasing all her negative energy and imagining herself a single white rose in the blue breeze of cosmic consciousness.

What's more, she had written for over two hours in her notebook, "Visualization Techniques For a More Creative You," she had listened to her tape "Getting in Touch With Your Higher Selves," and she had read and done all the suggested exercises in her guidebook "How to Become a Literary Genius in 30 Days or Else."

But still, there was no trace of Flannery O'Connor. Jennifer just couldn't understand it. Where the hell could she be? What could have possibly gone amiss?

To calm herself, Jennifer closed her eyes and began to meditate on the left and right hemispheres of her brain. She knew they needed to be in perfect balance before Flannery or anyone in the spiritual world could make contact. All her books had insisted on that.

"An unbalanced brain is a deterrent to successful communication with any of the higher realities," she had read. "An unbalanced brain becomes a pernicious maze in which higher consciousnesses may become lost and disoriented."

Jennifer tried not to panic. If Flannery O'Connor had gotten lost somewhere inside her brain, which Jennifer knew was anything but balanced, certainly she would be smart enough to find her way out again. After all, she had found her way out of worse things than Jennifer Grogan's brain, and besides, Flannery O'Connor was an expert on unbalanced brains. How else could she have written all those stories about misfits and perverts and Bible salesmen who went around shooting people and stealing their wooden legs if she hadn't understood and appreciated what an unbalanced brain was?

Jennifer knew it was all just a question of faith, of having confidence in one's own abilities, which is why she had chosen Flannery in the first place to be her muse and mentor out of all the great writers who had died and gone off to other dimensions. If anyone could give Jennifer confidence, and at the same time teach her to write, Flannery O'Connor could.

Except for talent, they had a lot in common, Jennifer believed. For one thing, they were both women and although Flannery came from central Georgia and she, Jennifer, came from northern Hoboken, they were still daughters of the American soil with a passion for truth and the written word. The only major difference as far as Jennifer could see was that Flannery O'Connor knew how to get her words down on paper while she, Jennifer, had to sweat wart-hogs just to complete a goddamn sentence. But that was all about to change now. Once she finally made contact with Flannery O'Connor, and their energy levels connected, Jennifer's days as an incompetent, inarticulate artist would be over. Words and ideas and sentences would pour down from the heavens like manna to the starving, and Jennifer would find herself going forth for the millionth time to encounter the reality of experience and to forge in the smithy of her soul the uncreated conscience of her race.

In the meantime, however, Jennifer knew she had to concentrate on the practical. She knew she had to locate Flannery O'Connor and find out what the hell was going on. She took a deep breath and began to type.

"Flannery O'Connor, this is Jennifer Grogan, author of "Rainbows in the Toilet," and "Reflections on a Dead Dog in a Hoboken Tenement." Can you hear me? Are you out there?"

She lifted her hands and waited. Nothing. Not even an aura. At the very least she had expected a voice, a flash of lightening, a pale shadow hovering above her hands, pushing her fingers across the keyboard, but instead she heard nothing, nothing except Spooky, her cat, scratching furiously in the litter box. It was incomprehensible.

She was simply baffled. According to everything she had read, she and Flannery O'Connor should have been half way through their first novel together.

Jennifer shoved back her chair and stood up, her arms at her side. Obviously this was a test of some kind; the type of thing Flannery loved to inflict on her characters. In fact, she was probably watching Jennifer right at that very moment, studying her the way she had studied the Grandmother just before the Misfit shot her, or poor Mrs. May just before that big ugly old bull came charging at her from across the pasture.

It was just the kind of trick Flannery liked to pull. Making believe everything was smooth as molasses and then dropping her poor, unsuspecting characters right smack into a circle of fire, face to face with the devil himself. No wonder she had died at 39. If she had hung on any longer, one of her characters would have come back and killed her.

Well, be that as it may, Jennifer was ready for her. If judgment day was at hand, she would rise up and converge with the best of them and prove to Flannery that she, Jennifer Grogan, despite all her rejection slips and unpublished stories, was worth every inch of her typewriter ribbon. Inspired, she sat back down and began to write.

***

Dear Ms. O'Connor

As you yourself once said, "You Can't be Any Poorer than Dead," so as far as I'm concerned you have got nothing to lose by coming down here and sharing a few of your fine literary ideas with a fellow writer like myself who still happens to be alive but suffering terribly from a bad case of stupidity. As you may no doubt remember from composing your truly great masterpiece, "The Life You Save May Be Your Own," no man is an island unto himself and he who helps others less gifted than himself wisely sows his own salvation.

With that in mind please realize that I am not asking for much. Just a few good sentences and images here and there and a couple of really colorful characters like Francis Marion Tarwater who got too drunk to finish digging his uncle's grave, or maybe Hulga Hopewell, the Ph.D.

who thought she knew everything and wound up losing one of her legs in a hay loft to a nutty Bible salesman.

According to all the books I am currently reading, you, as a highly creative energy awareness on the astral plane, should be more than willing to help.

However, if you do have any doubts as to my sincerity or artistic integrity, please remember that both our mothers were crazy and Roman Catholic and that both their names began with the letter R and ended with the long vowel--A--.

Yours truly,

J.G.

***

Jennifer carefully removed the letter from the carriage of her typewriter, folded it, and walked over to the window of her second floor tenement on Fourth and Adams Street in downtown Hoboken.

"May this affirmation be carried by the winds of Prana to the sacred Purusha of Flannery O'Connor."

With that, she opened the window, and began ripping the letter into dozens of tiny pieces, flinging them skyward.

"Hey, what the hell is goin' on, Lady? You think this is New Year's Eve or somethin'?"

It was the U.P.S. man standing in front of his truck. He was holding a clipboard and pushing a large cumbersome box wrapped in filthy green tissue paper and tied with a big red bow.

"Sorry," Jennifer smiled. "I didn't see you there."

"Didn't see me? What's the matter? You blind or somethin'? I've been struggling with this goddamn thing for over twenty minutes."

"I was releasing my invocations."

"Well, that's very nice, but would you also mind releasing the lock on your front door so I can shove this thing in?"

"Is it for me?"

"This is 401 Adams Street, isn't it? And you're J.Q. Grogan, right?"

"Yes."

"Well, this is yours then."

"But I didn't order anything."

Jennifer paused. Flannery? Was it possible? Had she finally made contact with Flannery O'Connor?"

She turned and ran down the steps to the tenement's front door, swinging it open. The U.P.S. man stumbled into the hallway, dropping the box heavily to the floor.

"Well, it's about time, lady. I could have gotten a rupture. This thing weighs a ton."

Jennifer took a step closer, peering into his face.

"You . . . you wouldn't happen to be . . . "

"Sign here, will ya, lady?" he said, thrusting the clipboard beneath her nose. "I ain't got all day."

Jennifer's eyes caught a flash of yellow beneath the dark brown sleeve of the man's jacket.

"That . . . that shirt you're wearing," she said. "It's yellow, right?"

"Yeh," he replied, taking a step backwards as if she were suddenly contagious. "What's it to you?"

"Does. . .does it have blue. . . blue parrots on it by any chance?"

"Yeah," he said, his mouth falling open like a hooked fish. "How the hell ya' know that?"

Jennifer smiled.

"She sent you, didn't she?"

"Who?"

"Flannery. Flannery O'Connor."

"I don't know what you're talking about, lady. I don't know any Flannely. My wife bought me this shirt. It was on sale in Mickey Finn's"

"Your wife?"

"Yeh. In case you didn't know it, I'm a happily married man."

"Your name is Bailey, right? Bailey from A Good Man is Hard to Find?"

"No, as a matter of fact, my name is Hiram. Hiram Purjinski. From Bayonne, New Jersey. Now why don't you just sign this thing so I can get out of this place."

"Did you get a peek at her?"

"Who? Who ya talkin' about?"

"Flannery. The lady who sent the box."

"What box?"

"That box," Jennifer said, pointing.

"Lady, I don't know who sent ya that box. I'm just delivering it. That's all."

"She's a very famous writer. She came back to help me."

"Came back from where?"

"From her disembodied state. She knew I needed her."

"Well, that's very nice. Now would you just sign here?"

He thrust the clipboard under her nose.

"Are you sure your name is not Bailey?" Jennifer asked, scratching her head as she stared up into his face.

"Now, Lady, look, what do you take me for? A jerk? Do I look like a jerk to you?"

"Why, no, as a matter of fact you look like Bailey."

"Bailey who? Christ, I don't know what the hell you're talkin' about."

"Bailey. The grandmother's son. The fellow who got killed by the Misfit."

"I'm sorry, Lady, I don't mean to be impolite. But I think you are seriously troubled. I think you need some real help. But in the meantime, why don't you be a good little girl and sign here. O.K.?"

"O.K., but you'll help me with the box, right? I mean, you won't leave until I open it, right?"

"Jesus Christ! O.K. O.K. I'll help you with this goddamn box after you sign this goddamn form. O.K.? Now sign."

Jennifer took hold of the clipboard and scrawled Flannery O'Connor across the bottom of the paper. Then she got down on her hands and knees before the large cumbersome box and began tearing off the brown wrapping paper.

"You get one end and I'll get the other," she ordered.

"O.K.," the U.P.S. man replied, kneeling next to her. "But I only got a minute and then I am out of here."

They took hold of the top of the box and ripped it open. Inside were three black bowling balls and a pair of white patent leather bowling shoes.

"What's this?" Jennifer asked, holding up one of the bowling balls. "Where did this come from? Who sent it?"

"How would I know?

"But I don't even bowl," Jennifer said. "And besides the shoes are too big."

Just then a man with silver rimmed spectacles and a long creased face who had been sitting on the curb in front of the tenement, entered the lobby and approached them.

"Hello," he said, smiling shyly at Jennifer.

"Hello," Jennifer said.

The man was wearing blue jeans and no shirt and carrying a large black hat..

"Don't you recognize me?" he said.

"No," Jennifer replied. "Should I?"

He remained silent, his eyes red-rimmed and defenseless-looking.

"Well I guess I'll be going," the U.P.S. man said, grabbing hold of his clipboard. "As they say, time marches on."

"I wouldn't talk like that if I were you," said the man with the silver-rimmed glasses. "It's not nice to talk that way in front of a lady."

"What the hell are you mumbling about, mister?" the U.P.S. man said, shaking his head.

"This building sure does attract the nuts, if you ask me."

He was about to turn and walk out the door when the man with the silver-rimmed glasses grabbed hold of his arm.

"Don't move."

From behind the large black hat he thrust a small caliber pistol into the U.P.S. man's face. Jennifer scrambled to her feet.

"Hey, now I know who you are. I finally got it. Talk about stupid. Shit, I can be pretty dumb at times."

"Be careful," the U.P.S. man cried. "Can't you see he's got a gun?"

"Of course, he's got a gun," Jennifer said, smiling happily. "He's the Misfit. He's got to have a gun. That's how I managed to recognize him."

She held out her hand in greeting.

"I'm so, so happy to meet you, Sir. You don't know what an honor this is. Coming face to face with Flannery O'Connor's Misfit. It's everything I have been wishing for. Maybe now I can become inspired just like Flannery and write real stories.

"You throw everything off balance," the man with the silver-rimmed glasses said, shaking his head and pointing the pistol at Jennifer. "You raise the dead and you ain't even Jesus."

"Call the cops," the U.P.S man screamed, dashing out the door. "Somebody call the cops."

"Flannery O'Connor is the best," Jennifer continued, "I mean, the very best writer of all writers. Why, when she described how you shot the grandmother and those two bratty kids, June Starr and John Wesley, because they recognized you, I knew in my very bones, in my very soul, there could be no other way of ending that story. It was perfect. Just perfect."

"No real pleasure," The Misfit said, pointing the gun at Jennifer's head. "No pleasure but meanness."

By the time the police and swat teams arrived, the man in the silver rimmed glasses was sitting quietly on the curb outside the tenement, wiping his glasses against his soiled trouser leg.

"She would have been a good woman," he mumbled as the police led him away in handcuffs. "But it ain't too smart to raise up the dead."+++++

M.I.A.

One morning after a long and fitful night of dream- drenched sleep, Helen Blake awoke and discovered to her astonishment that she had been transformed into a large and dazzling butterfly.

Surely this can't be possible, she thought, gazing first to her right and then to her left at what appeared to be two large, multicolored wings. Surely I must be dreaming.

Gone were her arms and legs, her head and torso, her hands and feet.

In their place, fluttering so tenderly upon the pillow where only a few hours before she had laid down her woman's head, was a lightness so lovely, a spirit so translucent, and so mysteriously linked with her own as to be almost unbearable.

"Dream or no dream, it sure feels strange," she said, eying the soft patterns of blues, yellows and purples etched like rainbows across her cool, trembling wings. "In fact, it feels as if I could almost fly."

She glanced over at her husband, Harold, who was stretched out and snoring beside her.

"Oh, but that's ridiculous," she said. "I'm a married woman. Of course, I can't fly. And besides, it's nearly seven o'clock. I have to wake Jennie up for school."

Immediately, her three new pairs of legs began scurrying across the pillowcase.

"But wait a second," she said nervously, peering up at the two stalk-like antenna quivering above her eyes, "how in the name of God can I do anything in this condition?"

She crept a few inches closer to her husband, hoping that he would wake up and give her a good shake, but he was sound asleep and worlds away.

She tried calling his name but that didn't seem to work. Like her body, her voice too had somehow changed overnight. It was so soft, so low, she could barely hear it herself.

After a few minutes of quiet reflection-something quite new to her-the thought entered her head that perhaps she should try flying onto her husband's face. For several minutes she sat quivering upon the pillow, wondering if such a feat were possible. Finally, she took another peek at her wings.

They certainly seemed capable of flying her through the air: they were large and strong enough. And, they certainly seemed willing, even anxious, to accommodate her, but since she had never really flown before, except in an airplane like everyone else, she was still just a wee bit hesitant. What if she crashed? How would she ever explain that?

After several more minutes of reflection, however, when nothing else seemed to be happening, she decided to give it a try.

To her surprise, it was quite easy. In fact, it was as if she had been flying for years. With just a few quick flutters, she was off the pillow and sailing through the air like a feather whisked merrily along by a playful summer breeze. In fact, it was so pleasant she was almost sorry when she landed several moments later atop the tip of her husband's long, pointy nose.

"I hope the poor dear doesn't mind," she said, gazing down at him with a smile, her antenna outstretched and trembling.

Gently she began to caress his cheeks with the soft silky ends of her wings. Every so often his nose would twitch and his head would toss from side to side, but like a perfectly graceful sparrow clinging to a twig of a long, swaying branch, she hung on tight, her wings, arched and alert.

Just as she was growing accustomed to his rhythms, however, her husband's eyes flew open, catching sight of her.

"Whoa," he cried, bolting upright and staring cross-eyed in her face. "What the devil--"

Without warning his right hand flew up, swiping the air above her head and barely missing the top of her left wing. Miraculously, Helen danced aside just in time, unscathed, but clearly startled.

Obviously he doesn't recognize me, she thought, hovering a safe distance above his head. I guess I'll have to do something.

But Harry was much too excited for her to do anything.

"Helen," he shouted, leaping out of the bed and looking around the room, "where are you? You must have left the window with the broken screen open again. We got some kind of a bug in here."

His hands kept snapping at her as if she were some nasty mosquito he was determined to crush.

Helen could hardly believe her eyes.

"Good God," she cried, "don't tell me he's never seen a butterfly before? Doesn't he realize butterflies don't hurt people. People hurt us!"

She paused.

What the hell was she saying? She wasn't a butterfly.

She was only dreaming she was a butterfly. Right?

Jesus, she was getting more confused by the minute. And to make matters even worse she could hear her daughter, Jennie, calling from outside the bedroom door.

"Daddy, is--is everything all right in there?"

She watched as the little girl stepped cautiously into the room, staring with wide curious eyes.

"Oh, Daddy," the child said, looking at the ceiling and breaking into a bright smile. "It's so pretty! So very, very pretty!"

"Where's your mother?" Harry asked. "Go get your mother. She's never around when I need her!"

Helen flashed her wings angrily. Harry could be so insensitive at times. There was no need for him to talk to Jennie like that.

"Where did it come from?" Jennie asked, staring up at Helen with rapt attention. "Can we keep it?"

"No," Harry said. "Bugs belong outside the house. Now please, go find your mother."

"But it's not a bug, Daddy," the little girl explained. "It's a butterfly. See? Its got real pretty wings."

"Do as I say," Harry ordered.

Jennie began to cry.

"Oh, the poor child," Helen said, dropping down a few inches from the ceiling and circling the room. "She's so, so sensitive. Why can't Harry see that?"

Almost as if he had heard her, Harry sighed.

"O.K., O.K. honey," he said, walking toward his daughter. "Don't cry. I'm sorry. The nice butterfly will be just fine. We'll open the window and set it free, O.K.?"

Jennie continued to sob.

"I don't want the butterfly to go free," she cried. "I like it. It's pretty. Pretty and nice."

"But, honey, butterflies belong to nature," he shrugged, pointing to the window. "They die when they have to stay locked up inside a house."

Jennie sniffled.

"Really?" she asked, through tear-stained eyes. "Is that true?"

"Cross my heart," her father said, walking to the window and opening it. "See? Now the pretty little butterfly can join all the other pretty little butterflies in the big world outside."

Helen shuddered. Was Harry serious? Did he actually want her to fly through that window?

She hovered fearfully about her daughter's head, wondering what she should do and how she might help her husband to recognize her. Before she could decide, however, she felt Harry coming toward her, violently shooing her in the direction of the window.

My God, this is awful, Helen thought, suddenly feeling terribly sorry for herself. Can't Harry see what he's doing? Can't he at least sense who I am?

Round and round the room they went, for hours it seemed, sparring like windmills in a dance of shadows, until Helen became so exhausted, her wings so heavy with confusion and sadness, that she found it almost impossible to fly. Like a black cloud brooding with rain, she suddenly broke and dropped to the ground, her legs and antennas limp with sorrow.

Thus, it came as no surprise when Harry finally reached down and picked her up by her left wing.

"See, Jennie?" he said, carrying Helen toward the window. "Why, the poor thing is just miserable inside this house. Of course it wants to be outside."

With that he flung his wife high into the air, slamming the window shut in her face.

As Helen tumbled through the open space, wind licking her wings and face, she managed to catch one last look at her husband who was standing behind the glass gazing out at her.

For some reason she felt very sorry for him. In only an instant, it seemed--the quick flick of a wrist--he had thrown away their love without even knowing it.

***

It took Helen some time, naturally, but eventually she got rather used to her new world. In fact, in many ways she liked it even better than her old one, although she still missed her daughter, Jennie. For one thing, everything she saw looked fresher, lovelier, more alive with color and texture. Each flower seemed sweeter, brighter, more mysterious than the next. Each day was an invitation, a journey of surprise through sunlight and freedom.

She spent hours clinging lovingly to a blade of grass and long afternoons breezing casually across sun-drenched meadows. Even when she got lonely at times, remembering her old way of life, there was always something to catch her attention and lighten her spirit--the warm, sweet scent of sticky nectar, the hidden softness of a yellow-tipped flower, the cool smoothness of a crystal dewdrop.

At night, drowsy beneath moon-lit skies, she drifted peacefully among the willow trees, her memories of the day lighter than the wispy tracings of her silken wings.

From time to time there were problems, of course. Little annoyances and frustrations, like the man with the long wispy net who tried to capture her one sunny afternoon as she sat dreaming atop a daisy. And the big black bird with the fierce beak that swooped down from an old oak tree and tried to swallow her as she lay bathing in a warm pool of sunshine.

But for the most part, she really couldn't complain. Despite all its dangers there was something wonderful and exciting about being a female butterfly. Winging about to her heart's content, she felt much freer than she had ever felt as a female human. Even on those soft spring nights when male butterflies pursued her for hours across long and lonely fields, she was not afraid. In fact, she rather enjoyed it.

She had come to know her power, the magic of her splendid wings. She knew how far they would carry her and to what heights, whenever her mood changed. She knew there was nothing else for her to fear ever again. Nothing else for her ever to lose. And so she was happy. Happy as a butterfly, catching every eye. +++++

THE DEAD

I was to be in charge of the burial. The coffin was small and very light so my father and I could easily carry it. We bore it through the lonely, deserted cemetery on the edge of town to the hole I had dug for it. Halfway to this spot, however, my father began to weep, causing the tiny box to tip and sway precariously.

He always felt terrible over the death of a child. I told him to leave the burying to me and go off somewhere to have a smoke. He left me and I lifted the white pine box into my arms and carried it until I reached the grave. It was necessary for me to dig out the top dirt that I had thrown in only hours before in an attempt to camouflage the gaping hole. I did so and when the grave was exposed once more and ready to accept its burden, I lifted the coffin and gently, ever so gently, laid the child to rest.

Whom I was burying, I did not know; that it was a child was all I could be sure of. Why I was chosen to perform such duties, I did not think of questioning. Furthermore, I didn't know whom to ask.

I stood brooding over the freshly turned earth, wondering if I would be ordered to do anything else. I was anxious to get home, to be among friends and familiar objects. I did not like unexpected events or strange, unsettling tasks and this one especially was more than I could endure.

Perhaps burying this child will free me, I said, staring into the liquid twilight of the grey cemetery, the digging spade still in my hands. Perhaps after this they will let me be.

Yet while I whispered these words, wanting to believe them so badly, I knew they were not true and that more would be expected of me.

"With them you never can be sure," my father warned many times. "You think they have gone away and then there they are again catching you within their worlds."

A deep silence had come and filled the space in which I stood. I wanted to leave and go looking for my father but my arms and legs had grown heavy and I lost the will to move. Night, like a claw, pressed upon me and held me in its grip. It is happening again, I said without protest.

In front of me shadows had begun to flicker and in the cool wetness of night I glimpsed the form of a young girl standing under a willow tree. Other forms were near but I could not perceive them clearly for they shifted and faded into grayness before I could apprehend them.

"Please don't be frightened," the young girl said in a gentle tone, taking a step closer to where I stood. "We are friends, you know."

"Friends?" I said, watching her closely. "How can that be? I don't know you.

"I am Mary Guilford," she said, tilting her head to observe me better. "You don't remember me?"

"Remember?" I stammered, "No. I'm sorry. I have no recollection of you."

She was silent, lost in the contemplation of my words.

"Why have you come to me like this?" I asked, staring at her.

"Because you have tried to bury me," she said simply.

She was a pretty child with long blonde hair and pale green eyes. As she spoke her lovely oval face seemed to change its shape like the moon.

"They made me," I explained as calmly as I could.

"They ordered me to bury you."

She seemed amazed by this, more curious than hurt.

"But this was my home," she said quietly, opening her arms to encompass the night and sky. "I loved it here. Why would anyone want to bury me?"

Tears gathered in my eyes and the world began to swim and dissolve into a green sea.

"Please don't judge me," I begged. "It was they and not me that buried you."

"No," said Mary, shaking her head patiently. "I am not judging you. You are my friend."

" But why are you here then instead of in there?" I asked, pointing to the fresh grave.

"Because I want to talk to you," Mary said, gazing at me from the darkness. "No one else understands me the way you do."

"But I tell you, you are a stranger to me," I protested. "A complete stranger."

She stood watching me, pale and mute like one betrayed.

"You have no right," I shouted. "No right."

"I cannot go back until you tell me why I had to be buried," she said softly, untouched by my anger. "That is why I've come again. You must tell me."

I thought of threatening her with my spade to make her go away, but she looked at me with such compassion and good will I could not harm her.

"Look, why don't you ask them?" I said, waving my hands indifferently into the distance. "They know more than we do anyway."

She began to laugh.

"No, I'm afraid that is not so," she said. "How simple it would be if that were true."

I felt a pang of terror in the pit of my stomach. I looked around for my father but he was nowhere in sight. I wanted to talk to him, to ask his advice, to see him step forth from the darkness that separated us. But something told me that he would not come again.

Mary seemed to have read my thoughts.

"We're really quite alone here," she said. "Are you frightened?"

Moonlight had fallen upon the cemetery. It lay thickly on the crosses and headstones, on the spikes of the black iron gate, on the barren thorns.

"It's hopeless," I said. "Can't you just go back and be done with?"

"You mean, stay buried?" Mary asked. "No. That is not possible. Not now, at least."

She walked to the grave and sat down on top of it, dangling her feet into the gaping hole.

"Have you anything to eat?" she asked, after a moment. "I'm very hungry."

"Stop pestering me," I said. "I'm not your mother. It's not my job to take care of you."

She began to laugh again.

"I'm sorry," she said. "But you say the funniest things sometimes."

I threw down my spade.

"Look. I've done everything I could here," I said, glancing around to see if anyone was listening. "I've got to get going now. Good luck, kid."

"Wait. I have to show you something," Mary said, springing to her feet.

She fixed her eyes on me.

"Come here," she whispered.

I hesitated.

"Come," she said.

Cautiously, I took one step forward.

We were standing in the living room of a very old house. The low-hanging ceiling was crisscrossed with heavy beams, the bark of chestnut trees still clinging to them.

"On cold winter nights I'd sit here," Mary said, taking my hand and leading me to a huge fireplace, where copper kettles and cast iron pots hung.

"It was so pleasant to feel the heat warm my toes and to listen to the happy, crackling music of the flames."

Before I could speak, she began pulling me away again, rattling on like a small wind-up doll come to life and rioting for sheer joy. We climbed a steep flight of narrow stairs--the steps much bigger than I ever experienced and I had to hoist my body up in great dramatic leaps before I succeeded in mounting them. Mary, however, flew over them with ease like a graceful bluebird.

"I will show you my bedroom," she said, once I had reached the top, breathless and panting.

She led me off to the left and pulled open a big wooden door. Inside, I discovered Mary's room was very much like my own when I was a little girl. I saw a long narrow bed, simple and strong, covered by a warm quilt.

I walked around the room sniffing and touching, rummaging shamelessly through Mary's closet and chest of drawers. I found an old, cracked hand-mirror, a clump of tangled thread, a crushed flower that crumbled between my fingers, and a small locked diary.

"Go ahead," Mary said, handing me a tiny silver key. "Open the diary up and read what it says. It's about us, you know."

Reluctantly, I took the key and inserted it into the lock. Almost instantly, the book flipped open.

I saw a maze of loops and circles and overlapping shapes, which at first glance, appeared to be nothing more than a childish, meaningless scrawl. However, as my eyes began to adjust, I was able to distinguish certain letters and words. Slowly and with great difficulty, I began to read sentences, paragraphs, whole pages.

I read of lives past and lives yet to come, of deaths that stalked like demons and deaths as soft as shadows. I read of faces I had worn, flesh I had borrowed, moments when time touched eternity and all was forgotten.

I read of the doing and undoing of all that was and all that would not be. Of parched winds and the coming of the rain. Of voices awakening and voices dying. Of young girls I would bury and old men I would love.

In the cracked and aging hand-mirror, I gazed at myself and saw Mary, a vision from a past long abandoned. In whose eyes I watched the flickerings of forgotten dreams and unlived days. In whose death I saw my own rebirth, my own beginning.

"Do you see now?" I said, turning to Mary who had been standing behind me. "Everything is as it must be."

But Mary was no longer there. I was alone. When I called her name, she did not respond. In a pool of silence I watched as the room dissolved around me.

In the distance beneath a cool wet evening and an ageless willow tree an open grave and a young girl stood waiting.++++

SYNGE'S GHOST

When judged by contemporary standards, Laura Blake might have been considered a bit odd. The only two things she wanted in life were her little red barn and her Irish Setter, Synge.

She had no desire to become a world traveler, a glamorous movie star, a rising young businesswoman, or a lady astronaut. Unlike her acquaintances from college who were busy accumulating careers and babies and infinite possibilities for their future, Laura was content merely to pass her days quietly, gazing at the barn wall and reciting her poetry to Synge.

When the mood came upon her, she would write thin melancholy verses about the sadness of autumn, the loss of youth, the calm tragedy of early death. Although these poetic attempts often lacked imagery and music, and died within the first stanza, they brought enormous pleasure to Synge and satisfied Laura's deepest, most secret longings.

Her own favorite poet was William Bulter Yeats and she dreamed of him often. In one of her dreams Yeats knelt before her in a shoe store lacing a pair of bright red running shoes about her feet while lasciviously stroking her knee. Later, as he sat beside her reading aloud "Crazy Jane on the Day of Judgment," her feet in the red running shoes disappeared through a nearby wall.

Laura's husband, Larry, never knew about Laura's dream or her special fondness for Yeats. In fact, Larry didn't know many things about Laura.

He met her in a laundromat and became captivated by the way her eyes were fixed upon the spinning dryers. Before his own dryer had come to a stop, he had fallen madly in love with her. Shortly thereafter, they were married.

A steadfast, dependable soul of immense faith, who knew nothing in the least about poetry, Larry often referred to Laura as his little recluse, and he would tease and make passing remarks that one day he would wake and discover her gone and Emily Dickinson in the bed beside him. In his heart of hearts, though, he was fiercely proud of her, and he dreamed of the day when she would blossom into a real poet. On the first night of their marriage he swore to protect her and her wistfully elusive little muse.

He brought her thick sweaters and woolen socks, and, for her jottings, fat white notebooks with silver-tipped fountain pens and tiny bottles of glossy black Indian ink. In the evenings when he sat watching her, fixed and staring like an obedient child over her books and papers and private visions, his soul would grow passionate and he would dream wildly of innocent, fair-haired women in glasses and caps, and plaid school jumpers.

When they were first married and still living in an apartment, Larry complained constantly of the cramped grey confinement, and he boasted of the day when he would discover for Laura a big old house in the country with endless rooms and doors and winding corridors on a quiet hidden lane in the middle of nowhere. At night in his dreams he saw Laura running naked through this house, holding aloft her clean white notebook and one dying red rose.

For months Larry went on scheming and dreaming of this house, and how happy they would be once he had found it. He pictured sunlit mornings cozy at the breakfast nook, lazy afternoons on the front porch with tea and biscuits, and long evenings before the crackling fireplace, frost thick upon the windowpanes, a sleeping dog snoring at the hearth.

But as life would have it, nothing seemed to materialize for poor Larry or Laura until the day, when out of the blue their house finally, almost magically, appeared.

Oh, it certainly needed plenty of fixing, this house. The porch sagged and swayed like tree limbs in a wind storm, the roof leaked, the bathroom pipes were rotted, bricks were missing from the bedroom fireplace, and the kitchen walls were oily and smelled of mice droppings-- but the moment Larry glided across the threshold he knew it was the place for him and Laura. It was almost as if some vaguely familiar presence had come out of the woodwork to greet and reassure him.

Together, Larry and Laura wandered through the entire house, Larry pointing excitedly to the old oak beams which hung low against the ceiling, to the wide board pumpkin floors that smelled of apples and pine shavings; to the stark shifting shadow cast by the gigantic maple tree outside the big bay window.

Later, trekking across the back field which was wild with strawflowers and fourfoils and knee-high meadow lilies, they saw the barn.

It was perched, like some waiting, patient host, upon a small mound of earth between two clumps of beech trees. Its front door flapped on one rusty hinge, a side window was broken and boards hung loosely around the foundation, but Laura was smittened. Dilapidated and lost among the ancient trees and wild foliage, the lonely, bewitching barn was immediately recognizable. She let go of Larry's hand and dashed toward it like one about to embrace an old friend.

Inside, she stood gazing at the thick cobwebs hanging from the heavy crossbeams, tracing her fingers across the grooved knots of the window ledges. In her mind's eye strange happenings began to unfold.

**

For weeks Larry worked at making the barn into Laura's private paradise. He built her shelves of polished oak from the floor to the ceiling to hold her books; in a nearby antique shop he found her the perfect writing table and reading chair; he installed leaded-glass windows and a tiny wood-burning stove to guard her against chill and freezing winter days. He even laid down a rug and hired an electrician to install overhead lights and glare-free reading lamps. He spared no expense, convinced that this barn, which Laura found so utterly intriguing, would help her embark upon her most interesting and creative period.

It did. Shortly after Laura began working there, she had the first of her many breakthroughs. As time went on, she had more and more. Eventually, she was spending more time in the barn than the house itself. Every morning she'd rise long before Larry left for work and steal out of the house in the barn's direction. She'd spend the entire day there, not returning until Larry came for her in the evenings.

He'd find her sitting peacefully in the shadowy corner of the room where the two rows of shelves formed a tiny but perfect triangle, a tranquil smile upon her face, her blue- eyes glowing in beatific calm.

Although he was always hopeful that one night she would open her notebook and show him what she had written, she never did, and so Larry never asked. He'd simply sit with her in silence for a while in the soft glow of the overhead light and try to follow her gaze upon the wall opposite them. He never quite knew what she found so fascinating about that wall, but he loved the way it made her eyes glow, and supposed it had something to do with poetic inspiration.

Later, when it was finally time to go, Laura would turn to him and nod and together they'd drift back to the house, arm in arm; Laura, perfectly at peace; Larry, blissfully expectant.

This went on for some time. Months, in fact, and Larry began to wonder if Laura's notebooks would ever be filled and if she would ever show him her accomplishments. At the very least he had hoped she would soon be asking for a new bottle of India ink.

A reasonable man, he had been more than understanding when Laura announced the need to spend entire days in the barn alone, but when she began sleeping there too, Larry grew lonely and just a bit depressed. He wandered the big old house changing light bulbs and filling up the ice tray racks just to keep himself busy. Later, he became preoccupied with the thought that his wife's delicate nature was somehow being affected by her work.

Although he never mentioned the incident to anyone, he had been thoroughly shocked one night when he arrived at the barn only to discover Laura's head and upper body wedged inside one of the upper bookshelves as her feet and legs dangled helplessly in mid-air.

Poor Larry, shaken to the core, was at last convinced that something had to be done.

Three weeks later Synge arrived.

He was the last pup left in a litter of scrawny Irish Setters bred to a mangy-haired russet bitch named Cornelia Clancy, and although Larry thought him rather bony and odd, he was determined to find as quickly as possible a pet and companion for Laura as a way of lessening her self-imposed isolation.

They called him Synge because Laura insisted he bore a striking, uncanny resemblance to John Millington Synge, her favorite playwright. Like the head of the human Synge, the head belonging to the dog Synge was exceptionally large and brooding. Moreover, both canine and writer possessed the same large, drooping mouths, and piercing, tragic eyes which to a poet were clear signs of an intense inner life.

To Larry's immense relief, Laura went crazy the minute she laid eyes on Synge, trapped and wiggling in Larry's large hairy hands as he stood in the barn assuring her that he had found her a most unusual animal who would provide loyal and healthy companionship.

As it turned out, Synge was the perfect companion for Laura, even though Larry thought him slightly demented. Let loose in the barn for the first time, he literally collapsed, his four legs splaying out from under him in four directions. When he came to, he broke into a wild panic, running madly in circles, whimpering and clawing at the walls and doors, and frantically leaping at the corners of the bookshelves. As Laura soothed and petted him, however, he began to settle down and eventually he fell into a heavy sleep at her feet. When he woke, he seemed a changed dog.

Totally devoted to Laura, he'd sit for hours beside her in military attention gazing intently at the same spot on the wall Laura seemed to have been so captivated by every time Larry arrived.

Larry would study them from the peephole of the barn door, barely breathing so as not to disturb them. He had no idea what was going on, but he supposed Laura was somehow trying to train Synge through unconventional methods. He would have preferred to see Synge learn some normal things like "Sit," "Heel," "Beg," and so on, but since Laura seemed to know what she was doing, he felt no need to criticize.

Sometimes, kneeling against the barn door in the cool evening air, his left ear pressed against the door jamb, Larry would see Synge leap toward the wall and begin to howl as if someone were there edging him on. Other times Larry would see Synge lie low against the floor and crawl playfully in the wall's direction while Laura sat mesmerized and smiling in her chair. Once Larry even saw Synge attempt to climb the wall, but since there was nothing he could grip his paws or hind legs on, he quickly plunged down again to the floor.

What really intrigued Larry, however, was Synge's digging. Out of nowhere, Synge would suddenly lean over some spot on the barn floor and dig like a crazed man unburying a beloved corpse. Larry supposed it was Synge's way of stretching, but since it left him so totally exhausted, Larry wondered why he bothered.

All in all, though, Larry was rather pleased with the way things worked out. Although Laura was still spending all her time in the barn, Larry felt she was happier and healthier with Synge as her companion, and even though he was slightly jealous of their relationship, he felt it in the best interests of Laura and her art.

Everything seemed fine, in fact, until the day Larry arrived at the barn and found Synge missing.

"Where is he," he asked, as Laura sat in her chair gazing at the wall.

"Who?"

"Synge. Your dog? Where did he go?"

Laura smiled and pointed to a tiny dark space between two bookshelves.

"In there," she said.

Larry got down on his hands and knees and peered into the small shadowy space. All he could see were spider-webs and dustballs.

"You must be mistaken," he said, wiping his trouser legs. "There's no one in there."

Laura shrugged, her eyes still fixed on the wall.

"I'll go look for him," Larry said nervously. "Maybe he slipped out the door when you weren't looking and ran off somewhere."

Larry searched until long after midnight. Although Synge had never been inside the house, Larry checked every room and every darkened corner. He combed the fields around the barn, and even drove along the nearby country roads in a vain attempt to locate Laura's missing dog, but Synge was nowhere to be found.

Heart-broken and weary, Larry returned to the barn to give Laura the bad news. When he entered, he saw Synge sitting upright in rapt, hypnotic attention, happily wagging his tail at the foot of Laura's empty chair, gazing starry-eyed into the tiny space between the bookcases.+++

GALATEA OF THE STRAWBERRIES

One morning in early June as Jennifer puttered in her garden, admiring her lettuce leaves and celery stalks, she stumbled across a woman's hand lying palm downward in the dirt between the squash and tomato plants. She was about to call the authorities when she noticed the hand begin to move. One by one it lifted its five long fingers, stretching and flexing them like a skilled pianist warming up before the keyboard. Then it raised itself and slowly crawled off through the strawberry patch and cucumber vines, disappearing under an umbrella of leaves where a tiny gray rabbit was busily feasting among the eggplants. "Where could it have possibly come from?" Jennifer asked, stumbling after it and trampling a string bean bush in her confusion. Its fingers were long and graceful, the palm cupped as delicately as the inside petals of a pink summer rose. "It's awfully attractive," Jennifer whispered, taking another step closer. "I wonder who owns it?" She looked around, almost expecting to see a tall, beautiful woman with satin skin and almond eyes emerge from behind one of the nearby willow trees, but the only things she saw were ribbons of sunlight shimmering across the green tops of her spinach patch. "Perhaps I should carry it into the house?" she thought. "It'll be much safer there. If it does belong to a woman, she'll no doubt want it back."

But the idea of bending down and touching it was too much for her. After all, it was still just a hand. There was no arm or body or face or anything else attached to it, and there was no way of knowing where it had been or why it had come into her garden in the first place.

She wished someone were there to help her. Someone who could reach down without a second's hesitation, snatch it up by the thumb, and carry it off. But there was no one there. No one except herself. Herself and the hand.

She gazed down at it again. It was rather appealing in a way. It seemed so small under the dark brooding leaves, so helpless like a little puppy sleeping on its back in the shade, its delicately pink stomach so innocent and trusting.

"I suppose it can't do me any harm," she said, taking a step closer. "After all, it isn't a head; it doesn't have a mouth. It certainly can't bite me."

She studied the nails. They were firm and tapering; the flesh beneath them--a rosy pink--healthy and glowing.

"What a shame someone had to go and lose it," she said, trying to picture the woman in her mind. "I wonder how it happened."

The hand was not cut, scratched, bloodied or damaged in any way, and except for the fact that it was detached, it looked perfectly normal in every sense.

"Maybe it wandered off while the woman was sleeping and got itself lost. Maybe she didn't feel a thing. Maybe she doesn't even know that it's gone."

Jennifer looked down at her own hands. They hung meekly by her side. Certainly she would know if one of them was missing. She would know instantly.

She brought her two hands up to her face. Perhaps, they weren't as pretty as the hand in the garden--the fingers were shorter and fatter and several of the nails were chipped and broken--but, nevertheless, they were good hands, dependable and loyal and extremely trustworthy. She was certain beyond any reasonable doubt that they would never desert her and go off wandering in a stranger's garden.

"It must be terrible losing something so precious," she said. "I bet that woman would give anything in the world right now to have her hand back again."

Except for the bees buzzing about the flowers, nothing in the garden, including the hand, moved.

"If it's sleeping I can probably just pick it up and carry it," Jennifer thought, "but if it starts to run away from me, we'll both be in trouble."

Quietly, she stepped over a row of beets and a patch of broccoli, wondering what it would feel like when her own fingers touched it.

"Why, I'm sure it'll be like holding someone's hand," she said, trying to reassure herself. "It'll be moist and warm and rather soft and . . . "

She took a deep breath and crouched down, too nervous to realize that the hand, which had been patiently awaiting her, was already crawling on its way toward her outstretched fingers.

It was a wonderful hand, a rare gift from out of the blue, far beyond anything Jennifer had ever hoped for. It slept with her at night and kept her company throughout the day. When she ate her breakfast, it sat atop the table playing with her fingers and patting her wrist. When she wandered out to the garden in the afternoon, it crawled after her, darting in and out of the flowers and plants. One day it even helped with the weeding and watering. At night when Jennifer sat in the tub splashing and relaxing among the soap bubbles, it scrubbed her back and brushed her hair, rubbing its fingers beneath her ear like a warm, loving friend.

In the morning when the sun poured through the patio windows it dashed about, carrying the tea cups and breakfast plates, the little butter knife and napkin rings.

Like Jennifer's own hands, it soon became inseparable from her. In fact, she grew so fond of it, she couldn't bear to think about the woman to whom it belonged. She feared that one day the woman would arrive on her doorstep like a bad dream and demand it back.

She tried to imagine what she would do if that ever happened. Would she lie and say to the woman that she had no idea what she was talking about, and that she--Jennifer—had never even seen a missing hand before? Or would she tell the woman that the hand had disappeared from her too, just the way it had arrived--without a trace?

Although in her best moments she tried to be philosophical--telling herself that it wouldn't matter in the least if the hand suddenly did vanish--she could never totally convince herself. At times, in fact, she became so fearful that her own two hands began to tremble and drip with sweat. Only in the evenings when she sat on the porch watching the sun die in a blaze of oranges and reds--the hand curled cat-like in her warm lap--did she allow herself to imagine that all would be well and harmonious.

One day, however, something totally unexpected occurred. When Jennifer and her hand were in the garden pulling out weeds, she thought she noticed one of her favorite tomato plants sagging pitifully to one side.

Pushing her sun hat above her eyes, she strolled over to investigate. For a brief second Jennifer thought time was running backwards. In front of her, trailing from one of the tomato vines, was a hand exactly like her hand, the one she had found weeks before among the eggplants--the one perched, at that very moment, on her shoulder playing with her hair.

In fact, so taken aback was she that for the first few moments she actually believed it was the same hand. That it had somehow duplicated itself and was magically occupying two spaces at the very same time. After all, it had the same lovely palm, and long, fine fingers, the same pink, healthy nails, the same delicate texture. The only difference really was the thumb, which pointed in a totally different direction. But other than that, the two hands matched perfectly.

"Like parts of a strange puzzle," Jennifer thought. "A puzzle I cannot for the life of me figure out."

***

Rarely did Jennifer let her two hands out of her sight. In the mornings she followed them out of the garden and into the house. In the afternoons, they went together along the paths, and at night she led them up the stairs and into her bedroom.

She slept with them atop her stomach, all their fingers wrapped tightly together, four hands rising and falling with each breath. Whenever she left the house she took them with her, securing them in a little cat box in the trunk of her car. On Sundays when she sat in church, she carried them in her pocket, feeling their fingers against her while her own two hands held the missal and anointed her head with holy water.

They were everything that hands should be--clean, well-behaved, dependable, unobtrusive, mature, hard-working, etc., etc. But more than anything else, they were elegant—the hands of a fine, exquisite woman.

Everything about them from the structure of their bones to the mystery of their appearance announced their aristocracy.

"She certainly must be very special," Jennifer said. "Someone I would love to meet if the circumstances were a bit different."

A few weeks later Jennifer found a woman's leg and foot among the basil leaves. At first she thought they belonged to a manikin or to a life-size china doll, so perfect were the toes, calf, knee, and long slender thigh, but when they began to walk toward her--so refined and wonderfully self-assured--Jennifer knew she was mistaken. Clearly, they had come from the woman, the woman she had been dreaming about ever since she had found the second hand hanging from the tomato plant.

She reached down and picked them up, holding the leg close to her breast.

"She must have been here," Jennifer said, glancing nervously around. "She must have come looking for her hands. But why on earth would she leave behind such a wonderful leg and foot?"

She took a few more steps deeper into the garden.

"Surely, she couldn't have gone very far without a leg and foot. She must be still here somewhere."

Then, just as she was about to step over the rhubarb and cabbage, Jennifer thought she heard something fall among the brussels sprouts.

Propping the leg, and foot beneath her armpit--the two hands beside her--Jennifer charged ahead.

There, crisscrossed under a stout stem dotted with tiny buds, were two long, lovely arms, paler than a string of pearls.

***

By mid-summer the garden was in full bloom. Every afternoon Jennifer would fetch her little wicker basket and go a-picking. There, among the tomatoes and yellow squash, the bell peppers and leek, she found a healthy harvest of pairs-- ankles, ears, elbows, eyes, breasts and buttocks.

And yet, despite all her efforts, she never managed to find the missing woman. To this day, though, she keeps on searching. Under the pea pods, the rosemary, the summer savory, the carrots, the parsley, the okra, the artichokes, the sweet marjoram, the turnips..+++++

AN OCCURRENCE AT SUCK CREEK

Marjorie P. Rainwater was miserable. Of all the people she could think of, she was the only one who had not been saved, the only person around in Suck Creek who had not seen God.

Everywhere she looked everyone was having the experience. Right and left, night and day people were keeling over unconscious with the Holy Spirit and dropping their drawers at the sight of the coming of the Lord.

Young children, decrepit old men, mangy farm dogs, bitten half to death with bloated ticks and fat fleas, were all being infused with the Holy Light and delivered up from the grave with the help of sanctifying grace.

Daily the newspapers carried stories of rebirths, miracles, transformations, religious conversions. They were the biggest thing to hit Suck Creek since the disappearance of Mary Lou Jackson's female cat, Boo, who was later found suffocated in a sink hole in the very center of Suck Creek's largest cemetery, Ambush Arbors.

Just why the Lord was appearing to so many people was anybody's guess, but some people insisted that since the end of the world was coming fast and furious, the good Lord had decided to return and see what he could do for all the decent hard-working, God-fearing folk of Suck Creek.

Apparently Marjorie was not included in this crowd, however. Her life remained pretty much the same old thing. Every morning she got up, washed out her teeth, drank her coffee, and then found herself so sleepy in an hour or two that she could barely hold her head up straight.

At night she rarely dreamed. Instead, her body just died, falling like a lump of heavy dirt into a dark hole. When she woke, she was more surprised than anyone at finding herself again.

Sometimes she would get very mad, convinced that God was playing mean tricks on her.

"Damn it, Lord," she would swear, popping tooth picks under her eyelids to keep herself awake. "What the hell is going on? What's taking you so long? All this waiting around for you is driving me crazy. Waking up every day to the same old thing, noisy chipmunks and soggy lettuce sandwiches and no decent miracles or heavenly visions to speak of. Why, a gal like me could go bonkers. Things are just too dull."

Every now and then she got so desperate, so despondent she took up hobbies--belly dancing, bowling, talking to parrots, painting her toenails--but nothing ever seemed to work. No matter what she did nothing seemed to fill that great big emptiness inside of her.

"It's like I'm missing an eye or something," she protested one day to her old bowling companion, Bobby J., who had experienced the coming of the Lord while driving to the local liquor store for a bottle of Hiram Walker in her Custom deluxe baby blue Chevy pick-up truck. "It's real strange. Kinda like how a bird might feel if it only had one wing, know what I mean?"

"Oh, I know exactly what you mean," Bobby J. said, grinning up at her friend. "Before I got saved, I felt the same way. Most times I felt like a pea without a pod lost in a big plate of turkey gravy, swimmin' all around without no direction and nothing to look forward to except gittin' swallowed up. But then the Good Lord came by and saved me, baptizin' me in the name of the Father, Son and Holy Ghost and snatchin' my soul back from the devil."

Marjorie had heard the story before--how the Lord had come bursting out at her from behind a Hostess Twinkie Cupcake truck which had been parked illegally in front of a fire hydrant, and how he had leaped onto her front fender and climbed the hood, his eyes and hands raised up to heaven like a man being robbed at gun point.

Nevertheless, Marjorie asked Bobby J. to tell it again, hopeful that this time she might learn something more about the mysteries of divine redemption.

"He came right through the windshield, he did," Bobby J. insisted. "Everybody says it's a miracle he didn't break it. But I say he wouldn't be God if he had to break the windshield. Just like he wouldn't be God if he had to fornicate with the Virgin Mary to get her to have a baby. God can do anything he likes. At least that's what I think."

"Well, you should know," Marjorie said, "After all, you've been saved. You've seen the Lord."

"Yep, that's right," Bobby J. said proudly. "I seen the Lord and to my mind there's nothing in the world like it."

"Nothing?" Marjorie asked. "Nothing at all?"

"That's right," Bobby J. insisted, crossing her heart with her right index finger which was painted a bright purple. "Nothing at all! Take my word for it. Nothing even comes close to it."

"That's what I figured," Marjorie sighed. "Boy, talk about getting screwed! I'm really missin' out, ain't I?"

"Well," Bobby J. shrugged, looking just a bit smug. "It's like they say. The Lord chooses and the Lord refuses. That's just the way it is. No sense getting pissed when the Lord passes you by."

"Who's sayin' he passed me by?" Marjorie exclaimed. "I'm only sayin' he hasn't arrived yet. But that doesn't mean he won't come sometime soon. After all, I'm not that bad a sinner. I mean, I'm doin' everything I should--goin' to church regular, readin' the Bible, visitin' the sick, buryin' the dead . . . ."

"Buryin' the dead?" Bobby J. interrupted. "Who you fibbin'? Ain't nobody you'd bury recently I knowed of."

"Well, you're wrong," Marjorie said quite indignantly. "Just last week I buried Jupiter."

"Jupiter? Jupiter who?"

"Jupiter, my pet skunk. He died after gittin bitten in the thigh by a beaver. I dug a big hole in the back yard and buried him under the old dead apple tree."

"Really?" Bobby J. said. "Well, boy, that's sure news to me cause I didn't know you even had a skunk."

"Well, I did," Marjorie said with mounting impatience. "And even though he was a big pain-in-the-ass scratchin' up my furniture legs and crappin' in my flower bed, I gave him a real fine burial. I'll show you the grave if you want."

"No, thanks," Bobby J. said, shaking her head. "Skunk graves give me the creeps."

"Well, O.K.," Marjorie replied, "but I was just trying to tell you I'm doin' my best, and that it ain't fair for the Lord to keep me waiting like this."

"Well, I don't know what to tell you," Bobby J. said. "I can't figure it all out either. But, frankly, if I was you, I'd keep my eyes open real good because the Lord has been known to work in mysterious ways."

"What do you mean?" Marjorie asked, looking a bit concerned.

"Well," Bobby J. said, "From what I've heard, sometimes he appears and people just don't recognize him."

"But why wouldn't they recognize him?" Marjorie said. "How could you not recognize God? You recognized him."

"Well," Bobby J said, scratching her head, "that's because he appeared to me as a person. You know, something normal. But some people claim that he changes his shape a lot, often times appearing to different people as different things. Sometimes he comes down as a white dove and sometimes he comes down as a burning bush and once or twice he's even been known to come down as a cow."

"A cow!" Marjorie gasped. "I never heard of that. Why would he come down as a cow?"

"I don't know," Bobby J. shrugged, "but that's what a lot of people claim. Especially the Indians."

"What Indians?" Marjorie said. "We got no Indians in Suck Creek."

"I know," Bobby J. said. "I'm talking about the Indians over in India. They think cows are God. That's why they don't eat them."

"Boy, I never knew that," Marjorie said. "I thought Indians didn't eat cows because they were all vegetarians."

"No," Bobby J said, shaking her head emphatically. "Being a vegetarian has nothing to do with it. This is purely a matter of religion."

"So what are you saying then?" Marjorie pressed on, her eyes gleaming with excitement. "Are you tryin' to tell me that the good Lord might come down and appear to me as a cow?"

"Well," Bobby J. shrugged, "considering you're not an Indian, I don't think that's too likely, but who knows? With God, anything is possible, I suppose. For all we know, he might come down as a big old skunk."

"Well, in that case, I guess I better keep my eyes open then," Marjorie said. "Cause it would be a damn shame if he decided to stop by and I missed him."

***

So, for the next two weeks Marjorie remained on top alert keeping an eye out for any sign of God. Once she thought she saw him in the A&P sharpening some carving knives behind the butcher counter and another time she could have sworn she saw him climbing up a telephone pole outside the Suck Creek Dog and Cat Kennel, but on closer inspection she realized she was mistaken in both cases. (The man behind the butcher counter was wearing a gold wedding ring and the man up the telephone pole was wearing a gold earring.)

Nevertheless, Marjorie remained undaunted. In fact, she was so optimistic that her salvation was at hand that she even made a special trip to the Suck Creek Library to get herself a book on the history of God and his many appearances throughout the world.

One bright sunny morning as she was sitting down looking at all the pretty pictures in this book, she heard a loud rumpus outside her kitchen window. At first she thought it was only Leo, the drunken postman, stumbling against the rear of the house as he did every morning. But when she began to hear loud snorting sounds similar to those of a horse choking on chimney smoke or some gigantic pig suffering from a severe asthma attack, she grew quite curious.

"I wonder what's going on," she thought, getting up from her chair and walking toward the window. "Leo must have a very bad cold or something."

Gingerly, she pulled the curtain aside and peeked out. A huge black bull with a snow white face, sharp, pointy horns, and long ragged tail was standing inches away from the outside of her window, staring in at her like some long-lost lover come back from the dead.

Marjorie froze, her face turning a sickly egg-white. For almost a minute there was no sound except for the loud snorting of the bull and the heavy pounding of Marjorie's heart, but then all at once the air exploded with a frenzy of male voices.

"There he is," someone shouted.

"Where?" said another.

"Over there. In that yard. He jumped the fence."

Three fat men in trucker's caps and plaid lumber shirts began scaling Marjorie's three-tier wooden fence. Reluctantly, the bull turned his head to gaze at them.

"Go easy," one of them said, approaching the bull slowly with both arms outstretched. "We don't want to let him get away again."

The bull lowered his head disdainfully and began to paw the dirt.

"We'll try to rope him," one of the men said. "It'll be easier to handle him that way."

Suddenly, deep within the pink, soft folds of Marjorie's sleeping brain, something exploded. Like a flash of lightning streaking across the night sky, or a whirling firecracker whizzing through a long, narrow tunnel, it lit up the darkness, lifted Marjorie clear off the floor, and tossed her smack into the kitchen window with a loud thump.

Startled, the bull leaped backwards, as if stung by an invisible bee. Then he sprung forward with the force of a cannon ball, charging full speed at the three men who dove helter-skelter into the safety of Marjorie's nearby petunia patch.

Marjorie dropped to her knees like someone who had been shot through the heart.

"Holy, Holy, Holy!" she began to wail, covering both her eyes with the palms of her hands. "Lord God of Hosts! I've been saved."

The bull, meanwhile, was bounding across the yard, smashing and crashing into everything within its path: trees, rocks, rusty chicken wire, garbage cans, three-legged chairs, iron posts, old mattresses.

By the time the three fat men were up on their feet again and out of the petunia patch, the bull had circled the entire property, ripping his way twice through Marjorie's old clothes line, and dragging her wooden clothespins, panties, slips, bras and flannel nightie behind him through the flying mud and trampled grass.

As the men stood watching him, wondering what to do next, the bull paused for the first time since his mad tormented gallop began. A pair of Marjorie's off-black pantyhose hung forlornly from his left horn. Like some grief-stricken old dog who has finally found its way home after a long journey, he stood quietly watching the house and the huge picture window behind which Marjorie knelt mumbling and rubbing her eyes.

Then, as if struck by some wonderful thought not his own, the bull raised his immense head toward the sky, sniffed the air happily, and charged for the window like a burning star ripping its way through black space.++++

TALES FOR CHILDREN

Trailing clouds of glory do we come
From God, who is our home
--William Wordsworth

OFFIE ASCENDING

It was a cold wet morning in late March when Offie Lee Johnson decided to go for a walk in the woods near his home. The earth was soft and moist beneath his feet and the air heavy and fragrant with the scent of pine needles and damp leaves. Among the ferns and fallen branches tiny rabbits with large frightened eyes and round white tails scurried in and out, pausing every so often to sit back and sniff the air like curious visitors in a foreign land.

As Offie watched them, he began to wonder what it would be like to live among the pine shadows and thorn bushes all winter long when icy winds and snow blew like a plague of loneliness across the dark deserted land.

And, as he trod over brambles and broken twigs that lay scattered across his narrow path, he pictured himself living inside a tree trunk for months at a time and then leaping from branch to branch on padded feet in the high noon spring sunlight.

At one point he even stooped to nibble on a long green shoot, imagining himself not as a boy, but as some wild creature lost and alone in a mysterious forest where night fell quick and bloodless. A creature who could roam at will, sleek and dangerous, and open to anything that might befall him.

Eventually he made his way down a small hill covered in fern and came to a stop at the mouth of a narrow rushing stream. It was there that he made his discovery.

It lay in the underbrush near a jagged rock, partially hidden beneath a thin covering of matted brown leaves and pine droppings.

Surprised, Offie rushed over, picked it up and began examining it. It was a very old violin, scratched and dirty, and missing two of its strings, but its soundbox was free from cracks and its neck and body as richly-grained as fine polished wood.

Offie ran his hand gently across the front and back panels, plucking the three strings that sagged slightly against the delicate bridge and fingerboard. They made a flat "plinging" sound that seemed to him like a muffled bell vibrating under a wad of cotton.

Brushing the dirt away as best he could, he tightened the tuning pegs, and then looked around for the bow. It appeared to be nowhere in sight. On his hands and knees, he searched the whole area, combing under tangled weeds and thick clusters of dark brush, but despite his efforts, he could not locate the missing bow.

Disappointed that he had managed to find only half a treasure, Offie tucked the violin under his arm and turned for home.

Although his mother was in the kitchen peeling apples for a pie she was about to bake, Offie did not stop to show her the violin but went instead directly to his room and put it on his desk. At first he thought the violin looked rather strange lying there among his old familiar schoolbooks and papers, like something from another time caught and held under a bright searching light, but after awhile he pretty much forgot it was there and began doing his homework without giving it a second thought.

In fact, Offie never even mentioned it to his parents during dinner that night, and later when he returned to his room and flung himself wearily across the bed, exhausted from his long trek through the woods, he fell immediately to sleep without even once glancing at it again.

Somewhere along about two-thirty in the morning, however, he woke very suddenly and heard a sharp, very high-pitched whine coming from the direction of his desk. At first Offie thought it was his radio buzzing with static, but just as he was about to get up and investigate, the whine died and a beautiful, but very melancholy refrain of music began to fill the room.

Offie jumped off the bed and walked toward his desk. There in front of him lay the violin gleaming like cut crystals in the moonlight as it poured forth its sad, haunting melody into the surrounding darkness. Amazed, Offie thought at first that he was still back in bed dreaming, but the longer he stood in front of his desk, watching and listening in his cotton pajamas, the more he was convinced the violin was actually playing without its bow.

Careful not to touch the fingerboard which was vibrating like a tuning fork, Offie picked up the violin by the scroll and carried it over to his bed.

Placing it gently on the pillow beside him, Offie lay back down, determined to solve the mystery, but before he could begin, lulled by the soft, sad melody that played only inches from his ear, he fell into a deep sleep and began to dream.

He dreamed of a young, dark-haired woman, whose face he did not recognize. She sat quietly at the foot of his bed staring up at him. Directly behind her was a man dressed all in black, save for a stiff white shirt whose collar was buttoned high against his neck.

As Offie looked on, the man, without a word or glance toward the woman, walked toward the bed and picked up the violin.

Almost immediately the woman began weeping, her cries rising and falling like broken, half-formed notes.

Offie jumped from the bed, trying to console her, but as he began to speak, he discovered that neither she nor the man could hear him. Frustrated, he tried to get her attention by standing in front of her and waving his arms, but when she continued to ignore him, Offie gave up.

He watched in silence as the man caressed the violin and plucked at its strings, running his fingers up and down the neck and bridge-board.

Every night thereafter for weeks to come Offie dreamed of the man and woman. Like beings resurrected from a forgotten time, they came to him with their tears and sad melody. But despite the fact that he, Offie, could see and hear them, he remained always separate from them, unable to enter fully into their darkly mysterious world.

Only through the music of their shared violin was he able to enter what seemed to connect them both. Hearing it in his dreams and while he was awake in his room beside his desk, Offie knew it was something he could share with no one but himself. In fact, despite their questions--his mother especially wanted to know why he was spending so much time in his room--he never told his parents anything about the music he heard. Instead, he kept everything to himself, taking out the violin only when he knew it was time for him to listen. And, although the music made him sad, sadder, in fact, than he had ever been in his life, somehow he knew he had to listen.

One day as Offie sat in his room beside his open window looking at the violin and waiting, a tiny bird flew into the room and landed atop his desk. Before Offie could react, the bird leaped onto the violin and disappeared into its sound- hole.

Offie tried to coax him out by whistling and turning the violin from side to side, but when the bird refused to come, Offie decided to wait and see what would happen.

For hours the bird remained inside Offie's violin, silent as a ghost. Not once did he cry out or scratch against the case. Offie wondered if he were sick or possibly dead. Several times he tried to peer inside the narrow opening, but he could see nothing. He began to wonder what might happen if and when the music began. He hoped that the bird would simply fly away and not injure or possibly kill itself trying to escape the swelling high-pitched sounds.

Eventually Offie grew so tired he convinced himself the bird would not appear. Wearily, he took up the violin and carried it to his pillow as he had done every night.

Just before drifting off, however, Offie heard the notes. There were three of them and they were as clear and distinct as pebbles dropping down a marble stairway. He pulled the violin closer and closed his eyes.

At first everything seemed the same. The woman, the man, the dream. She sat on the bed, her face in her hands; he stood behind her, plucking away on the violin. As always Offie watched in silence.

Only the violin appeared different. It was glowing with an unearthly light, a light so splendid Offie could not bear to stare directly into it.

As the man started to play, however, Offie began to realize that the music too was different. It was clearer, lighter, more balanced and harmonious than any melody he had ever heard before. Lost in the beauty of its sound, he paid little attention to the small bird that was peeking its tiny head out of the narrow sound hole. As the man continued to play, however, this time turning and facing the woman as if the notes were for her ears alone, Offie caught sight of the bird and watched in awe as he lifted his wings and flew from the violin with effortless grace. He circled the room twice, lingered for a moment above the heads of the man and woman as they slowly and cautiously began to dance, then vanished out the open window.+++++

LALI AND OMEGA: A CHILD'S TALE

The children of Kali, where the sky touches the white shoulders of the surrounding hills and brings a blue mist, soft as the eyes of the sea, gather under the warm breath of Unga every evening to hear Althea, the story- teller, weave her tales of mystery and magic.

On one of these nights, as the moon watched from the heavens and sky hawks drifted wingless against the horizon, Althea told the story of Lali and Omega, two friends who passed their days in great joy and happiness, sharing the earth and all of creation with their companions, the wild beasts and flying birds.

Lali and Omega were unlike any humans that were to live after them, Althea told the listening children. Tall and graceful with limbs as smooth as lake water and eyes the colors of burning coals, they lived like the winds: free and spirited, drifting north, south, east, and west.

Half boy and half girl they romped in their splendid nakedness through the hills and valleys of Uaker Country, dancing to the music of the seasons and loving each day for its light and soft shadow. In the morning when dew sat atop the green earth and silver-tailed rabbits crept from their holes in search of food and warm sun, Lali and Omega would stretch their healthy brown limbs, look into each other's eyes and touch their lips in joy to a new dawn, their arms wrapped around each other in great love and compassion.

Diving into the clear blue waters of their favorite mountain stream where deer and lion came to satisfy their parching thirst, Lali and Omega would splash and sing and hold their happy faces up to heaven in blessed thanks for their very being.

Later, they would walk hand in hand to their breakfast under the thick hanging trees where cool shade and lovely breezes teased their bodies and sharpened their appetite. Lali would share goat's milk with Omega and Omega would give Lali sweet berries and spicy apples.

PATRICIA E. FLINN

After feasting, Lali and Omega would play with their friends the spotted horses and sloe-eyed deer, the speckled trout and red-tipped butterflies.

As they ran over the earth and held their faces up towards the light whence all goodness came, music would descend upon their souls and every beast and living thing would join in the songs of creation.

Some days they would sing of love and friendship; other days their songs would be of great adventures in far off lands where any thought became a burst of light and any kiss a flower of desire.

Never were the songs sad or dark, for Lali and Omega and their world as it existed knew nothing of sorrow and unhappiness. "Grief" was a word that would come later.

In the evenings when the sun went to sleep in the sky and the moon came out to brood and dry her hair for the coming day, Lali and Omega would light a fire of passion and beauty and tell their visions in words and stories. Lali, laughing and smiling, would tell of flying through the air like the night birds of the mountains who were bodiless and free. Omega, sitting very close would share tales of winged horses and flutes playing lovely music by themselves.

Soon black night like a warm blanket would enfold them and Lali and Omega would drift asleep wrapped in each other's arms like the swaying branches of trees high above them. All was pure and wondrous and a dream that knew no end.

But one day, as all things go, a heavy figure dressed in Darkness entered the lives of Omega and Lali. It appeared from out the hills one morning as they were finishing their breakfast of tangy nuts and warm blueberries. They watched it, bearing down upon them, silent and quick as night.

"Look, a friend," Lali and Omega sang, springing to their feet, for everything that betook of life was friend to them and blessed.

The figure lifted its dark presence and gazed at them.

"Welcome," cried Lali and Omega. "Welcome to our home of love."

"Only fools welcome what they don't know, " the figure said.

Lali and Omega, who did not understand, only smiled.

"I have come to open your eyes, to show you that your life is nothing more than a pleasant delusion of the senses."

138

Before Lali and Omega could speak, a blackthorn cudgel, dripping with icy blood, swung through the air and smashed into Lali's lovely face.

Twisting in pain, she fell, gasping for air. As Omega watched in horror, Lali's life blood fed itself into the silent earth. Omega fell to the ground, wrapping Lali inside arms that had suddenly come to know weight and darkness.

Everything split in two. Winter descended unto the land and every beast, bird and living creature separated into its shadow. As quickly as it had appeared, the figure vanished, returning to whence it had come— from a region of endless tears and burning griefs, a region where lost souls wander in search of the light they have lost and the faith they have forfeited. And so it was. Omega sat beside Lali's grave, wan as a living ghost, dead even to grief. Nothing, not even a wish to destroy the dark being that had brought such misery, touched her heart.

Omega wanted only to enter the earth where Lali lay and die unseen and forgotten in Lali's cold embrace. And so, time passed, and season followed season. Omega's tears, however, would not cease. They fell like silent spears upon the land, piercing the very heart of what had once been paradise. But one night, long after Lali had ceased to be, when the moon was full and watching, a star appeared in the northern sky, unlike any the heavens had known. It cast a ray of light so pure and bright even Omega looked up from tears and gazed at its radiance.

"Oh, Star," Omega cried, "You are so beautiful. If only Lali were here with me to share your loveliness."

"Cease your tears, Child of the Earth," advised the star. "You will be with your Lali soon."

Omega rose, trembling.

"My Lali?" Omega cried." You have come with news of my Lali?"

"Lali waits in a place where sea and sky touch, beyond the borders of your dreams," the star said. "In a realm where greens and golds sing, and love begets only love."

"Please take me to her," Omega begged. "It is for Lali, I live."

"Put away your tears then and wrap yourself in thoughts of joy for no one with grief and sorrow in the soul may enter the place where Lali waits," the star warned.

Omega obeyed, stepping outside a skin of sorrow like a silkworm shedding its cocoon.

"Now dance beneath the moonlight and sing songs of what is possible," the star continued." When you are ready I will carry you to Lali."

Omega danced and sang while the moon watched in a flame of desire.

Blue and green and purple worlds spun in whirling cacophonies of sound, echoing across the universe as Omega was carried towards infinite beginnings and endless futures.

Round and round Omega spun, flinging soul and self open to the mysteries of the galaxies, free of the grasp of shadows and dark circles.

"You are ready," whispered the star. "Go and find your Lali and forever be one."

And so Omega went forth, singing Lali's name and sharing her memory with the spirits of past, present and future.

When it was so ordained, Lali was found. Omega spotted her sitting beneath a green thought waiting to be born. Lali was smiling.

Today, when Althea, the storyteller, talks of Omega and Lali and of their great love, she talks of green thoughts, for therein dwells all creation.+++++

A CHILD'S VIEW

The child was playing under the kitchen table when the old man knocked on the door. She knew it was the old man because he was the only one who came by to visit them at that hour of the day. Hidden safely behind the long creamy white tablecloth that cascaded down almost to the floor, she watched her mother's feet go by as she walked over to open the door.

"Why, good-morning, Mr. Sills," she heard her mother say. "Come in. Come in."

He was a funny, old man with grey, sad, wrinkly skin and rough, sharp whiskers that bit into her face when he sat her on his lap and talked to her. Under his long black coat which he wore even on hot days when the sun was shining brightly through the windows there was always a strange smell. Sometimes she thought it smelled like the cellar when it rained and water got into the big cardboard boxes her daddy kept next to her old baby carriage and her blue and red tricycle. Other times she thought it smelled like Hermit, her brother's white hamster who lived in a cage on the green fire escape outside the kitchen window.

It was a smell that made her feel very dark and cold inside. Like watching the rain come down on all the grey empty streets on days when there was nothing to do except pretend and draw pictures on the smoky windowpane with her warm breath.

"Sarah," she heard her mother call again, "Where are you, darling? Mr. Sills is here. Come say hello."

The old man's dull black shoes came toward her. They were like big waves down at the seashore when a bad storm was coming. Or like ink marks that her brother's leaky fountain pen left on white paper. She inched her way backwards where it was dark and secret.

"Sarah, honey! Where are you?"

Sometimes when she looked into the old man's eyes she thought of the inside of the big yellow cup with the wide crack that her mother gave to her some mornings when it was time to eat her eggs and buttered bread. Sometimes she had no appetite for eggs and her mother would get very angry. But on other mornings breakfast was nice and she really liked it when the kitchen grew warm and began to smell of good things like coffee and oatmeal and cinnamon toast.

Then she would have no trouble at all eating her breakfast, and her mother would be very happy, telling her what a good little girl she was and how pleased her daddy would be when he got home that night. She wished her daddy was here now.

"Sarah!" her mother snapped, her face hanging upside-down beneath the table. "What are you doing under there? Didn't you hear me? I said Mr. Sills is here. Now come say hello."

Her mother reached for her hand and dragged her out into the light.

Mr. Sills' long black coat was only inches away from her nose. She did not look up at him. Instead, she clung to her mother's hand, hoping she would not go away and leave her. Sometimes when her mother wasn't there and Mr. Sills put her on his lap, the long black coat enfolded her and pressed her so tightly that she could barely breathe. But when her mother came back into the room, the coat would open again and release her.

"Sarah," her mother said, nudging her forward. "What's gotten into you today? Don't just stand there. Say hello."

Mr. Sills held out his hand. It looked grey and bony.

"Hello, Sarah," he smiled. "How's my favorite little girl today?"

Sarah lowered her head and thrust it into her mother's belly which was round and soft like a pillow.

"My, she's gotten awfully shy all of a sudden," her mother said, patting her gently on the shoulder. "You feel O.K., honey? Anything wrong?"

Sarah shook her head, keeping her eyes on the white swirls within the green linoleum.

"Maybe she wants a candy?" Mr. Sills said, coughing into the big white handkerchief that he pulled from his coat pocket. "Do you want a candy, honey?"

He spat loudly into the handkerchief before folding it up carefully and putting it back into his pocket. When his hand emerged again, it was holding a small blue package of peppermint Life Savers.

"Here, sweetheart. Come take one."

Sarah buried her face even deeper into the soft warmth of her mother's cottony belly.

"Maybe her tummy is a bit upset," her mother said, glancing up at Mr. Sills. "Maybe I should take her temperature."

"Yes," Mr. Sills nodded. "Could be that she caught a little cold. It's that time of year, you know."

"Yes, that's right," her mother agreed. "There are lots of viruses going around."

She pulled out a chair for Mr. Sills and beckoned him forward.

"Here, you have a seat, Mr. Sills," she said, "I won't be long. Have a cup of coffee while I get the thermometer."

Sarah clung to her apron.

"Now, honey, you sit down here too and be a nice little girl and talk to Mr. Sills. I won't be a minute."

She watched as her mother turned to the stove and lighted the burner under the big aluminum coffee pot.

"Feeling a bit under the weather, sweetheart?" Mr. Sills said, as her mother exited the room.

His teeth were brownish-yellow, the same color as the face of Miss Grogan, the lady who lived in the apartment next door to them. Like Mr. Sills, Miss Grogan lived all alone and liked to come visit too. Sarah remembered her mother telling her never to be unkind to Miss Grogan because she was very sick and had no one else in the whole world and would die very soon all alone and forgotten.

Sarah wondered if Mr. Sills was sick too. She wondered if that was why he was always coming around to visit them. Maybe he had no one in the whole world either. Maybe he too would die very soon all alone and forgotten. In that case she would have to be very nice to him too.

Shyly, she glanced up at him. He was smiling at her, patting his lap and beckoning for her to come sit on top of it.

"Come on, honey," he whispered. "Let me give you a big hug. You're such a sweet little thing."

Sarah didn't really want to sit on his lap. She didn't want to feel the long black coat closing around her or smell the funny smell that rose up like wet cardboard boxes from beneath its dark secret folds, but she didn't want to be unkind either. She didn't want to be mean to someone who was sick and all alone. Someone who had no one and who might die very soon all alone and forgotten.

She slipped off her chair and slowly walked toward him.

"That's a good little girl," he said, reaching out both his arms and lifting her up onto his lap. "I knew you still liked me."

Sarah nodded, keeping her eyes on the thick lump that went up and down inside the grey stubbly flesh of his long wrinkly neck.

"Your mommy says you may be sick," he whispered, feeling her forehead with the palm of his right hand. "Are you sick, Sarah?"

Sarah shook her head.

"You don't feel sick," he said, rubbing his chin across the top of her head and squeezing her tightly. "You feel like a nice little girl. The nicest, sweetest, little girl in the whole wide world."

With one hand he began to unbutton his coat and wrap it around her.

"In fact, you feel even better than a little girl. Did you know that, Sarah?"

Sarah stuck her thumb in her mouth and shook her head.

"Well, it's true. You feel just like a little bunny rabbit. The softest, cutest, sweetest little bunny rabbit in the world wide world."

The long black coat began to swallow her up, just like one of the big black waves down at the seashore.

"The most adorable, lovable little bunny . . . . "

Sarah did not like the way the black coat felt against her legs or the way Mr. Sills' hand suddenly went under her dress and in between her panties. She knew that was naughty. She knew her mommy would not like that if she saw it. She wanted to get away. She wanted to get down and hide beneath the table again where no one would see her.

"Sarah!"

All at once the long black coat loosened its hold and Sarah was thrust onto the floor.

When she looked up, she saw her mother standing very still in the doorway, holding the little silver thermometer in her right hand.

Then all at once her mother was running past, shouting something at Mr. Sills. She was very angry. Her face was red and terribly twisted. Sarah watched as her mother took hold of Mr. Sills' arm and pulled it. Then Mr. Sills got up from the chair and backed away, his black shoes moving very quickly.

"Get out and don't ever come back here," her mother shouted, pushing Mr. Sills out the door. "You should be ashamed of yourself. I've a good mind to call the police."

Sarah picked herself up from the floor and ran as fast as she could beneath the table. She was more afraid than she had ever been in her life and she wished with all her heart that her mother would not come back into the room and yell at her too. She hadn't meant to be bad. She hadn't meant to be naughty. It was all so confusing.

In the darkness she kept on thinking, hugging herself, wishing for her daddy to come home.+++++

TO BE CONTINUED . . . .

Once upon a time in a lovely summer garden beneath a blue open sky and a lazy old willow tree a tiny yellow-orange flower began to grow on the stalk of a young zucchini plant. It was a pretty flower, soft as a baby's hair and tender as newly ripened corn.

Shaded from the burning sun by broad, cool green leaves and nourished in a bed of rich moist soil, it lived happily and contentedly without a care in the world, completely unaware that one day it would cease being a flower and become, instead, a full-grown zucchini. Unlike the gardener who had planted it, the pretty flower existed only for the moment, never once giving a thought to the future. Every day it grew bigger and more lovely, delighting in all the strange sights and sounds that surrounded it.

In the morning, long before the sun rose high and golden in the blue-pink sky, it would awaken to the soothing kiss of dew drops and the wing-tipped caress of silky butterflies fluttering gently over the basil and parsley patch.

In the afternoon, when the sun was glowing a fiery purple, it would listen to the soft drone of busy honeybees circling curiously above its head, and watch the traces of their delicate wings fall in shadows across the grass. Come twilight the tiny yellow-orange flower would lie awake listening to the wind play among the tomato plants and the birds whistling and singing as they made ready for bed.

"Oh, how wonderful life is," the flower would exclaim in bursts of pure joy. "How beautiful!"

One night, however, just as the flower was curling itself up to sleep, the air began to vibrate with a strange new sound. It was low and haunting like a heavy thought trying to break forth.

At first the flower did not know if it were hearing the rustle of leaves swaying together in the night wind, or the echo of a cry floating ghost-like across the nearby open meadow.

Gradually, however, the sound became a voice, deep and menacing as a darkness descending onto a bed of rock.

"How foolish you are, little flower," the voice laughed. "You think your life will go on forever, but you are sadly mistaken. Your flower days are numbered. Soon there will be nothing left of your pretty petals."

"What do you mean?" the flower asked, gazing down at itself. "There is nothing wrong with my petals."

"They will be gone," the voice cried. "All gone. And there's nothing you can do about it. It's your destiny. Understand?"

"No," the flower said, beginning to tremble. "I don't understand."

"Look," the voice continued, "you're not really a flower. That is only a stage. You were made to be something else entirely."

"Something else entirely?" the flower repeated. "But what else can I be? Certainly I am not a bird or a butterfly or the sun that beats down upon my head every day. What else can I possibly be except a flower?"

"You will be a zucchini. A full-grown zucchini that people will cut up and eat for their dinner."

"Eat?" gasped the flower. "What do you mean eat?"

"Chew up and swallow," the voice said, laughing loudly. "And if you are as delicious as most zucchinis, you will be eaten pretty quickly. Take my word for it. People will swallow every last morsel of you until there isn't one speck left. And then you will be nothing. Absolutely nothing. Not a flower or a zucchini."

With that, the voice vanished into the surrounding shadows. The poor flower was so horrified its petals began closing tightly like a clenched fist. For the first time in its young life it began to weep and despair.

All through the night and long into the next day, the flower continued to cry, lost in a sadness and confusion so deep the earth itself could not contain them.

"Oh, how can it be?" the flower asked, desperate to discover some answer, some insight into the terrible chaos engulfing it. "I am a flower, not a zucchini. A flower!"

But sure enough when the flower looked down at itself again, it saw for the first time that it was turning green and that its petals were somehow being mysteriously transformed into the long thin body of a young fuzzy zucchini plant.

"No," the flower cried. "This is not possible. It's just not possible."

Frantically the flower began struggling, determined to free itself from the strange, new creature that it was becoming, but no matter how hard the flower fought, it could not separate itself. The little zucchini seem to cling to its very soul, growing bigger and fatter by the hour.

"My God, this is terrible," the flower wailed as it grew heavier and heavier, hanging and swaying like a weary head only inches above the dark loamy earth. "I'm dying and there's nothing I can do about it. Soon I will be gone."

But come next morning as the sun began to rise bright and golden in the soft pink sky, the flower discovered to its amazement that it had changed shape.

"Somehow I've become a zucchini," it said, gazing down at itself in wonder. "A full-grown zucchini with the heart and soul of a flower!"

"Awfully strange, isn't it?" said a pretty blue butterfly who had been looking on from the stem of a nearby cauliflower plant. "Makes you sort of curious, doesn't it?"

"What?" the zucchini asked, looking up in surprise.

"Who said that? Who's there?"

"Oh, only me," answered the butterfly. "Don't get nervous. I was just passing by and I thought I'd stop and say hello."

"But--who--who are you?"

"Well, right now I suppose I'm a butterfly," the butterfly shrugged. "But who knows what I'll be this afternoon. Yesterday I was a caterpillar."

"A caterpillar?" the zucchini said, swaying back and forth on its short stubby stem to steal a peek. "My God, doesn't anything ever stay the same around here?"

"Oh, not for very long," the butterfly smiled, twitching its lovely wings. "At least nothing that I can think of."

"Well, that's terrible," the zucchini cried. "Just terrible. That's what makes life so awful!"

"Awful?" said the butterfly. "Why is it awful? I think it's very interesting."

"Oh, that's easy for you to say," replied the zucchini. "You don't have to worry about being eaten as I do. You can fly from flower to flower without a care in the world. But once I get eaten, I become nothing. Nothing at all."

"Oh, poppycock," said the butterfly shaking its wings. "Where did you hear that nonsense? You don't become nothing just because you get eaten. Didn't you know that?"

"No," said the zucchini, looking mighty surprised. "I didn't know that. I heard that--"

"Don't believe everything you hear," the butterfly said. "You can really get screwed up that way."

"Yes, but--but I still need to know," the zucchini persisted. "What happens?"

"You mean if you happen to get eaten?" the butterfly asked.

"Yes. Please tell me. I really need to know."

"Well, use your common sense," the butterfly said. "What do you think happens? You become part of the person who eats you."

"What?" said the startled zucchini. "What on earth do you mean? That doesn't make any sense. Any sense at all!"

"Who cares?" the butterfly smiled, "Making sense is not that important. As long as something is true, it doesn't have to make sense."

"Yes, but how can I tell it's true?" the zucchini protested. "I mean, I won't really know for sure until after I'm eaten and by then it might be too late."

"Too late for what?" the butterfly said, twitching its wings impatiently. "What on earth are you talking about?"

"Too late to escape my fate," the zucchini wailed. "Too late to avoid becoming a nothing."

"Look," the butterfly said, "I'm telling you once and for all. You've got nothing to worry about. Once you're a something, you can never become a nothing. Things just don't work that way. Take my word for it."

And with that, the pretty butterfly lifted its wings and flew off into the horizon.

But despite the butterfly's reassurances, the worrisome zucchini continued to fret.

In fact, so caught up was it in the deep and perplexing questions of fate and fortune that it didn't even notice the chubby white-tailed rabbit who was stealing its way through the garden gate and heading hungrily in its direction.

***

By the time the rabbit had finished nibbling the lettuce and the broccoli and was on its way home, hopping merrily through the tall grass with the zucchini nestled securely in its belly, the zucchini was already on its way to becoming part of the rabbit's big white tail.

What happened to it after that, however, is still somewhat debatable.

Some people say it grew into a tree, and others say it went back to being a flower. No one seems to deny, however, that it did become something. +++++

TALES ON THE DARKER SIDE

The clouds that gather round the setting sun
Do take a sober colouring from an eye
That hath kept watch o'er man's mortality
                    --William Wordsworth

THE TEMPORARY AND THE AXOLOTLS

Whenever anyone asked Margot how she was, she would always say she was temporary. Most people would stare at her blankly for a second or two and then snicker, mumbling something like "Oh, that's nice" or "What'd ya know?" while gazing off glassy-eyed into the distance beyond her shoulder. Only rarely did someone have the curiosity or interest to ask for further details.

"Temporary? In what sense?"

"Why, in every sense," Margot would reply matter-of-factly. "What a silly question!"

Bill, Margot's husband, always got mad when he heard Margot talking this way.

"Cut that out," he would scold. "And quit calling yourself temporary. It makes me feel like I married a goddamn rainbow or something."

Margot would shrug her shoulders and say she was sorry, but deep down inside she never really understood why he got so upset.

What's wrong with being temporary? she would ask herself. It's a perfectly reasonable occupation and surely it does no one any harm. In fact, it's really rather interesting. Almost like sleep-walking or riding an escalator, you might say.

How Margot became temporary is really hard to say, but even she admits she certainly didn't plan it, that's for sure. Actually, it just kind of happened. Like winning a lottery or a trip to Bermuda. As a little girl, she had a perfectly normal childhood. She jumped rope, played with dolls, made mud pies. All of that. Not once did she ever suspect she would grow up and be anything but permanent.

Margot's mother, Sarah, however, who considered herself nothing but permanent, thought that Margot first began showing signs of being temporary when she was about four.

"That girl was simply wild over caterpillars," Sarah recalled. "She used to stare at those dirty varmints scrawling back and forth across the front lawn and ask me all sorts of questions no normal child would ever think of asking. She'd want to know why a caterpillar turned into a butterfly, and what the butterfly turned into when it got tired of flying around being a butterfly and on and on. I tell you, that child was enough to drive me looney. Where she ever came from I don't know, but she was too much for me to handle at times, that's for sure."

Margot's father, Sam, however, saw it a bit differently.

"I never remember Margot asking any questions about caterpillars," he said. "My wife is nuts! The only thing Margot was interested in at that particular time of her life was lobsters. She used to have us buy them at the A&P so they wouldn't be killed, and then she'd bring them home and raise them as pets. They were always crawling all over the bathroom floor. I stepped on one once late at night when I was half-asleep, and it almost took my toe off. Other than that, though, Margot was pretty much of a normal kid. She was certainly nothing like her mother, I'll tell you that."

Margot's teachers from grammar school remember her mainly as a quiet little girl with a rather strange penchant for collecting light bulbs.

"Oh, she was a lovely little thing," one of the teachers recalled. "But she was always unscrewing something or another to get those bulbs-- lamps, flashlights, her mother's crystal chandelier, you name it. What she did with them I don't know, but I'll tell you wherever that child went darkness seemed to follow."

Bulbs, caterpillars and lobsters notwithstanding, Margot actually showed no overt signs of being temporary until after she married Bill. They met in a dog and cat beauty salon in Somerville, New Jersey, where Margot was working at the time as a part-time shampooer.

"I had gone there with Jumbo, my German Shepherd," Bill later told his friends. "Jumbo had all these big ugly hair-knots, round as golf balls all over his fur, and I wanted to get him cleaned up. So I wandered into one of the back rooms and--zingo--who do I see but little Margot, wearing those long rubber gloves and washing this funny-looking poodle in a gigantic tub. She and the poodle were both covered with soap. Lots of soap. I tell you it was something. Right then and there I knew Margot was the girl for me."

Three weeks later they were married. It was Bill's fourth and Margot's first. Not many people thought it would last

"Aren't you concerned about his children?" her friend asked her. "We heard there are six of them."

"Seven," Margot corrected. "We count the twins as two."

"But don't you think all those children might be a problem?"

"Problem?" Margot replied. "In what way? They're all very nice people. They take after Bill's former wives. And besides, I'm not going to have any children. I'd make a terrible mother."

For their honeymoon Bill and Margot went to Disneyland with three of Bill's children, Larry, Eddie and Bobbie. While Bill and the boys rode the monorail all across the park, Margot took a tour of Underwater World. It was there that she first encountered the Axolotls. For some reason they intrigued and fascinated her. For over two hours she stood in front of their tank, pressing her head against the cool thick glass, as she watched and studied the Axolotls' delicate little bodies with their long transparent fins, whip-thin tails, and almost human feet--she counted five actual toenails on each Axolotl's foot. Try as she might, though, she simply couldn't get over the fact that the Axolotls were so still, so fixed and motionless, so seemingly calm and indifferent to everything surrounding them.

From the tiny pink placard hanging on the side of the tank Margot learned that Axolotls were the larval stage of a species of North American and Mexican salamander of the genus Ambystoma.

"Unlike most amphibians," the placard read, "Axolotls retain their external gills and become sexually mature without undergoing metamorphosis. What's more, they possess an extraordinary capacity for surviving on dry land during periods of drought, or under water during a rainy season."

"I'll be," Margot said, loud enough to alert one of the security guards who had been carefully observing her for most of the two hours she had been standing before the tank.

"Is there a problem?" the guard asked, frowning and taking a step closer.

"I'd like to buy one of these," Margot said, pointing at an Axolotl. "How much are they?"

"I'm sorry," the guard replied, shaking his head, "but this is not a pet shop. The Axolotls are not for sale."

"No?" said Margot. "Why not?"

"Because," said the guard. "they belong to this aquarium. They're one of our most popular and permanent attractions."

Shortly after Margot and Bill and the children returned from Disneyland, Margot's mother underwent an extraordinary change.

"She just stares at me," Margot would tell Bill after arriving home from the institution each afternoon. "No matter how much I try talking to her she won't say a word."

"What's the use of going then?" Bill would ask. "It sounds like it's a big waste of time."

"Well, some days she seems to recognize me and other days she doesn't."

"Then," Bill would reply, "go only on those days when you think she recognizes you."

"But I'm her daughter; she's my mother."

"Look at it this way," Bill would shrug. "Sometimes you are and sometimes you're not. So figure out who you are and what you are and play it from there. O.K.?"

After a while Margot saw Bill's point. When she felt like a daughter she went; when she didn't, she didn't. Actually, it worked out quite well.

Bill's children lived several months of the year with Bill and Margot and several months of the year with their respective mothers, Nancy, Ruth and Katherine, Bill's former wives. Nancy's children, Tommy and Janet, arrived in January and stayed till April; Ruth's children, Ricky and Sally, came in May and remained till August and Katherine's children, Larry, Eddie and Bobbie, appeared in September and hung around till just before Christmas. The rest of the time Margot hopped from job to job doing a little bit of this and a little bit of that. Sometimes she worked as a check-out lady in the Path-Mark, sometimes she sorted mail and licked envelopes in the post office. For several days until they hired a full-timer she was the chief stacker of aluminum cans in the recycling plant behind the town dump.

Her favorite job, however, was manikin dresser and undresser at Macy's Department Store. She loved standing inside the front display window watching all the people on the outside watch her as she took off and put on the manikins' hats, shoes, skirts, blouses, slips, bras, etc., etc. On good days she even got a chance to unscrew a manikin's hands, arms, and legs and replace them before the delighted eyes of spectators with the hands, arms and legs of another manikin.

"It's such a wonderful, powerful feeling," Margot explained to her friends, "to be standing up there with a leg in one hand and an arm in the other, knowing I'm the one to put them all back together again."

But. . . . like everything, the job at Macy's did not last.

One day Bill came along during his lunch hour and saw Margot crouching in the window, unscrewing the left leg of a partially-clad, one-armed manikin while a cluster of passers-by looked on, trading lewd jokes.

"I don't want you to go back there," he told her that night over dinner. "You hear me? If you need to work,--and God knows you got enough to do around here--get yourself a decent job. Something normal like other women, for Christ sake."

Although at that point she was finally beginning to suspect it, it was really the manager of the employment agency who first convinced Margot that she was a temporary.

Margot had gone to the agency the morning after her discussion with Bill looking for a job in an aquarium.

"I'd like to be in charge of the Axolotls," she said. "That's the job that I would like."

The woman who was interviewing Margot--a tall, bony blonde in her late forties with pop eyes, stared at her for several moments without saying a word and then got up to fetch the manager.

When they returned, the manager, a short fat man in a dark, rumpled suit, sat down opposite Margot.

"The nearest aquarium is over 100 miles away," he said. "How far are you willing to travel?"

"Oh, a mile or two, I guess," Margot replied. "You see, my hours are a bit limited. I have other responsibilities. From time to time I'm a mother."

"From time to time?" the manager asked, looking from Margot to the blonde. "I'm afraid I don't understand."

"The children--they come and go," said Margot. "Three here. Two there. They vary with the season."

"But how many children do you have in all?" asked the manager.

"At the very most," said Margot, "seven."

The manager began leafing through a small notebook

"I see," he said, "I understand now. What you are is a temporary and temporaries, unfortunately, are usually very hard to place. Also, because of the limited distance you are able to travel, the aquarium job is out of the question. But, if you're interested I can probably find you something in a pet shop or an animal clinic. They're always looking for temporaries."

"Fine," said Margot. "That sounds wonderful."

Depending upon what month and day of the week it was, and what time of the morning or afternoon it happened to be, Margot either got in her car and drove to the Elephant's Nose Pet Shop, where she took care of the Axolotls, or remained at home puttering about the kitchen, where she fed and looked after the children.

"Where's Daddy?" Eddie, Bobby, Sally, Janet, Ricky, Larry or Tommy would sometimes ask as she stood, whipping up their flapjacks or waffles.

"Oh," Margot would shrug. "I suppose he's off somewhere doing something or other."

The fact that she had become a temporary wife was totally reasonable to Margot. Like the rising and setting of the sun, it was, she believed, only natural.

Much like the Axolotls, in fact. Every week or so she brought another one home with her. The owner of the pet shop, Mr. Quigley, told everyone later he thought she was in some kind of business.

"I thought she had a zoo or something. I mean, Jesus, she was my best customer. She was working practically for nothing. How was I to know?"

Some people claimed that was what did it. They said it drove Bill away.

"No man in his right mind would have put up with that kind of thing," they said. "That woman had to be crazy doing something like that."

Other people, mainly women, took Margot's side.

"I wouldn't doubt it if she did the whole thing out of spite," one said. "She might have suspected something. After all, Bill always did have an eye for the ladies. He was a hard man to tie down. Maybe she just couldn't take it, like his other wives. Maybe he sort of drove her to it."

What people didn't realize, however, was that Margot just liked her Axolotls. She couldn't bear it when someone came in to buy one. Even the thought of leaving them alone in the store at night upset her. So it was really perfectly understandable when she began to take them all home.

When Bill complained about the smell, she tried to reassure him.

"You'll get used to it, dear," she told him in the beginning. "It's only temporary. Pretty soon you won't even notice it."

She was right too. It was only temporary. After a while Bill didn't notice a thing. He just stopped coming home altogether. After a couple of months, the house was practically overrun. The mailman said he saw twenty on the front porch alone. On the morning the Board of Health officials arrived, Axolotls were seen hanging from the windows and door-sills. Margot was fast asleep in an upstairs bedroom. Like the Axolotls she barely ever rose before late afternoon. One of the men who led her from the house was very gentle.

"Don't worry, miss," he told her, patting her arm. "We're just taking you over to the hospital for a quick check-up. It won't last very long, believe me."

"I know," said Margot, smiling up at him. "Nothing ever does. Does it?" +++++

LIFE SUCKS

I got my dog Charlie on the same day my mother burned her apartment to the ground and suffered second and third degree burns over half her body.

It was three months after my father's death and I suspect my getting a new dog and my mother setting herself on fire were--in some crazy way--a statement of how we both felt about the future and my father's untimely passing.

He was a great guy and far too decent to go the way he did, dying on the toilet seat in the middle of the night when we were all sound asleep and snoring.

We always thought he'd go much more dramatically since he was a heavy gambler and up to his neck in debts with the local loan sharks who'd think nothing of breaking a man's legs or tossing him into the Hudson River, but after finding him in the can like that, alone and with his pants down, we knew the loan sharks had nothing to do with it.

Still, it was a great shock naturally, and for the longest time none of us could use the bathroom without thinking about him and remembering how sad it was when the Hoboken ambulance people came to take him away to the city morgue.

Nobody could get his legs straight--one of the doctors told me later that rigor mortis had already set in--and so they had to carry him off on the stretcher with his legs and feet sticking up in the air like some weird wooden manikin that had fallen over backwards in a store window.

I started worrying that the people in Serenity Funeral Home would have trouble fitting him into the casket, but my brother reassured me.

"Oh, they'll fit him in," he said. "You don't have to worry about that. They'll just break his legs if they have to, but they'll get him in, believe me. They do it all the time."

As always my brother was right. Everybody who came to see my father at the wake said his legs looked straighter than two long-stemmed roses lying side by side in a flower box.

Which made my mother happy, naturally. She was always a great one for worrying about what the neighbors thought. In fact, it positively delighted her when several people commented favorably on the choice she had made for my father's suit and tie.

"I bet you paid a good penny for them," I heard the daughter of one of her close friends whisper into my mother's ear as we stood in front of the casket. "I bet ya ten dollars to a donut, quality like that didn't come from Mickey Finn's Bargain Basement."

"Oh, you're right," my mother beamed. "I wouldn't dream of sticking Charlie into something from Mickey Finn's. Not on this day, at least. That's real wool. One hundred per cent real wool."

Shortly after the funeral, however, my mother's spirits began to slump quite noticeably. For weeks she refused to eat anything other than salted peanuts and pastrami sandwiches--two things my father had always loved and used to order whenever he happened to be in Mueller's Deli on Fourth and Park where they make delicious German potato salad and the best rice pudding you ever tasted in your life.

I'd come home from work every day and find her sprawled on her Easy-Boy recliner in front of the T.V., her eyes blank as paper plates, the floor littered with greasy, empty bowls and little white napkins smeared with mustard.

"Hey, Ma, what's goin' on?" I'd say, trying my best to communicate. "You crackin' up or something?"

She'd mumbled a bit, give a little sigh, and then lapse back into another long, icy silence.

"Look, Ma," I'd say. "You've got to face it. Pop's gone now. There's nothing we can do about it. We got our own lives to live now, right?"

But she wouldn't listen to me and as time went on, she continued to get worse. She began to lose weight. She started smoking Camel cigarettes, and she'd spend hours sitting on her bedroom floor rummaging through moldy cardboard boxes of old family photographs and my father's World War II medals. One day she stopped talking altogether.

"Relax," my brother tried to reassure me. "Let her alone. It's just her way of grieving. She'll be O.K."

But she wasn't O.K. Some days I'd find her talking and laughing to herself in the toilet where my father had died. Other days she'd leave the house long before dawn and not return until way past midnight, offering not a word or one single shred of information about where she had been.

"Look, I can't take this anymore," I told my brother one night after I came home and discovered my mother kneeling on the floor in front of a lighted, brightly glowing statue of the Blessed Virgin. "You don't live here like I do. You don't know what goes on. Ma is carrying this mourning crap too far. She's losing her head."

"So what d'ya want me to do about it?" he said, shrugging his shoulders. "I've got my own problems. Life goes on, as they say."

"Well, I just want you to know I can't take it anymore. I'm leaving. I'm moving out. Understand?"

"Moving out?" my brother repeated, looking really surprised. "But where will you go? Who'll look after Ma?"

"She'll have to look after herself," I told him. "I'm goin' find an apartment somewhere, that's all."

"Look, you're making a big mistake," he warned, staring me straight in the eye. "A big mistake. You'll be as lonely as hell living all by yourself in an apartment. And besides you'll have to pay rent."

"I won't be lonely," I said. "I'll get a dog. I always wanted a dog. I'll get a real nice dog who'll keep me lots of company. It'll be a fresh start. The beginning of a whole new way of life."

"You can't keep a dog in an apartment nowadays. Supers don't allow it. They'll kick you out."

"I'll get a real quiet dog. The kind nobody will notice. I'll take him out at night when there's nobody around."

"It won't work," my brother said, shaking his head. "I'm telling ya, it won't work. Landlords don't allow dogs in apartments nowadays. You'll be out on your ear before you know what hit ya."

"Wanna bet?" I said. "Wanna put your money where your mouth is?"

"Yeah," my brother replied, thrusting up his thick chin into my face. "How much you wanna bet?"

"Twenty bucks," I said. "Twenty bucks I find a place."

Three weeks later I found an apartment, four flights above a seedy-looking drug store with a big, colored advertisement for rat poison and a sign saying No Dogs in the front window. It was a cold-water dump on Fourth and Jefferson Street in downtown Hoboken with no shower and no tub, and a hallway that reeked of urine and moldy mop water, but since it was relatively cheap and within walking distance of the Lackawanna Railroad station where I hopped the Path train to work in Manhattan every morning, I decided to grab it.

Once I was safely moved in, and relatively free from the nosy scrutiny of the landlord--a short, hairy little guy with a shiny bald head and lots of gold teeth who lived in the apartment opposite me--I was determined to go shopping for my dog.

I wanted a nice, calm, reliable mutt. Nothing expensive or fancy or snotty like some of those little dogs you see on Fifth Avenue who go parading around with ribbons in their hair and are always shivering and growling and sneaking nips out of people's ankles. As far as I was concerned, those kind of dogs were for the birds. They were spoiled, neurotic, and really hard to handle, and since I was fed up with neurotics, having spent the past few months living with my mother, I wanted no part of that scene.

I just wanted a real laid-back, Steady-Eddie-type-dog who would fetch my slippers, lay his head on my knee, and make me feel like any other normal person who looks forward to coming home every night.

To my surprise I didn't have to search long. I found just the dog I was looking for in the Hoboken pound. He was a tan and white mutt who seemed a cross between a fat sheep and a wet pig. The dog warden led me to him right away when I told him what I was looking for.

"This guy's so calm you can set a bomb off under his rump and he won't bat an eye," the warden assured me. "See what I mean?"

The dog lay sprawled and panting in the middle of his cage, his large flat head hanging sleepily between his two enormous paws, his pink tongue rolled out and drooling.

"Well, he sure does look calm alright," I told the warden. "In fact, he looks so calm he seems comatose."

"Comatose?" the dog warden repeated. "What are you talking about? This dog's fine. He's just sleepy, that's all."

"But don't you think his eyes look kinda glassy?" I asked, taking a step closer to the cage. "They're awfully shiny."

"Look," he said, "I'm telling ya, he's fine. He's a perfectly healthy, calm dog, and he's the dog for you. You just look around here. You won't find a calmer, quieter, more relaxed dog than him, believe me. Here. I'll show you."

The warden opened the mesh wire door of the cage and clipped a small cloth lease to the dog's collar.

"Come on, boy," he yelled, trying to tug the animal to its feet. "Come on. Come on."

The dog did not budge. He just sat there, looking dazed and sleepy, a large fat lump, drooling spittle down the front of his furry chest.

"See?" the warden said, turning to me with a smile. "How much calmer can you get than that? Anything calmer and this dog would be dead."

He thrust the leash into my hand and stepped away from the cage.

"Go ahead, talk to him," the warden said. "See for yourself."

"Hello, doggie," I said, cautiously stooping down and petting the dog on his wet nose. "How's things?"

The dog stared up at me blankly, gave a little snort, closed his eyes, and tumbled over."

"See?" the warden said. "What did I tell you? He loves you."

I began dragging the dog out of the cage.

"You think I'll have a problem getting him home?" I asked. "I mean right now it doesn't look like he's in the mood for walking."

"I'll drive ya," the warden said. "Don't worry about a thing. I'll have the two of you home before you know it."

***

Charlie--I decided to name the dog in memory of my father--slept all the way home in the car. I had the warden carry him up the three flights of stairs in a big blanket just in case the landlord was snooping around. However, even after we got Charlie into the apartment, and I placed a bowl of hot hamburger meat before his nose, he still continued to sleep.

"Well, at least he isn't goin' to be any trouble," I said to myself, stepping back and forth over his large, inert body as I made my way around the tiny kitchen. "At least no one will know he's here with me."

And no one would have known either if my damn mother didn't decide to go and torch herself that very same night. Around two in the morning, just about the time Charlie and I were getting used to one another, someone began banging on my apartment door. Charlie didn't even bark, God bless his heart. I got up and opened the door. There were two cops standing there.

"You Hope Stirling?" one of them asked, staring down at my bare feet.

"Yeah," I said, trying to speak softly so as not to wake up any of the neighbors. "What's up?"

"Your mother's in the hospital."

"What's she doin' there?" I asked, grateful that Charlie was keeping a low profile behind me and not growling up a storm like some other dogs I happened to know.

"She fell asleep with a cigarette apparently. Set the place on fire."

"Holy Jeez," I said, spotting the landlord's door beginning to open. "Of all the rotten stinking luck."

I thought of pulling the cops into my apartment, but I didn't have time.

"Is there a problem?" the landlord asked, eying me and the cops as he stepped out into the hall. "Is something wrong?"

"Oh, no" I said. "Just a little personal matter, that's all. Something concerning my mother."

"Your mother?" the landlord asked, sniffing the air suspiciously. "I didn't know you had a mother. She doesn't live here with you, does she?"

"She's in the hospital," one of the cops said, cutting him short. "Fell asleep with a cigarette."

"Oh, how awful," the landlord said, straining his neck to see into my apartment. "I hope there was insurance."

He spotted the bowl of chop meat on the floor.

"What's that?" he asked, pointing above my shoulder.

"That?" I said, trying to block his view.

"Yeah. That."

"Nothing, Just a bowl of chop meat."

"What's it doing on the floor?" he asked, looking at me closely. "You don't have an animal in there, do you?"

"Look, we better be goin' now," I said, turning toward the cops. "For all I know my poor mother may be dying right this very minute."

"Stop!" the landlord insisted. "Before you leave I must know if you have an animal in there. Now do you or don't you?"

"Look, fella, hit the road," the burlier of the two cops said. "This lady's had a terrible tragedy in her family. Where's your respect?"

And so that night Charlie and I were let off the hook. But not for long really, because the next day the landlord came back after I had returned from visiting my mother in the hospital. Despite my protests, he insisted on inspecting my apartment. He found Charlie snoozing under the kitchen sink, which was dripping terribly.

"Either he goes or you go," the landlord warned, not mentioning one word about my poor mother's precarious condition.

"You're cruel," I said. "You have a heart of stone."

"I'm a landlord," he said, shrugging his shoulders. "What do you expect? Life is tough."

The next day I took Charlie back to the pound. I certainly didn't want to, but what choice did I have? I mean, I couldn't very well lose the apartment, could I? Especially since I knew I would never be able to find another one so convenient and so cheap. And I certainly couldn't go home again, thanks to my mother. There was no home. So what else could I do? I had to survive, didn't I?

"What the hell are you doing?" the dog warden asked when he saw me dragging Charlie through the front door of the pound. "He didn't bite you or anything, did he?"

"No, he was just great," I said, trying not to get all choked up and sentimental as I bent down to kiss Charlie good-bye. "He was the best friend I ever had. Slept continually the entire time we were together."

"So what's the problem then?" the dog warden asked. "I don't understand. Why are you bringing him back?"

"I'm bringing him back because I've got a rotten landlord and a fruitcake of a mother in the hospital," I said. "That's why."

"Gee, that's too bad," the warden replied. "I'm really sorry to hear that. You and that dog seemed made for one another."

"Well, I guess that's the breaks," I told him, "but as they say, life sucks, right?"

"Yeah, I guess," he sighed.

I took one long, last look at Charlie as I edged my way out the door.

"Well," I thought, "at least I saved twenty bucks."+++

TILL HUMAN VOICES WAKE US

They saw the truck as soon as they left the main road and began walking down the narrow, rock-strewn path, carefully holding onto one another and lifting their feet above the tangled clumps of sandy grass and old knotted tree stumps. In the soft twilight it looked like a bluish grey thumbprint smudged across the orange and gold horizon.

"Do you think it's all right we're here?" the woman asked timidly, gazing around with wide watchful eyes. "I mean, you're sure it's no one's private property?"

"Of course, I'm sure," the man said, taking hold of the woman's elbow and guiding her off the edge of the path and onto the beach. "You don't see any homes, do you?"

"But what about that truck? What is that truck doing there all by itself? Where's the driver?"

"How should I know?" the man shrugged. "Maybe it's an abandoned truck. Or maybe the driver is just off taking a swim somewhere."

They stopped, their eyes methodically scanning the long expanse of blue-green water that lay smooth as a mirror beneath the softening pink sky. Except for several seagulls circling noisily above their heads and a few clumps of broken driftwood floating peacefully in white foamy waves at the edge of the water, the beach was still.

"Beautiful, isn't it, Alice?" the man said, tossing back his head and inhaling a deep breath of the fresh salt air. "Sure beats being cooped up in that damn car."

It was the last day of their vacation. They had been driving since dawn, trying to cover as much ground as possible before heading to Portland to return their rented Oldsmobile. In the morning they would board the plane back to Jersey.

"Yes, Paul, it's very nice," Alice said, casting another quick glance around. "But let's not stay too long, O.K.? Before we know it, the sun will be gone and we're be stranded here in the dark."

For over two weeks they had been on the road, traveling across Northern California and up along the Oregonian coastline. Now Alice was tired. She had grown weary of motels and road-side restaurants. She longed to be back home, where everything was warm and familiar.

"You worry too much," Paul replied. "The dark won't matter. The dark can't hurt us."

"But Paul," Alice pleaded, "be reasonable. If it gets dark, we'll never be able to find our way back up that path."

They had seen the path and the small patch of wild beach from the car window as they drove along the two-lane scenic highway. Paul had insisted they stop, arguing that he needed the break. Now Alice was sorry they had.

"Relax, will ya?" Paul said, bending over to pull off his white tennis sneakers. "There's going to be a full moon tonight. We'll find the way."

"But Paul, what if . . . ."

"What if what, Alice? What are you so keyed up about? You've been like a jittery cat all day long. Why can't you just relax?"

"I don't know," Alice shrugged. "I just have this feeling, that's all."

"Feeling? What kind of feeling? You're not getting sick, are you, honey?"

"No," Alice smiled. "It's nothing like that. I'm just nervous, I guess."

"Oh," Paul sighed. "Well, in that case, let's go for a swim. The salt water will be good for us."

"Swim?" Alice exclaimed, her eyes widening. "Here? Now? Why, Paul, you can't be serious."

"Of course I'm serious," Paul said, zipping open his trousers and pulling them off. "I don't know about you but I'm as stiff as a corpse sitting all day. I need to stretch."

Before Alice could protest, Paul was out of his socks, shorts and shirt.

His nakedness, blotchy white and grey against the fading pink and orange horizon and the burnt-yellow sand came as a genuine shock to her.

"Come on, honey," Paul said, holding out his arms. "What are you waiting for? Take off your clothes. A little exercise will do you good. The salt water will help you unwind."

"Paul, you're being ridiculous," Alice said, picking up his shirt and glancing nervously around. "Someone may see you. Someone may come by. Put your clothes back on, please."

"Who's going to come by?" Paul protested, waving away the trousers that she held out to him. "Nobody's around. Nobody can see us."

"Paul, please. It's getting dark."

"Look, I've already told you, Alice, I need to stretch. Now will you stop acting like a child and come on in the water with me? It'll only take a minute."

"Paul, I beg you, please. . . . "

"O.K., O.K.," Paul said, throwing up his hands. "We've been married too many years. I give up. Do whatever you want to do. But as for me, I'm going in for a swim. I'll see you in a few minutes."

He turned and walked quickly away, his soft, pale buttocks and long skinny legs floating stark and white above the scattered driftwood on the gleaming wet sand.

For what seemed an eternity, Alice stood, sentry-like, on the beach watching the small rounded haze of her husband's head bobbing up and down in the darkening waters. She watched as it drifted farther and farther away from her into the distance, fading like a pinpoint of light against the vanishing horizon, beneath the large black wave curling high atop the rushing waters like some huge terrible tongue. Long after her eyes grew weary with the shifting shapes and strange phantasmagoria of the deepening moon-drenched night, she continued to watch, warmth draining from her body like air from a punctured balloon.

***

For a moment she thought she was dreaming. But then she heard it again. Sharp and clear as the call of a country-morning rooster. It sounded so close, so absurdly familiar she almost laughed. Quickly, she glanced around. A tall, thin man and a large, scrawny bird, his long, skinny neck fastened to a rusty leash, were standing a few feet away at the spot where Paul had shed his clothes.

"Howdy," the man said, lifting the bird, a red-eyed rooster, high into the air where it screamed and bucked like an angry child. "Hope my friend Zero here hasn't disturbed you any. It's hard keeping him quiet sometimes."

173

The man's hair was red, long and matted; his face covered by a thick bushy beard. He took a step closer and held out his hand, his eyes burning two small holes into Alice's ashen face.

"Zig Zag's the name. Please to meet you, Ma'am."

Alice hesitated, her eyes darting in the direction of where she had last seen Paul. Now all she could see was blackness. Even the massive rocks rising out of the dark sea had disappeared.

"I'm--I'm Alice," she said, forcing herself to accept the man's outstretched hand which felt raw and bony like a sharp toothless gum. "Alice Montgomery. My--my hus-band, Paul, is in the water, but he should be right back. He left a little while ago."

"I know," the man grinned, looking down at the pile of clothes lying in the sand. "Me and Zero here saw him go. Didn't we, Zero?"

He grabbed hold of the rooster's tethered neck and twisted it backwards.

"Don't care much for swimming myself, have to admit. Tide can be real dangerous sometimes. Especially for strangers who don't know no better."

"Yes, I--I suppose," Alice said, struggling to keep her voice steady.

"But my--my husband is very strong. He's--he's a really strong swimmer."

"Being strong means nothing, Ma'm," the man said, shaking his head as the rooster struggled furiously to free himself. "Not when it comes to that tide."

"Yes, but--"

"Where you folks from?" he asked, keeping his eyes firmly on the rooster.

"New--New Jersey," Alice said, "Northern New Jersey."

"Never been to New Jersey," he shrugged, tossing the bird high into the air and laughing as it plummeted to the sand. "Been to lots of other places, though. Portland, Seattle, Vancouver . . . . . You name it."

Alice looked down at the man's hands. In the thick darkness they seemed to glow.

"Yes," he continued, "Me, Zero and that truck of mine up yonder have seen a lot of things over the years. In fact, that's why I call myself Zig Zag. I'm always zig-zagging around seeing something or other. Some of them good and some of them not so good."

He glanced up at her and smiled. "How 'bout you, Ma'm? You seen anything good lately?"

Alice shook her head, staring up at him blankly.

"That's too bad," he said, clicking his tongue against the back of his teeth. "Maybe I should lend you my truck. Trucks are real good for seeing things. Plenty of spying goes on in trucks, did you know that, Ma'm?"

"No," Alice whispered, her legs brittle as glass.

"Well, it's the truth," the man said. "Take my word for it. In fact, maybe you should think about getting yourself a truck someday. Might help you keep an eye on that there husband of yours."

He cocked his head in the direction of the sea and laughed. Then he bent down, picked up the rooster and began to stroke it.

"Mind if I ask you something, Ma'am?"

Alice's stomach lurched.

"Your husband likes to swim in the nude, don't he?"

She felt the blood drain from her head.

"Oh, I want you to understand it makes no difference to me, Ma'am," he said, digging his left toe into the sand. "I got no complaint with people doing that sort of thing if that's what they like. I'm just curious. I mean, 'specially since you didn't seem to want to yourself."

Alice looked off into the distance, her thoughts forming and fading like the waves she heard in the distance.

"Oh, you don't have to explain, Ma'am," the man said, staring at her fixedly. "That is, not if you don't want to. You see, I know things like this can be embarrassing to a lady. Especially if she's talking to a strange man. Like me."

Dazed, Alice gazed down at her husband's clothes. The right leg of Paul's trousers was buried deep in the sand.

"But I'm harmless," the man continued. "Honest, I am. I don't believe in all that violence you see going around nowadays. Killin' and murderin' and rapin' and all that. I believe in love and peace and that kinda stuff. Don't you?"

He paused, his eyes steady and expressionless.

"I--"

"And I believe in letting people do what they want to do. Even if it means going naked."

With the tip of his shoe he began kicking sand atop the pile of clothes.

"No," Alice said faintly, her voice trembling.

"And besides," the man continued, "going naked is really nothing. Not after all I seen. Not after all that."

Confused, Alice got down on her knees and quickly began picking up her husband's clothes.

"Once I seen a cat cleaved in two and once I seen a dog fried alive and once--"

He paused, gazing down at the back of Alice's head.

"Once I seen a man floating naked in the--"

Alice began to sob, her breaths coming sharp and irregular.

"Hey, what's the matter, lady?" the man asked, gazing at her as he squatted down beside her. "Something wrong? You don't like sand? You don't like it when I play in sand?"

Alice shook her head.

"Sand never hurt nobody," he said, running a handful of it through his open fingers. "Sand ain't like that tide out there that kills people. Sand feels good. Real good. See, I'll show you."

He took hold of her hand and thrust it roughly beneath the sand.

"See," he said, his eyes gleaming like a cat's in the dark. "Ain't nothing wrong with sand. Ain't nothing wrong at all."

Alice jerked her hand away and scrambled to her feet, her husband's clothes thrust against her breast.

"I--I have to go now," she gasped, her eyes blinded by tears.

"Go?" the man said, lifting his face up to the sky. "Go where?"

The rooster let out a fierce cry, his filthy wings flailing the air wildly.

"Home," Alice said, backing away. "My—my husband is waiting. He's--he's calling me. Can't you hear him?"

"Home?" the man cried, yanking the rooster backwards by the leash. "Home where? You ain't got no home. Not any more."

"Good-bye," Alice called, her voice breaking.

"Wait," the man shouted, rising to his feet after her. "You're crazy. You hear what I'm sayin'? You don't got no home. Not anymore. You got nothing. Nothing at all."

Alice turned, stumbling blindly in the heavy sand.

"Hey," he shouted. "You hear me? You hear what I'm saying?"

Alice began to run, dropping pieces of her husband's clothing as she went along. By the time she reached the water, her hands were empty.+++++

MY MOTHER'S BRAIN

For the past couple of months now I've been thinking a lot about my mother's brain. It's sort of an obsession, I guess, because no matter how hard I try, I can't seem to get the damn thing out of my head. Even at work down at the General Store I think about it, when I'm slicing people's cold cuts and wrapping up their ham sandwiches. Twice I got so confused I almost cut three of my fingers off in the goddamn slicing machine. And once when the place was packed to the rafters with customers, and I was doling out bowls of clam chowder, I got so upset seeing it hovering in front of my eyes that I knocked the pot off the stove and almost scalded myself.

At night I even dream of it sometimes. It's always floating up and down in some cloudy, greenish water inside a big thick jar that looks a lot like the jar Steve, my boss, keeps the pickled pigs feet in. Sometimes it looks so real, I can almost smell it. Sort of a combination of formaldehyde and decaying skunk. Once or twice I even woke up with my eyes burning.

Joe, my boyfriend, thinks I should see a shrink. He says I must have a lot of guilt locked up inside me. Guilt that's eating away at my subconscious because I let those doctors do that damn autopsy on her. But personally I think Joe is full of shit. He means well and all, but if you ask me he doesn't really know what he's talking about. It's just all that psychology stuff he's always studying in school. His head is filled with it, and sometimes he sounds like a real jerk, especially when he starts quoting Freud, or one of his stupid teachers, or something from one of his dumb textbooks, which he's always underlining in ugly yellow ink.

In all honesty, I really don't pay any attention to him. I just let everything he says go in one ear and out the other. Life's a whole lot easier that way, I think.

But still, I have to admit, sometimes it does make me nervous. I mean, dreaming about my mother's brain so much and all. It's not natural. After all, she's been dead for almost a year now and life's pretty much back to normal again. In fact, except for her brain, I really don't think about her at all. And, to be quite frank--which I know must sound rotten--we were never very close to begin with. Even as a kid, I thought she was a pain in the ass. Always complaining and feeling sorry for herself and moping around like her butt was about to fall off. It used to drive me crazy. Especially when I'd come home from school all happy and find her sitting in the dark against the wall like some goddamn old owl.

"Gee, Ma," I'd say, looking up at her with my big sad eyes. "Why can't you be like those moms I see on television? You know, moms like Donna Reed and Jane Wyman and Harriet Nelson. They're always so happy. Always smiling and baking cookies and going off to P.T.A. meetings and stuff. Why can't you be like them, Ma? Huh, why can't ya?"

Sometimes she'd get so mad she'd come at me with the carving knife.

"You little bitch," she'd scream at the top of her lungs. "You goddamn little bitch. I don't know why I ever had ya."

Ah, but what the hell? I really ain't complaining. I understand. Being a mother in those days must have been a real bummer. And besides, I was no little angel, that's for sure. But as they say, that's all water under the bridge now anyway, right?

I mean, all that stuff has absolutely nothing to do with what I'm talking about or why I let those doctors do that autopsy on her. That's a whole different matter entirely.

Honest.

Back then, I just wanted some facts. Some information. Some basic insights into why my mother died, and what went on inside her head all those years, and whether or not it was anything I might catch one day. You know, like Parkinson's Disease or varicose veins or something.

And besides, how was I to know what would happen? I mean, it wasn't my fault. I always thought autopsies were performed the same day the person died. How was I to know those doctors were going to stick my mother's brain into some jar and then put it into storage for over a month? I thought they were kidding when they told me that.

"I'm afraid there's going to be some delay," the doctor said. "Your mother's the only brain we got here in the lab right now."

Which was really a surprise to me since no one had ever referred to my mother as a brain before.

"We got to keep her on ice until we get a couple more."

"A couple more what?" I asked.

"Brains," he said. "We need at least three."

"Three?" I said, trying to understand. "Why? So they can keep one another company?"

"No," he laughed, thinking I was joking. "To make it worth the pathologist's time to come round to do the work. He won't do it for .just one brain. There's got to be at least three."

"But what if there aren't three?" I asked, getting a bit queasy over the idea that long after my mother's body would be buried under six feet of dirt, her brain would still be floating around in some hospital lab only a mile away from my apartment waiting for some half-ass doctor to show up. "What happens if nobody dies?"

"Oh, I wouldn't worry about that," he said. "This is a hospital. Somebody's always dying here. Even the ones you least suspect."

And so, what was I to do? I mean, at that point the damage had already been done: the autopsy was over, my mother's brain was already in the lab, and her body was already in the funeral home, waiting to be viewed that very night. I couldn't very well ask for her brain back, could I?

I mean, what the hell would I do with it? Stick it in her coffin under the satin pillow when nobody was looking? I tell you, I was really confused. The whole situation was so ridiculous. For the first time I was actually sorry I ordered the damn autopsy.

"Look," I told that doctor. "It ain't right. After all, my mother's dead. She deserves a little respect now. Can't we just force that pathologist to come to the lab? I mean, that's his job, fer Christ's sake. That's what he's getting paid for."

"Look, Miss, I'm telling you. He won't come unless there's three brains here. He's a very busy man. He travels all over the state."

"But she's my mother," I insisted. "I can't let you just stick her brain up on some shelf all by itself like that."

"And why not?" he asked. "Nothing's going to happen to it."

"How do you know?" I said. "I mean, isn't it possible that someone might—might steal it?"

Now in all honesty, I knew nobody in his right mind would want to steal my mother's brain, but I figured the doctor wouldn't know that.

"Look, relax," he told me. "There's no need to worry about your mother's brain. It's in very good hands now. We're going to take good care of it, and as soon as the other two brains come in, we'll get right to work."

Since I didn't say anything, he probably thought I was upset because right after that he told me I was perfectly welcome to stop by and chat with him anytime I liked.

"It's against laboratory regulations naturally, but if you want, I'll even take you to where we keep your mother's brain. You might enjoy seeing it. I mean, knowing that it's O.K. and all."

"I think I'll pass," I told him. "I'd much rather remember Mom the way she was."

"Suit yourself," he said. "But just remember, it'll be around for a while in case you change your mind."

"What'll happen to it after that?" I asked. "Will you bury it or what?"

"We'll incinerate it," he said. "That is, unless you're willing to donate it to us for further use."

"What kind of use?" I asked.

"Oh, research and all," he replied. "You know, the usual stuff. After all, this is a teaching hospital. We're always in the market for good brains."

Right then and there I knew he was out of luck, but I didn't tell that to him naturally. I just said that I would have to think about it and then get back to him. But as it turned out, I never did get in touch with him. In fact, I never even read the pathologist's report when it finally came from the lab two months later.

I mean, after so much horseshit, how was I to know that they didn't mix things up down at that lab and send me the report of one of those other two brains? Christ, can you imagine if I had read the lousy thing and it said something like, "We're very sorry but after extensive analysis and evaluation, we have come to the conclusion that your mother's brain was 100% healthy and perfectly normal given the circumstances of her life and environment."

Jesus, that alone would have made my hair stand up. After all, it's one thing knowing that your mother's demented because of medical reasons, and another thing realizing she's just cracked. But even besides all that, I had had it at that point. I just wanted to forget all about those doctors and that goddamn autopsy. It was just too nerve-racking. Too depressing. Sitting around thinking about that jar. About my mother's brain. All alone like that on that shelf. In that laboratory. Waiting for that doctor and those other two brains to show up. It just wasn't right. Even if she was a pain in the ass.

Still, no matter how much I try, I can't seem to shake her. In fact, if you want to know the truth, she's even more of a problem now than she ever was. Before, she just used to call me on the telephone. Now her brain follows me around most of the time, floating in and out of my head like fog or some bad dream when I least expect it, and throwing me for a loop.

It drives me crazy sometimes, even though I'm sure one of these days, it'll all end and she'll go away and leave me in peace. But who knows when that will be?

In the meantime, however, I guess I'll just have to be patient and keep on doing what I've been doing—slicing people's liverwurst and salami down at the General Store, bringing them their bowls of clam chowder and pea soup, and staying clear of the jar of pickled pigs feet.+++++

JESUS IN REVERSE

For the longest time Sarah Spinello had been waiting patiently for three things: the death of her cat, Spooky; the death of her dog, Tomorrow; and the death of her mother, Faith.

Every morning she'd wake up convinced that before noon she'd have a corpse on her hands, but no matter how promising the day looked--Spooky had refused to eat; Tomorrow had collapsed in the back yard; Faith had been given the last rites by Father Donovan--by nightfall they had all miraculously rallied again, dashing Sarah's hopes to pieces.

"You'd think it was a conspiracy or something the way they're hanging on," Sarah confessed to her girlfriend, Joan.

"I mean, Christ, what do they want from me? What did I ever do to any of them?"

Joan, who was a very practical person--she rarely answered any of Sarah's questions directly--shrugged and told her to see a psychic.

"After all, a psychic is supposed to be able to see into the future, right?"

"I suppose."

"Well," said Joan, "Maybe you'll at least find out which one of them is going first and when."

"You really think that's possible?" Sarah asked.

"Sure," Joan replied. "Getting hold of that kind of information is easy for a psychic. They do it all the time. It's like turning on the television set or something."

"But what if . . ."

"What if nothing. At the very least you'll have something to look forward to. Right?"

"I guess."

"After all, let's face it. You got nothing to lose, right?"

"No," Sarah said, shaking her head. "Nothing except one dog, one cat and one mother."

It wasn't that Sarah didn't like her cat, her dog, and her mother. It was just that they had been dying for so long now that she was getting kind of sick of it.

Every time she turned around one of them was having another "crisis."

Spooky, who was nearing her twentieth birthday, had had five major cardiac arrests in a six-month period; Tomorrow, who was blind, deaf and arthritic, had been hit by a car twice and poisoned by an angry neighbor; and Faith, who was over 90, had already approached medical history by being the first woman ever to undergo more operations in one year than a cadaver in a training lab for student morticians.

Yet in every case, against all the odds, they had managed to pull through. It was more than Sarah could figure.

"Look at the statistics," she would tell her friends. "If it had been any ordinary dog, cat, or mother, they'd have all been goners by now, right?"

Her friends had to agree. The facts were on her side. On at least five different occasions the vet, Dr. Glowfleck, had insisted on putting Spooky and Tomorrow out of their misery, but always at the last minute— sometimes seconds before the fatal shots were about to be injected—the two would undergo a startling and miraculous change for the better, confirming Sarah's worst fears that their time, alas, had simply not come.

Her mother's case was slightly different, however. Since no one obviously had ever considered giving Faith a fatal shot, Sarah knew there was nothing she could do except let nature take its course.

Still, the ups and downs of Faith's slow extinction were more than exhausting at times.

"A person can only take so much," Sarah told the psychic whom she found listed in the Yellow Pages under "Desperate," a grim young woman with a glass eye who worked in an insurance company during the day and sold scented candles from the back of her Chevy station wagon in the evening. "I mean, let's be honest. After awhile, even dying can get to be pretty boring."

"Boring or not, what's to be is to be," the psychic advised, holding up the three hair-balls belonging to Spooky, Tomorrow, and Faith that Sarah had bought along in the pocket of her beige coat because of their strong vibrational frequencies. The psychic was convinced that strong vibrational frequencies were essential aids for contacting the future.

"One simply cannot change one's karma. You must remember this."

"But my God, I could be an old lady before all this ends," Sarah protested. "These are the best years of my life. I'm in my prime."

"That may be true," said the psychic, "but prime or no prime, karma is karma."

"Look, I agree," Sarah replied, "Karma may be karma, but can't you at least tell me how long this karma stuff is going to last and whose karma is going to be used up first? That's all I really need to know."

"That I cannot do," said the psychic, staring into the hair-balls. "The laws of nature forbid it."

"Forbid it?" Sarah persisted. "But I don't understand. That's why I came here in the first place. I thought that--"

"It is for your own good," the psychic said. "Ask no more questions, please."

"But--"

"And remember, no matter what happens, karma is karma.

Sarah's love life was a mess.

She hadn't been out with anyone since the night St. Jude's Hospital called to tell her that her mother had been removed from the intensive care ward and put on the "stable" list.

"You think they would have had the decency to at least wait until the morning," Sarah told Joan. "I mean, do you have any idea how distracting it is when you're listening to someone giving you a blow by blow account of your mother's bowel movements?"

Joan said she never believed in hospitals. Especially Catholic ones.

"So they kill you, so what?" she said. "They tell the family it's God's will. How do you fight something like that?"

"They told me it's God's will my mother is still alive," Sarah replied.

"See. Either way they got you."

"Well, maybe I can sue them for emotional suffering. You know, the way they do in divorce cases?"

"Are you crazy? How can you do that? They saved your mother's life."

"That's my point."

"But, Sarah, use your head. Nobody, and I mean nobody, ever sues a Catholic hospital and wins. Especially if the patient survives. It would be a waste of time. You'd be better off finding yourself a good faith healer."

"Faith healer? That's the last thing I need."

"No, I mean, a faith healer that would work the opposite. You know, instead of praying for a fast recovery, he'd pray for a quick end."

"But won't somebody like that be hard to find?" Sarah asked. "What happens if I run into another fraud like that psychic woman?"

"I'll help you this time, " Joan replied. "You won't have any trouble. All we got to do is put an ad in a good newspaper."

Sarah did her best to word the ad discreetly.

"Now remember, it's important we attract the right sort of person," she told Joan. "I got enough problems on my hands already. I don't need crackpots calling me up all hours of the day and night."

"No, you sure don't," Joan agreed. "We've got to be subtle. I mean, we just can't write-- Wanted: Dog, Cat and Mother Exterminator."

"That's right. The whole thing has to be very professional. Our aim, after all, is to find somebody who's good."

"A person who knows his job."

"A pro."

"Someone whose best interests are for Spooky, Tomorrow, and Faith."

"Right."

"After all, they were good to you all these years."

"Yes, very dependable. That's for sure."

"It's the least you can do for them."

"I agree."

"O.K. then let's get to work."

***

The ad ran for one week under Personals sandwiched between a prayer to St. Anthony for the return of a missing diamond brooch, and a 1-800-number for Dial-A-Joke- International.

Wanted: Loving Person to Assist Dying Dog, Cat and Mother. Needed immediately. Call 913-6116.

The calls were quite varied. Some people wanted to know what kind of dog, cat and mother. Others wanted to know what they were dying from.

"If it's one of those contagious diseases I won't touch it," one man said. "I ain't dying for no dog, cat, or mother. No way."

Still, other people wanted to know what "to assist" meant.

"If it means emptying a bedpan for some sick old lady, well, that's no problem, " one woman said, "But I'll be damned if I'm going to clean up for two smelly old fleabags."

Only one person actually understood what Sarah was talking about when she explained what she meant by the phrase.

"Oh, I get you," the man said. "You're looking for a sort of Jesus in reverse, right? Somebody who buries rather than raises the dead, correct?"

"Correct," said Sarah.

"Well, lady," he replied, "Search no more cause I'm your man."

His name was Dave Orny Anderson, but he told Sarah she could call him D.O.A. for short.

"Best to keep things simple," he said, winking at Sarah as she sat down opposite him at her kitchen table. "Shoot your mouth off too much and you're apt to wind up behind the eight ball, right?"

"When's the last time you used your hands?" Sarah asked.

For a moment D.O.A. looked confused.

"My hands?"

"You know. For praying. Like we talked about on the telephone?"

"Oh," said D.O.A. "Now I get you. Well, let me think The last time? Well, just recently I prayed for a man--a real big fellow--who happened to be suffering from a boil in his ear. Ugly old thing. Looked like a big old prune pit. Anyway, I did all I could--prayed my heart out--but nothing worked. In fact, the poor fellow was howling in pain by the time I left."

"Would you say your praying made him worse or do you think that was just a coincidence?"

"Oh, I'd definitely say it made him worse. No question about that."

"Could he have died by any chance?"

"From a boil?"

"No, from your praying. I mean, if you kept at it."

"I suppose. He was in bad shape. Really bad shape."

"So he might have died, right?"

"Yes. I think that's a reasonable assumption. A couple of more minutes and I would have finished him off. Yes. That's right."

"Now one more thing," Sarah continued. "Have you any objection to working with animals? I mean, animals and mothers?"

"No, Ma'm. No problem there. I love animals and mothers. Have all my life."

"So you won't mind working with all three of them then?"

"Do you mean at the same time?" D.O.A. asked, scratching his head.

"Oh, well, that would be entirely up to you," Sarah replied. "I wouldn't want to interfere with your usual method. I mean, you could pray over them separately or take them on all together. Whichever you prefer."

"I can't recall ever having done that," D.O.A. said. "But that's no problem cause I sure am willing to try. As far as I'm concerned, there ain't nothing like an exciting challenge."

***

Sarah had a rough time getting Tomorrow into the portable doggie carrier. Every time she touched one of his legs, bent and crippled with arthritic tumors, the animal would let out a frightful screech and begin clawing the air like some huge overturned cockroach.

"Maybe I should just wrap him in a blanket and carry him under my arm," Sarah asked, looking up at Joan who was in the process of tucking Spooky into a box of kitty litter. "He might be less noticeable that way. In fact, the guard might think he's a baby or something."

"No," Joan said. "I wouldn't take any chances if I were you. Suppose you drop him?"

"Well, maybe, but trying to sneak a big doggie box like this one into that hospital is going to be pretty difficult."

"I know, but getting this cat past the front desk is not going to be a cinch either. What happens if she lets loose with some blood-curdling scream right as we're walking into the goddamn elevator?"

"She's too sick to scream. Look at her. She's half dead."

The cat, his legs splayed out like a dying squid, was lying face down and unconscious in a pile of Meow Mix Kitty Chow.

"Yeah, but she's been known to have bounced back, remember?"

"I know. I know. But let's try to think positive, O.K.?"

"And D.O.A.?" Joan asked. "What does he think?"

"He's pretty optimistic," Sarah replied. "He told me there's a one-in-three chance of one of them going."

***

Sarah was to the right of the bed, cradling Tomorrow; Joan was on the left, rocking Spooky. D.O.A. stood opposite the pillows, holding Faith's bone-grey hand high above her head.

"Ashes to ashes and dust to dust. "

"What's he doing now?" Joan whispered.

"I dunno," Sarah replied.

"Going once, going twice, going. . . . "

"Sounds to me like he's trying to auction your mother off."

"Could be."

"It doesn't seem to be working, though."

"No."

"She's still breathing."

"I know."

"They're all still breathing."

"Right."

"In fact, they all look pretty good.

"It's still early. Give him a chance."

"We've been here for over four hours."

"These things take time."

"My left leg's fallen asleep."

"Shake it."

"I'm shaking it. It's dead."

"Really? Then keep your fingers crossed. Maybe he's finally making some progress."

***

When it happened, nobody could believe it. Least of all Joan. It all happened so fast. So unexpectedly. One minute Sarah was fine and the next she was. . . .

Naturally, hospital officials wanted to know the whole story--how Joan and Sarah and D.O.A. had gotten past the guard on the first floor without obtaining passes; what the three of them had been doing around Mrs. Spinello's bed; why a dog and cat were present in a critical care unit, if the deceased had ever been subject to sudden seizures, strokes, heart attacks. . .

Considering the nature of the circumstances, Joan was more than cooperative.

"Sarah was my best friend," she said, sobbing into a pink Kleenex outside the hospital's morgue. "My very best friend. There was nothing the matter with her health. Nothing. Who could have dreamed. . . . ?"

"Now, now," the doctor said, trying to reassure her. "Tragedies like this happen all the time in hospitals. There's just no telling when it comes to matters of the heart."

"But there was absolutely nothing wrong with her heart," Joan said. "She was in the prime of her life."

"Prime or no prime," the doctor replied. "When your number is up, your number is up."

"But it doesn't make sense. Sarah wasn't even sick."

"That's usually the case. Well, perhaps the autopsy will prove something."

"The autopsy?"

"To determine the exact cause of death and to rule out any foul play."

"But she died while praying? How could there be foul play?"

"These days anything is possible."

"But. . . "

"Are there any surviving family members besides the victim's mother?

"Just her dog and cat."

"Excellent. Then we'll get started immediately. I mean, there's no sense delaying these things, right? As far as I'm concerned, there's nothing quite as painful to our loved ones as dragging out a damn burial."+++++

ETCHED IN STONE

Hypatia Hubert, who worked as a go-go dancer in Dante's Inferno, a late night hangout in downtown Philadelphia, knew absolutely nothing about higher mathematics. Therefore, she was more than a little surprised when she began to dream a series of rather intense, vivid dreams involving weird geometric shapes and strange, incomprehensible configurations. What was even stranger, however, was the fact that in these dreams she always saw herself as one of these shapes or configurations, usually spinning out of control in a vast sea of burning blue sky. One night she would be an upside-down triangle trapped inside a falling circle; another night she would become a tiny point of light moving outward like a ray of sunshine toward an open, limitless horizon. On one occasion she even saw herself as a huge plane of glass tumbling gracefully through the air like an empty window frame, perfect in its symmetry except for a small missing piece of itself in one of its corners. Why she should dream such dreams made absolutely no sense to Hypatia, and because they left her so baffled and unsettled she began to talk to Paul, the weekend bartender at Dante's who had been to college and was now studying computer science.

"You dreamed of a gnomon," he told her. "When you saw yourself as that plane of glass with the missing piece, you were dreaming of yourself as a gnomon."

Hypatia, who was nude save for a couple of leather strings and patches of pink silk across her breasts and pelvic area, asked what a gnomon was.

"Well, let's see," Paul began, wiping the bar and flinging down a couple of coasters. "How can I explain this? Do you know what a parallelogram is by any chance?"

Hypatia shook her head.

"It's a miracle I even recognized the triangle and circle," she said, glancing nervously at her watch. "I told you, school and I didn't get along. We parted company when I was sixteen."

Ten minutes more and the bar would be opened for the evening's first customers. She was scheduled to dance five sets—twenty minutes each starting at nine—in the cages above the rear of the bar. Fortunately, she still had enough time to put on her face and body make-up.

"Well," Paul said, "if you don't know what a parallelogram is, it's kinda hard to explain what a gnomon is, but let's see."

He paused, scratching his head.

"Do you know what the word 'parallel' means?" he asked, waiting for her reaction.

"Of course," Hypatia said." I'm not that stupid. Parallel is what railroad tracks are, right?"

"Right," said Paul, slapping the bar. "So now picture four railroad tracks, two going this way and two going that way—he gestured vigorously with his hands—coming together to form something that looks like this."

He picked up a nearby napkin and drew Hypatia a picture. "This is a parallelogram," he said, pointing to the figure he had drawn. "And this is a gnomon—that part of the parallelogram that remains after a similar parallelogram has been taken away from one of its corners. Understand?"

Hypatia looked down at the napkin and then up at Paul. "Sort of," she said, frowning as she gazed down again at the drawing. "It's kinda like an ex-pregnant woman whose belly is gone because the kid is no longer there, right?"

"What?" Paul asked, startled. "What the hell are you talking about?"

"I don't know," Hypatia shrugged. "Don't ask me. I'm still trying to figure out why I would dream of myself as something I never even saw before."

"Maybe your subconscious is trying to tell you something," Paul said, crumbling up the napkin and dropping it into a nearby waste basket.

"My subconscious?" Hypatia asked, looking at him curiously. "What do you mean by that?"

"Your hidden mind," Paul replied, tapping his head. "The voice of your inner self, as some might say. We all have one. Maybe yours is trying to tell you you've been dancing in those cages too long. Who knows? Go ask a shrink. "

"A shrink? Me?"

"Well, it can't hurt. After all . . ."

"Look," Hypatia said. "I ain't seeing no shrinks. Not on your life."

"Makes no difference to me," Paul said. "I just thought that . . . "

"Let's just forget all about it, O.K.?" she said, backing away from the bar. "Let's not even give it another thought. It's really not that important anyway. Honest."

Paul nodded.

"Suit yourself," he said. "After all, it's your life." Of all the women he knew, Hypatia certainly had to be one of the strangest.

An hour later she was all motion. A spinning, whirling, kicking, jiggling mass of motion. Legs, arms, tits, you name it—she had them all, and they were flying and feeling good, so why the hell should she care? Screw her goddamn dreams. Screw her gnomons and triangles, Screw her hidden mind. There was nothing the matter with her. Nothing.

Paul was nuts. He had meant well, but he was wrong—dead wrong—for implying she needed some kind of help. Who did he think he was anyway?

She didn't need his advice. She was free, free and strong as a tornado ripping across a mine field. She didn't need anybody's help or advice.

Round and round, up and down she went, oblivious to everything but the beat, the steady beat of music hammering, pounding against her like fists in the night.

"Go baby, go," several of the men at the bar yelled up at her. "Break it open , doll. Strut your stuff."

It didn't bother them any that she dreamed of gnomons and triangles. They could care less. She could dream of devils disappearing down sinkholes or moons exploding and tearing out her eyeballs as far as they were concerned, just as long as she was up in her cage, shaking her ass and wiggling her tits every Friday and Saturday night.

She liked them for that.

In fact, she was extraordinary grateful. They, at least, made her feel real, real and solid. They, at least, made her feel like a woman.

She had been dancing at Dante's for over a year. Despite some of the crap that went along with the new job—the creeps who tried to climb inside her cage, the weirdos who laid in wait for her in the parking lot, the misfit-types who wrote their telephone numbers and numerous four-letter words across her dusty windshield—she didn't mind it so much.

For one thing, she was finally earning herself a halfway decent buck which gave her the right to come and go as she pleased. With money in her pocket she could tell any creep to go screw himself if he started acting up and punching her around as Charlie, her ex-husband, had done when he was in one of his moods.

Dead broke, she had put up with Charlie's shit for over two years. When the job at Dante's came along, however, she took off like an angel out of hell.

In many ways she was really lucky getting herself hired there over so many other women. Especially since she hadn't danced in years.

"Relax," one of the guys who hired her said after her audition. "You're a natural. A real natural."

For as far back as she could remember she had always wanted to become a dancer.

As a little kid she used to close her eyes in bed at night and dream of herself as a tall, beautiful ballerina leaping across immense white spaces and towering blue-green hills. Even after she got a little older and began to realize that her hips and breasts were a bit too big for her ever to become a ballerina, she continued to think of herself as a dancer—a Ginger Rogers or an Isodora Duncan type who could make men dizzy with the mere sweep of her gorgeous arm and hand. Although things hadn't exactly worked out that way—bouncing her ass up and down at the Inferno was a lot different than waltzing through Hollywood with Fred Astaire or Gene Kelly on her arm—she wasn't complaining.

Dancing was, after all, good exercise and a lot more interesting than being a goddamn punching bag.

***

In Hypatia's dreams there was always some kind of music playing. Not the kind of music she danced to in her cage and not the kind of music she heard on the stereo driving back in her car to her apartment from the bar at three, sometimes four, in the morning along the lonely black strip of highway, but a kind of music she could not explain in words very well. It was more like delicate pieces of fine glass tapping against each other in a warm breeze, or crystal wind chimes swaying in harmony to the rise and fall of sea waves. It would begin just at the time she found herself dissolving into her circles and triangles and tumbling parallelograms. At first it would be very soft, almost unnoticeable—more of a quasi-sound like the distant hum one hears by pressing a seashell against the ear—but gradually it would increase in intensity, flowing outward and upward until the whole atmosphere was alive and singing with its fullness and vibrancy.

Although it lacked the regular beat of most of the music she knew, there was a rather strange rhythm to it which, oddly enough, seemed to flow from her mood. Floating along without arms, without legs, without any of the old familiar parts by which she was so often identified and by which she identified herself—she was, after all, just a configuration of lines and dots having neither mass, weight, nor solid dimension—she discovered to her amazement that she could will the music into any rhythm and pattern she desired by just thinking about it or feeling it.

Regular, irregular, harmonious, discordant—it was all up to her. Whatever she felt, it became. When she was down, the music seemed to collide against her like bumper cars ramming together in an amusement park; when she was blue, the slightest sound became a broken music box slamming shut on somebody's fingers.

"Maybe you're just horny or something," one of the women at Dante's had suggested. "Maybe you ain't getting laid enough. Maybe that's your problem."

"Getting laid?" Hypatia had replied. "What's getting laid got to do with anything?"

As far as she was concerned getting laid had nothing to do with nothing. Even goddamn Charlie had taught her that.

Sometimes, after waking up from one of her dreams—a low, mysterious melody still playing in her head—Hypatia would throw the covers aside and look down at herself in the bed. For a moment the sight of her own body, lying there pale and still in the soft light cast by her bedside lamp, would startle her. Toes, feet, hands, thighs—they seemed to make no sense. They did not belong, somehow. They were outside, remote, alien—things that had been dropped upon her in the night by some force she could not imagine or even hope to understand.

Frightened, she would lie back down and close her eyes, clutching the sheets beneath her fingers as she fought against an overwhelming, unbearable sadness.

Later, when she was feeling better—like her old self again, as she described it—she would try to figure out where this sadness came from, whether it was part of her dream world, her real world or that other world in between when she didn't know where the hell she was.

Although she thought about this a lot, she could never come up with any answers. The only thing she knew was that it left her feeling lopsided and alone, as if some vital, secret part of herself had been torn away and sent spinning into nowhere.

It was an incredible feeling of emptiness. The total opposite, in fact, of everything she had ever experienced in Dante's. Which, again, was another reason why she liked the place so much. At least there she could count on things being halfway normal.

***

He was sitting by himself at the far edge of the bar, running the fingers of his right hand round and round the top of his beer glass when Hypatia first saw him. For a moment she thought he was a woman, a short-haired dyke from downtown come to watch the fun, as the guys in the back room would say.

He was small, almost fragile-looking, with soft, delicate features and high, prominent cheekbones. As she got a little closer, however, Hypatia noticed the light stubble of a beard and the heavy thickness of his forearms and hands. They seemed incongruous, somehow, with the rest of him.

What's more, they were restless hands, driven by an internal energy that seemed to be lacking in the lower half of his body, which sat rigidly still upon the narrow barstool.

Hypatia was so intrigued by his hands that she almost missed seeing the napkins. There were at least seven of them scattered randomly on the bar in front of him, all of them covered with pencil drawings of sharp lines and box-like shapes, merging and intersecting like pairs of crooked crosses and open wings.

For a moment Hypatia was stunned. Something inside her head seemed to click slowly, like the shutter of a camera closing in a dark, spiraling tunnel.

She began to say something, then stopped. Although someone was speaking to her, she found it almost impossible to take her eyes away from the napkins.

"Boy, you really can dance, do you know that?" the voice was saying. "I've been watching you all night."

When she looked up, she realized the voice belonged to the man she had been observing.

"I'd really like to buy you a drink, if I may," he said. "It'll be my way of saying thanks."

"Thanks?" Hypatia asked, puzzled. "Thanks for . . . for what?"

"For what you've given me."

"I . . , I don't understand," Hypatia said.

"Well, " he grinned. "In that case I guess I'll have to explain myself."

He picked up the napkins and handed them one by one to Hypatia, who gazed down in amazement at their swirling lines and half-formed figures.

"What do you think?" he asked. "They're my impressions of you. Of the way you move, the way you look, the way your body looks, way up there in that cage against all that emptiness."

Hypatia's eyes followed his finger. "You fill it all up. All that space. You fill it up with something beautiful. The way an artist does. The way I do."

He pointed to the napkins again.

"Shapes, lines, shadows—they're my life. I live them, I dream them, and I create them."

Hypatia began to tremble, her face shifting expressions like a turning mirror.

"But this is all so. ,. . .strange," she said. "It's almost as if . . . . "

"Artists always know," he said, laughing softly. "It goes with the territory, as they say."

***

His name was Mark. Mark Framington. And he was different from any man Hypatia had ever known. There was no question about that. The way he talked, the way he treated her. The way he looked into her eyes and smiled whenever she shrugged her shoulders or hugged herself against the cold.

He was a man she could trust. She knew that. Someone she could come to respect.

After awhile they began going out together. Sometimes they took walks; sometimes they went to dinner. One afternoon they went to a museum. Mark was particularly fascinated with the statuary, especially the bronze and marble heads.

"Yes," Hypatia had said, turning to him with a smile, "they're all very nice, but in all honesty what I would really like to see is your work. Do you think that would be possible someday?"

"Oh, very possible," he had replied, taking hold of her hand. "In fact, I imagined I would be showing it to you right from the beginning. I guess I was just waiting for the right moment, that's all."

***

The right moment came one night when Hypatia left Dante's and found Mark waiting for her in the parking lot.

"Are you ready?" he asked.

"Ready?" Hypatia repeated. "Ready for what?"

"To see my work. You said you wanted to."

"But now?" Hypatia said, glancing at her watch. "It's almost four o'clock in the morning."

"I know," he nodded. "This is the best time. No one will be there now."

She heard it as soon as they stepped inside the gate. Her music. The music she had heard in her dreams. At first it was soft, almost unnoticeable, but gradually it increased, flowing upward like sea waves. Overhead the moon shone cold as stone.

Silently they walked along, past the crucifixes, the flying wings, the dark blocks of heavy stone.

"It's what I saw," Hypatia whispered. "In my dreams. All these shapes, these terrible, geometric shapes."

"Shapes I've created," Mark said, turning to look at her. "Worlds I made with my hands, my eyes, my mind."

"But they're all tombstones. You spent all your time making tombstones."

"They're not just tombstones. They're living monuments to the living dead."

He led Hypatia across several graves to an immense angel with one wing standing guard over a grey mausoleum.

"Look at that face. I made it. See how real it is. It's breathing. It's absolutely beautiful. The way you're beautiful. The way you're real.

"No," Hypatia said. "No."

"And I can make you part of it. Your face. Your body. You're my missing piece. My next angel. An angel to fill the emptiness.

He began stroking her lips, her cheeks, her forehead. Hypatia closed her eyes, dropping backwards into the void. +++++

REMEMBERING THE DEAD

Three months after Janet Thompson's father died of a sudden, massive heart attack, her best friend, Paula, who was working on her M.F.A. and who liked to think of herself as an artist, presented her with an original, portrait-size oil painting of the dead man.

"Surprise!" Paula said as she unveiled the canvas for her friend and Robert, Janet's husband. "I hope you like it. I mean, your father was such a nice man and all. I really wanted to capture him on canvas."

For the first few seconds Janet didn't know what to say. It was not her father. Not at all. She did not want to hurt her friend's feelings—Paula had probably spent some time working on the portrait—but she did not want this to be her memory of her father. Confused, she just stood there, gazing at the painting.

Like her late father's, the face in the portrait had ruddy brown skin, wispy, grey hair and a smooth high forehead. The long straight nose and prominent high cheekbones were also like her father's. Even the shape and color of the eyes were the same—a soft transparent blue so light they seemed to disappear if one stared into them for too long.

But unlike her father's, the face in the portrait had no chin. And hardly any mouth. Just a thin red and orange line traced like an after thought beneath the nose. It was more like a scratch across the bottom half of his face which seemed to just drop away, fading into the murky shadows of his mottled brown neck like a long twilight sinking into night.

Nevertheless--and this was why she supposed she found the portrait so odd and unsettling--a vague resemblance was there, brooding within the thick dabs of oily paint that formed the contours of his head and face. Anyone who knew her father even slightly could see that. They would be able to recognize the similarity despite all the differences.

"It was a real challenge for me," Paula said."I learned a lot, especially since portraits can be so difficult."

"I think it's great," Robert said, glancing over at his wife who still hadn't said a word. "I think you really got the old man down. Right, honey? Doesn't Paula have the old man down?"

"Well," Janet hesitated, "there is a slight resemblance."

"Only slight? Robert replied. "I think it looks just like him."

"No, I'm afraid not," Janet said, taking a deep breath, "I'm sorry to say this, but it's just not him."

"Well, of course, it's not him," Robert laughed. "It's a painting, for heaven's sake."

"Oh, it's all right," Paula said, patting her friend's hand. "I understand what Janet is saying. A map is not the territory, that's all."

"Yes, " Janet said, "I guess that's what I mean."

"Oh, pay no attention to her, " Robert insisted. "I think your painting is just great, Paula. It's Jack, all right."

"No, it isn't," Janet repeated. "The chin in this portrait just disappears. It just drops away."

"So did Jack's chin " Robert said. "I remember his chin exactly."

"Now, isn't that nice?" Paula said

"And my father's lips were thicker, more . . . . more alive."

"Alive?" Robert repeated. "His lips? What are you talking about?"

"No, you're right," Paula sighed. "It's hard to paint real lips."

"Those are your father's eyes though," Robert continued, pointing a finger toward the center of the canvas. "You can't argue with that. They're the same color and everything."

"No," Janet said, shaking her head. "His eyes never really looked like that."

"Eyes and chins are hard too," Paula said, after a moment. "They're really difficult. No matter how much I work on them I can never seem to get them right."

"Well, maybe they're not perfect," Robert hedged. "But they're certainly not bad. Not bad at all. In fact, I think they're fine. I think they look really good on Janet's father."

There was another awkward silence.

"I mean, I know I couldn't have painted them. That's for sure," said Robert.

Paula took a step closer to the canvas.

"What's strange is that I painted that portrait from a photograph. I mean, naturally I remember your father's face and all, but when it comes to portraits you don't want to rely just on memory."

"No, that's right," Robert agreed. "Memory can play awful tricks sometimes."

"Photographs never did my father justice," Janet said, holding her voice soft and steady. "They always made him look dead."

"I always thought they made him look fat," Robert laughed. "But I guess he was sort of fat."

"He wasn't fat," Janet insisted. "He was never fat."

"Oh, come on now, Janet. He weighed over two hundred pounds."

"But he was very tall and muscular. All his weight was muscle, not fat."

"Love is blind," Robert said, shaking his head. "What can I tell you?"

"My father was a tall man."

"Janet, your father was only about five foot nine. That isn't very tall."

"He was almost six feet," Janet said softly, "I should know. He was my father. I know him as he really was."

"Oh well," Paula said, coming between them and taking both their arms. "It's no big deal, really. Everybody remembers a person differently."

"It's not a question of remembering," Janet said. "It's a fact. My father was a tall, muscular man who was definitely not fat."

"Do you think I made him look fat in the portrait?" Paula asked softly.

"Yes," Janet nodded. "That man in the portrait is much fatter than my father ever was. I'm sorry, but it's true."

"It's not true," Robert protested. "Don't listen to her, Paula. She's just being crazy all of a sudden, that's all. "

"Well, I probably did make him heavier than he actually was. Janet should know. Right, Janet?"

"Yes, that's right."

"Well, if you ask me I think memories suck," Robert insisted. "They play tricks on us all. What's important is the here and now."

"The here and now plays tricks too," said Janet, turning away from the painting and staring out the window.

"Nothing stays."

"Oh, pay no attention, Paula," Robert said, grabbing hold of the painting. "I'll find a good spot in the house to hang this. A spot that will do it justice. You just wait and see."

"It's hard when you lose someone you love," Paula said softly. "Very hard. Janet's father meant a great deal to her. They were very close. I understand that."

"I understand that too," Robert said, glancing over at his wife. "He was a really great guy and we had a lot in common. A whole lot in common. And--and if you ask me I think he'd love your painting."

***

Janet did her best to try and forget the painting, which Robert had insisted upon hanging in their bedroom. She tried to imagine that it was just another picture on the wall: a splattering of color thrown haphazardly across an empty canvas; a vague impression of a shadowy figure who held no connection and stirred no memory. But after a short time she discovered that this was quite impossible.

For one thing, she was always conscious of the face in the painting. It seemed to stare out at her, following her every movement around the room, pleading with her in some secret, anguished way. It was a stranger's face with a stranger's mouth and chin, but within its mute silence she saw her father's face buried there. The face she had known and loved. The face she fought to hold within her mind's eye, safe from the shiftings of time and the hands of others; safe from the terrible blankness and erasure of death. This face, the real one, called to her like a dream, echoing from some dark well of sleep, crying out for life and release.

Even at night when she lay in bed in the darkness next to Robert she could sense this face hovering above them, speaking to her. The way her father had spoken to her so long ago when she was a little girl before time and memory had shifted and his face had faded into that of a stranger.

Every morning dressing for work Janet would try to keep her eyes on the floor or the mirror above their oak bureau while Robert chatted on about work or the weather or what they would do that weekend. But eventually her eyes would drift--almost beyond her control, it seemed-- toward the face in the portrait. Each day she watched, silent and grieving, as her father faded farther and farther away, until one day he vanished completely, leaving her with nothing but the haunted eyes of a chinless, painted stranger.

To Robert, however, the portrait seemed no different than the day he had hung it, although he had to admit he rarely noticed it. To him it was just a very good painting of his dead father-in-law, the way he would always remember him. +++++

TALES OF RELATIONSHIPS

All you need is love

--John Lennon

PERSON-TO-PERSON

There was something very strange going on in Martha Thompson's life. It seemed that everywhere she turned someone was trying to save her immortal soul.

On otherwise deserted street corners Jehovah's Witnesses would pop out at her from behind the sharp corners of red-brick buildings and thrust damp copies of the Watchtower into her unsuspecting hands. In the noisy subway station where blind old nuns collected pennies for the starving poor in Ethiopia, Hari Krishnas would dance toward her, chanting and drumming their tambourines in spasms of spiritual ecstasy. Even at home on her very own doorstep among the milk bottles and clay pots of geraniums a never-ending stream of self-proclaimed Saviors-- Young Baptists for A Sinless World, Born-Again Christians, Meaningful Methodists for a Better Tomorrow--would arrive regular as the morning, ringing he doorbell and knocking at her windows to offer their versions of truth and salvation.

At first Martha couldn't understand why she--out of so many other people she saw all around her--had suddenly become the object of so much religious attention.

"What can they possibly want from me?" she asked herself, slamming her front door one mild spring evening in the pale face of a young Jesus-Freak who had begun to read to her from the Book of Revelations.

"Why can't they just leave me alone? You'd think from the way everyone is carrying on, that I was some fallen, terribly wicked woman or something."

Having just returned home from a long, exhausting day of drawing blood from pre-op patients at the hospital where she worked as a lab technician, she was in no mood to stand around chatting about the coming Armageddon with a Bible-toting twenty-year old dressed in a Mickey Mouse T-shirt. Wearily, she headed for the kitchen where she poured herself a glass of wine.

"Maybe it's these goddamn bags under my eyes," she said, pausing for a moment to stare at herself in the oval mirror above the bookshelf. "They make me look desperate. Like a lost soul or some loose woman who spends all her day in bed and is headed straight for hell. Christ, I should be so lucky."

Sighing, she lifted the wine glass toward her reflection. "To you and your devil," she said. "May you some day meet and find eternal happiness."

Just then the phone rang. It was a Mr. Burke T. Burke calling long distance person-to-person for a Miss Martha Thompson.

"But I don't know any Burke T. Burkes," Martha protested to the operator. "You must have the wrong Martha Thompson."

"Not at all," said a deep male voice into her ear. "You're just the Martha I have been looking for."

"Who is this?" Martha asked, wondering where the operator had gone. "Who are you trying to reach?"

"You," said the voice, "as is everyone else. I hear you're quite the popular lady now. Very much in demand. Well, that's to be expected naturally at this stage, but still I do hope I'm not too late?"

"Too late?" Martha said. "Too late for what?"

"To win your heart," the voice said softly.

"Now wait a minute," Martha said. "I don't know who you think you are, or why you're phoning me but if this is another one of those crank calls I've been getting late at night, I'll have you know . . . "

"I've already told you who I am," the voice said. "I'm Mr. Burke T. Burke. A secret admirer who has been observing you for some time now. I'm phoning you simply to warn you that I'm on my way."

"On your way?" Martha repeated. "On your way where?"

"On my way to you," the voice said. "Straight to your very soul."

Martha was a nervous wreck. In the course of two hours she had dropped three vials of blood, and broken off the head of a needle in the beefy forearm of a Polish-speaking longshoreman who was suffering from the flu. Try as she might, she just couldn't stop thinking about this Burke T. Burke character and where he might be at that very moment. She had absolutely no idea who he was or what he wanted from her. She didn't know what he looked like, where he was coming from, or what he might do when he arrived.

At first she thought about going to the police, but when she realized that she had nothing really to report, she decided against it. Then she wondered if she should at least tell someone at work that a strange man had called, threatening to come visit her. But when she began to think about how she might sound talking about strange men calling in the night when she—as everyone at the hospital knew--hadn't been out with a man since the day her ex-fiance, Ralph, eloped with her best friend, Barbara, she decided against it.

"I'd rather take my chances with some nut than be laughed at again by those damn nurses and doctors who are forever gossiping about something," she said to herself with a touch of self-pity.

She began to wonder whatever happened to all the normal men in the world. Men she used to know and find so attractive. Men who would invite her up to their apartments for a drink and then carry her off to bed. Sadly, they seemed somehow to have vanished from the face of the earth.

"And now here I am again, hounded by some maniac who tells me he's on his way from out the blue to capture my heart and soul. Good Christ, will it ever end?"

***

A dozen long-stemmed roses were lying on the kitchen table when Martha arrived home from work later that night. However, she was so tired, so worn out from her dash up the front steps past three puny Presbyterians who were carrying a six-foot crucifix covered with lamb's wool and aluminum foil that she failed to notice the flowers at first. In fact, it wasn't until she had kicked off her shoes and poured herself a glass of wine that her eyes actually lighted upon the roses in their shiny narrow white box lying amid the breakfast plates.

"To the One Woman I have desired for all Eternity," read a small pink card atop the box.

"Good Christ," Martha said. "What the hell. . . "

Suddenly there came a loud knock at the front door.

"Yoo-hoo, Martha, it's me. Burke T. Burke. Open up, darling."

Martha dove toward the door.

"I don't know who you think you are," she cried, sliding the pull chain securely into place, "but you better leave me alone because I'm about to call the police."

213

"Police? Martha, don't be absurd," Burke T. Burke said. "Why would you call the police? Didn't you get my roses?"

"Yes, and I don't know how you got into my house," she said, beginning to tremble, "but if you don't go away I'll have you arrested."

Burke T. Burke began to chuckle.

"You're a most unusual woman," he whispered, his face close to the door. "Unfriendly, suspicious, rude. I like that. It shows real character. Real character."

"Go away," she screamed. "Do you hear me? Go away."

"Not before I at least talk to you," Burke T. Burke said, rattling the doorknob. "After all, I've come so far, and what I have to say to you is so, so important."

"Then write me a letter or something, but I'm warning you, you're not getting into this house."

"But it's extremely important that you see me," Burke T. Burke replied. "Can't you at least open the door a little and take a quick peek?"

Martha hesitated.

"Why should I do that? I don't have to see you. I don't want to see you."

"Oh yes you do," said Burke T. Burke. "That's probably one of the most important things of all. You must see what I look like. That would make everything so much easier."

"I have no idea what you're talking about," Martha said, "but I swear, if you don't go away immediat--"

"Look, you don't even have to open the door, if you don't want. I'll just stick my face up close to the window and you can look at me from inside your house. O.K?"

Before Martha had a chance to reply, a thick shadow darkened the window of her living room. She hesitated, wondering what to do, then grabbing hold of the heavy frying pan atop her stove, she tiptoed nervously toward the window.

There, to her amazement, hanging upside down outside the glass and staring back at her, was her own face, save only for a thick black moustache and heavy five o'clock shadow.

"I told you that seeing me would make all the difference," Burke T. Burke said, fanning Martha slowly back to consciousness with a thin paperback he had found on her desk, Everything That Rises Must Converge.

"It's like they say, 'one picture is worth a thousand words.' Right?"

"I--I can't believe this is really happening," Martha said, groggily, trying to lift her head from Burke T. Burke's lap. "How did you--?"

"Get inside here past all those locks? Oh, it was nothing really. I have my ways."

"I must be dreaming," Martha replied, "I have to be. Or maybe I'm just losing my mind."

"Well, some people might say you're doing a little of both, but who cares? What's important is that I finally found you."

"But this is so . . . so strange. So weird."

"You mean our getting together like this? No. I don't think it's strange at all. It just took time, that's all."

"But don't. . . don't you think that it's strange that we . . . we look so much alike even though you're a . . . a man and I'm . . . I'm a woman?"

"No, not at all. We are alike, save for a few differences. And, as they say, Vive la difference!"

He looked at her and smiled.

"You know, I find you very attractive."

He was about to kiss her, but Martha quickly pushed him away.

"No, stop," she said, struggling awkwardly to her feet. "This is awful. Awful."

"Awful?" asked Burke T. Burke. "Why?"

"Because, well, because, it's. . . I mean. . .it's not right."

"What's not right?"

"It's not right that. . . that . . . you and I are . . . are so."

"So wonderfully attracted to one another?"

"No!" Martha cried, backing away. " I didn't mean that at all. I don't find you attractive. I . . . I find you repulsive."

"Repulsive?" Burke T. Burke laughed. "Now isn't that a bit strong? A moment ago you told me we looked alike."

"I . . . I was wrong"

"No, you weren't wrong, darling. You were just afraid, that's all," Burke T. Burke said, rising to his feet and walking toward her. "But once you get to know me, you'll find me very exciting. Very appealing. I promise."

"Stay where you are," Martha cried. "Don't come any closer."

"But honey, be reasonable. Think of how lonely you've been all these months."

"Lonely? I haven't been lonely."

"Yes, you have. Terribly lonely. Your life has been a real bore. Admit it."

"I'll admit nothing of the kind. How dare you!"

"In fact, that's why you called me. You knew you needed some excitement. Some passion."

"Called you? Why I never . . ."

"Since Ralph took off, the only men in your life have been those misfits who come ringing your doorbell with their Bibles and prayer books."

"That's not true! Why I . . . I . . . "

"You need a real man. Someone to love. Someone who is able to understand you completely. Possess you completely. Your soulmate. Me."

"You?"

"Me. The one and only Burke T. Burke."

You're insane."

"Yes, insane with love. I have been for centuries, but you kept putting me off, remember?"

"No! I don't remember. How could I? This is the first time I ever met you."

"That's not true," he said, taking several steps toward her. "We've been together since the beginning of time. Why, we even shared the same protoplasm together."

"Stay where you are," Martha said. "Don't you dare touch me."

"I have to touch you," he smiled. "I can't help myself. You belong to me. We belong to one another."

He lunged toward her, pinning her against the wall

"Help!" Martha screamed. "Somebody help me."

"Face it," he whispered, planting a kiss on her cheek. "This thing is bigger than the both of us."

"Like hell it is," she roared, lifting her right foot and bringing it down full force upon his left instep. "Take that, you bastard."

As Burke T. Burke sprung back in pain, grabbing hold of his foot, Martha let loose with a powerful left hook which landed squarely against the base of his nose.

"My God," Burke T. Burke cried. "You're killing me."

"You ain't seen nothing yet," Martha cried, taking a frenzied dive at his knees and bringing him smashingly to the floor. As Burke T. Burke screamed in terror, Martha climbed atop him and began beating his head against the leg of a nearby chair.

"Take that," she said. "You. . .you beast."

"Please," Burke T. Burke began to moan. "I give up. I swear. Just stop. Please stop. I can't take any more."

"What?" Martha said, her fury at last beginning to subside. "What did you say?"

"I said I can't take any more. Please. Just stop. Just let me go. Please."

Startled, Martha looked down at the figure beneath her. Eyes thick with terror stared back at her.

"Oh. . . oh," she said, overcome suddenly with a new and powerful wave of emotion. "Did I--?"

Gently, she touched his nose which was bruised and bleeding.

"I'm . . . I'm sorry, so sorry," she said, leaning down as if to kiss him.

Terrified, Burke T. Burke closed his eyes. For a moment Martha too saw darkness.

"I'll . . . I'll get you some ice," she said, running her hand along the left side of his face.

"No," Burke T. Burke said, slowly raising himself upon one elbow and rubbing his head. "I'd. . . I'd rather you didn't. I have to go now."

"But you're hurt. You can't go."

For a moment Martha couldn't believe what she was saying. It was as if she had been suddenly turned inside out, upside down.

"I . . . I mean you've come so far. . . so very far and now . . . "

"And now I got to be getting along," he said sheepishly, inching his way across the floor. "As you can imagine, our little encounter was not exactly what I had in mind."

"Nor I," said Martha.

"But still it has been interesting to say the least. If I'm ever in the neighborhood again I promise to give you a buzz. O.K.?"

"Fine," she replied. "I'll be looking forward to it."

With that he was out the door and down the steps in seconds, galloping across the street like a devil straight from hell. Martha watched him disappear among the reflecting shadows of the windowpane, wondering what the T in his name stood for. +++++

QUEEN OF THE ROAD

Linda Ellison had just left her mother's room at the Fair Acre Nursing home in Hopewell when she heard the commotion at the end of the corridor.

"Look, I am not an animal, some dog you can tie to a pole. I'm a human being. You hear me? A human being."

"Now, now, Rose. Keep your voice down. We don't want to upset the other guests here, now do we?"

Rose, a gray-haired woman with bright blue eyes and sunken cheeks, gripped the arms of her wheelchair, desperate to lift herself.

"I'll keep my voice down when you untie this rope from the wheel of my chair."

"It's for your own safety, Rose. You know that. We cannot have you flying up and down this hallway in that wheelchair. You're liable to hurt yourself or one of the other guests."

Linda hesitated, wondering if she should walk past them or remain where she was.

"Flying? You call rolling a wheelchair down a hallway flying?"

The nurse, a practical woman long accustomed to following rules despite the natural promptings of her heart, smiled good-naturedly.

"Rose, if there were a traffic cop around he would give you a ticket for speeding. I know. I've seen you."

"I am not going to sit here all day long trapped to a hand rail like some prisoner. I gotta move around a little."

"When you want to go somewhere you can call the nurse. She can push you. But we can't have you roaming about in that thing whenever you feel like it, barging into other people's rooms, poking your nose into the nurses' station, chasing after visitors."

"I do not barge into other people's rooms and I do not chase after visitors. I simply enjoy a little conversation every now and then with someone who can still speak. What's wrong with that? You want me to shrivel up and die like these other corpses I see wandering around?"

Embarrassed, Linda slipped back into her mother's room. Seconds later the nurse turned and began writing something down in her clipboard.

"There are plenty of things here to keep you busy," she said with patient detachment. "You can listen to the radio, you can watch television, you can sit in the solarium and play Bingo."

"Play Bingo? What in heaven's name do you take me for? I suffer from arthritis, not a mental disorder."

"Oh, Rose, you're a handful. I just don't know what we're going to do with you."

"For a start you can untie me. I promise I won't budge an inch."

"Sorry, Rose," the nurse said closing the clipboard and smiling, "but I don't trust you. Once my back is turned, you'll be off in the Grand Prix again."

"But what happens if I have to go to the bathroom or something? I won't be able to move."

Linda turned and looked at her mother who was sitting slumped in a chair by the bed, staring glassy-eyed into space.

"You can ring for the nurse."

"This is horrendous," Rose said, squirming in her seat, as if she might suddenly rise up and fling the chair and table both out a nearby window. "Never in my life have I--"

"I tell you what," the nurse said, interrupting, "if you're a good girl and you behave yourself the rest of this morning, I'll give you a ride down the hallway myself this afternoon after I make my rounds. O.K.?"

She patted Rose briskly on the shoulder, then marched off down the hallway, clipboard in hand.

"I'm warning you," Rose shouted after her. "Either you untie me from this thing or else. Do you hear me?"

For a moment Linda didn't know what to do. To get to the exit she would have to pass the woman in the wheelchair. It would be terribly embarrassing if the old lady stopped her and asked her for help.

Although she sympathized with her, the last thing she wanted to do was to get involved in her problem, or in anyone's problem for that matter. She simply had too many of her own, especially now with her mother so sick.

What's more, she was tired. She longed to get home, kick off her shoes, and relax. She certainly did not want to spend her time alienating any of the nurses by interfering with their patients. Her own mother's welfare as a patient was at stake, after all, and under no circumstances would she jeopardize that.

Nevertheless, she was reluctant to simply ignore the old woman. As one human being to another, she would have to say or do something if she decided to walk past her.

But in all honesty what could she do? If she helped the woman untie the wheelchair from the hand rail, more than likely the nurse would be furious. If she simply chatted with the woman, and then took off, she would feel guilty.

The only reasonable thing she could think of was to wait inside her mother's room. Maybe the old woman would eventually fall asleep, or somehow free herself. Or maybe somebody else would come along and distract her long enough for Linda to slip by unnoticed.

Whatever was to happen, she wished it wouldn't take too long. Being trapped inside a nursing home was certainly not her idea of a good time.

***

Nobody could really say for certain what was wrong with Linda's mother. Some doctors said that she was suffering from Alzheimer's disease and others claimed that she had had a stroke, but when the reports from her CAT scan and EEG test came back from the lab, there was no evidence of any organic disease.

All Linda knew for sure was that her mother had become, within a matter of months, a woman broken in body and spirit, totally incapable of caring for herself, and totally oblivious to everything and everyone around her. Lost in her own silence, she would sit hour after hour, gazing blankly into space, a mere shadow of the woman she had been.

"Do you know," one doctor had asked, "has she suffered any severe trauma or anything of that nature?

"Well," Linda had replied, hesitating. "She did lose her husband, my father, a few months back, but in all honesty, I never thought they were very close."

"In any event," the doctor had explained, "his death may have been quite a blow to her. In fact, it's quite possible that her immune system was adversely affected by the shock. If that were the case, without a strong will to live, she would suffer a severe and rapid decline, both physically and mentally, once an infection did strike."

It was so ironic, but apparently it was true. For all her seeming indifference, her mother had, it appeared, lost her will to live after her husband's death. Like some helpless animal who had crawled off to a hole to wait for death, her mother too had disappeared into a hole of silence and despair.

All that remained of her was a shell, gray and brittle like a broken pearl--what Linda saw every time she went to the nursing home to visit her.

***

At first Linda thought she had wandered into the wrong room. Close to the left of her mother's bed, sitting upright in her wheelchair, was Rose, the woman she had seen arguing with the nurse on her last visit.

"I . . .I . . "

"It's all right," Rose said, matter-of-factly. "Come on in. You've got the right place."

Sure enough, Linda's mother was lying face up in the bed, her eyes closed, her thin arms by her side.

"I was going by her room when I heard her moaning. I thought I'd better come in and see what was going on."

Quickly, Linda moved to the bed, reaching out to touch her mother's forehead.

"Moaning? What kind of moaning?"

"Oh, you know. Like she was whimpering or something."

"Maybe I should get the nurse," Linda said, looking anxiously into her mother's face. "Maybe she's sick."

"Oh, I think she's all right," Rose said. "She was probably dreaming or something. That happens sometimes. I wouldn't worry. She's been quiet for some time now."

"Well, it . . . it was very nice of you to check on her like that," Linda said. "I really appreciate it."

"Ah, it's no big deal. Something like that keeps me occupied. Most of the time I'm bored to death sitting around this place doing nothing."

"I guess in one sense my mother is pretty lucky then. She doesn't know where she is or what's going on. She's been out of it for some time now."

"Well, she's pretty much like everybody else then, wouldn't you say?"

"I suppose," Linda laughed. "Nowadays lots of people are confused."

"Take my husband, for instance," Rose said. "I've been here for close to a month now and the bum still hasn't come to visit. In fact, he probably doesn't even know I'm gone--thinks I'm still in the bathtub or something."

"That's too bad. I'm sorry."

"Ah, I'm used to it. No skin off my tail."

Outside the door a nurse passed, returning almost instantly to poke her head back into the room.

"Rose! So that's where you are. I've been looking all over for you."

"Why? Did I win the lottery or something," Rose asked.

"How on earth did you manage to get into that wheelchair again? You know the doctor told you to stay in bed."

"Ah, the doctor is an ass," Rose said. "A genuine first-class ass."

"Oh, you naughty lady," the nurse scolded, giving her a playful tap on the shoulder. "How can you say such a thing?"

"Because it's true. The first time that man ever saw me, he told me I'd be in this place for the rest of my life. He said that my arthritis would probably never get better."

Rose turned to Linda.

"Can you imagine anyone actually saying such a thing to a person? And a doctor to boot? A doctor who should know better? The man has to be an ass."

"Rose, you're impossible," the nurse said, grabbing hold of the two back handles of the wheelchair and pushing it toward the door. "You're always finding fault with something."

"Hey, let me alone," Rose shouted. "What are you doing? Where are you shoving me off to? I was right in the middle of a nice conversation with my friend here."

"It's time for your medicine," the nurse said, winking at Linda. "Your friend will understand that, I'm sure."

"Why don't you let my friend speak for herself?" Rose said. "She's got a brain, right?"

Linda blushed, careful to avoid the nurse's eyes.

"Good. . . good-bye, Rose" she said, waving shyly. "And thanks again for your help."

"No problem," Rose said over her shoulder as the nurse began wheeling her down the hall. "I'll try to keep an eye on your mother whenever I get the chance."

"Thanks."

"And remember, if you feel like it, drop in and see me the next time you visit. I'll fill you in on what goes on in this place if they don't have me muzzled by then."

***

One week later after returning from a sad and wordless visit with her mother, Linda found herself sitting next to Rose in the solarium.

Although the wheels of Rose's chair were tied with a long rope to a hand rail running across the rear wall of the room, for once Rose didn't seem to notice. She was too busy peering down into a huge paper map of the world she held in her lap.

"Ever been to India?" she asked, as Linda stared out the window into a gray maze of bare winter branches.

It was one of those mild late February afternoons that hint of early spring and the promise of bright, warm days and hyacinth-scented nights.

"India? God, no," Linda said. "What would I do in India?"

"Same thing you'd do anywhere else. See the sights, meet the people. Live a little."

"India doesn't appeal to me."

"Really? Why?"

"It's too depressing. All that poverty and those sacred cows and skinny people wandering about. I'd find it horrible."

"But what about the Taj Mahal? Wouldn't you find that interesting? And how about the holy temples and the great works of art and the beautiful mountains and breath-taking rivers? You got to take them into consideration too. You can't reduce a whole country to a couple of cows. What's the matter with you? Don't you have any vision?"

"Vision?"

"That's right. Vision. You know, imagination, passion, energy."

"In all honesty, no. At least not right now. Not after visiting my mother for over an hour."

"Why? She say something you didn't want to hear?"

"Say something? Are you kidding? My mother hasn't said a word in months."

"Well, maybe she's got nothing to talk about."

"She wants to die. I know it. She's had it with life. I can see it in her eyes. There's nothing there anymore."

"That happens sometimes. I know. It happened to my son."

"Your son?"

"My son, Charlie. He committed suicide when he was 18."

"God, I'm . . . I'm. . . "

"Oh, that was a long time ago. I was a young woman. In my late thirties, I'd say. A lot of things have flowed under the bridge since then, believe me."

"But you must have felt terrible at the time?"

"It was no picnic, but I got over it. You just have to learn to adapt, that's all."

She was running her right index finger, bent and gnarled with arthritis, along the coast of Kashmir.

"How about Afghanistan? Think you'd be interested in going there? Maybe see a few camels?"

"There's a war going on in Afghanistan."

"I know, but maybe it will be over by then."

"Rose," Linda smiled, "Something tells me you're an optimist."

"Why be gloomy? It ain't practical."

"I wish my mother thought like you. It would be a lot easier on everybody."

"Well, each to his own, but as far as I'm concerned, nothing's getting me down. Including this place. I'm leaving."

"Leaving? How? When?"

"First chance I get."

"Did your doctor say it was O.K.? Did he . . . "

"Of course not. He told me my arthritis was getting worse. That the medicine they were giving me wasn't working and that in a couple of months I might be bed-ridden."

"Do you agree with him?"

"In a sense, yes. I probably will be bed-ridden, but only if I remain here and do what they tell me to do. I mean, let's face it. With arthritis you gotta move. You can't stay cooped up. Look at me. They got me tied to a wall, for Christ sake. No wonder I'm getting worse."

"But where will you go? What will you do?"

"I'll go home and do what I've always done. Take care of myself. Hope for the best. Then when I'm feeling better I'll do some traveling. With a little luck and a few bucks, I'll be O.K."

"But what about your husband? Doesn't he have to sign you out of here? What if--"

"What if the world ends? Jesus, for a young woman, you sure worry a lot. Learn to take one step at a time. You won't age as fast."

"But--"

"And besides, my husband may be in Florida by now for all I know. The bum never was reliable. If I waited for him to sign me out of here, I'd be stiff as a poker."

"Well, I . . . I wish you luck. I hope things work out for you."

"Thanks," Rose said. "They will, if you help me."

"Help you?" Linda gasped. "How?"

"By giving me a push out of here and a ride to Bayonne. I live on 23th street. It's not too far."

"But . . . but I . . . I can't do that. That . . that would be like kidnapping."

Don't be silly. You can't kidnap someone who's willing to be kidnapped."

"But . . . but . . . "

"You'd be doing me a favor. And besides it would be good for the two of us. Every now and then you got to do something exciting."

"But what if the nurses--?"

"Look, just untie this damn rope and give me a little shove. There're no nurses around. They're all having coffee and watching the soaps."

"I'm . . . I'm scared," Linda said, her hands trembling as she reached for the rope. "I've never done anything like this in my . . . my life."

"That's because you're still young. What do you expect? Give yourself a chance."

"There . . . there are just too many knots. I . . .I can't--"

"Take your time. Just--"

"No!" Linda said, backing away from the chair as her eyes welled with tears. "I can't do it, I'm sorry but I just can't do it."

Rose looked at her for a moment and then shrugged. "It's O.K. I understand."

"I'm . . . I'm really sorry," Linda said, edging her way toward the door. "It's . . .it's just that I have my mother to think about. I wouldn't want to get her in any trouble."

"Sure, I know. Blood is thicker than water, as they say."

"Maybe if you were already outside in the parking lot by my blue Volkswagen--license plate number AJT 193-- I could . . . could help you. You know, drive you to Bayonne and all. But to actually roll you out the front door past so many nurses, I . . . I would be too afraid."

"Oh, well, now that makes sense," Rose said, eyeing the loose rope that Linda had managed to untie before her panic attack. "I understand that very well. Nurses do have a way of intimidating people."

"All my life I've been afraid of people in authority," Linda said, glancing over her shoulder. "Doctors, nurses, teachers, judges, police officers. . . ."

"God help you," Rose said, gripping the wheels of her chair and looking both ways up and down the hallway before rolling out the door after Linda. "You'll have to learn to get over something like that or you'll be doomed. Doomed. Do you hear me?"

"Oh, I'm . . .I'm trying," Linda said, hurrying down the corridor with Rose in hot pursuit. "Believe me, I'm trying."

"Well, that's good then," Rose replied, as the two of them sped out the front door and down the ramp to the parking lot, "because then you've got nothing to worry about. Do you understand? Do you hear me? As long as you try, you've got nothing to worry about. Nothing at all."+++++

THE WOMAN IN THE OFF-BLACK PANTYHOSE

A most extraordinary thing happened to Angela Atwood one day at the Tunesboro Foodtown supermarket.

It was one of those late afternoons in early spring just before twilight when time seems to crystallize and the whole world sparkles with an unearthly luminosity when Angela, feeling a rather odd emptiness in the center of her heart, stepped from her car and walked slowly across the parking lot. At the front of the store she took hold of one of the shopping carts that were lined up neatly against the wall.

Almost instantly her eyes caught sight of a small piece of paper lying at the bottom of the wagon. She sighed as she bent to pick it up. If there was one thing she couldn't stand, it was other people's litter. Gum wrappers, old candy boxes, torn sheets of paper, crumpled coupons or debris of any kind at the bottom of her cart never failed to irritate her. When she went shopping, she liked her wagons nice and clean. It was a matter of principle.

If only people would learn to pick up after them selves, she thought, glancing down at the paper which was bright pink and finely grained, an expensive sheet, no doubt, from someone's personal stationery. It was covered with large black letters that curled and looped across the entire page.

How odd, Angela wondered. Who would use expensive stationery to write a grocery list, and in calligraphy, no less?

Her eyes ran across each item--a pair of off-black panties and pantyhose, a bottle of ketchup, a jar of kosher dill pickles, a package of Thomas's English Muffins, mascara, Kleenex, lipstick.

She turned the paper over.

Against a pale and raging moon
When all the world lies hushed
I lie alone upon my bed
And dream again of you.

The silence of your secret eyes,
The arms I knew so well,
The tender lips and burning thighs
That speak the soul of you,
Darleen, sweetheart, meet me at 9 sharp.
You know where. I'll be waiting.
Wear your black bra.

For a moment Angela was stunned. It was almost as if a stranger had come out of the darkness and embraced her. She glanced around nervously. There was no one in sight, except a young boy in a large cowboy hat and boots who she knew worked for the store and was in charge of rounding up the stray wagons.

Angela read the note again, trying her best to imagine where it had come from and what kind of person could have written it. She brought the paper up to her nose. It smelled faintly of perfume. Obviously it belonged to the woman who had come to the store in search of panties and pantyhose and pickles and—what? Angela took another quick look around before her eyes fell onto the paper again.

I lie alone upon my bed
And dream again of you.
The silence of your secret eyes
The arms I knew so well—

Was it some type of joke or what? Darleen was a woman's name and yet the poem had apparently been written by a woman, a woman who was calling another woman sweetheart and asking her to wear a black bra. What on earth did the whole thing mean?

Angela glanced to her right, then to her left. A tall attractive woman in a bright yellow dress was strolling across the parking lot toward her. Angela watched as the woman approached. Had the note been intended for her? The woman passed by without a glance, disappearing into the doorway of a nearby bookshop.

Angela took a deep breath and tried to think. She didn't know whether to stick the note back into another cart or simply drop it into the nearest waste bin. But suppose someone sees me, she thought. She might think the note was for me.

She closed her eyes, trying to imagine why anyone-male or female-would write such a thing on the back of a grocery list and then leave it behind in a public shopping cart for anyone to find. Was it possible that it was all perfectly innocent, the absent-minded scribbling, say, of some bored but highly imaginative person trying to pass the time on a long check-out line? Or had she actually stumbled upon the real makings of some secret and passionate assignation involving two women? The question left her somewhat lightheaded, especially since nothing like this had ever happened to her before.

She stood there, fingering the note, wondering what she should do. After a few moments, however, she found herself thinking about the women. She tried to imagine what they were like. Where they lived. How they had met. Whether they were young or old, married or single, attractive or not.

Despite herself, strange and unsettling scenarios began flashing through her brain: A young, very beautiful woman in a lacy black bra was walking along a rain-splashed street; a tall, slender woman with thick auburn hair was slipping her lovely hips into a pair of tight black panties; two women, fair as moonlight, were embracing in the shadows of a thick lush garden.

Angela shuddered. Years before she had had such dreams of women. Dreams that had left her vaguely uncomfortable and somehow unsettled, but that had been a long time ago when she was much younger. A girl, really. Certainly long before she had married and begun raising a family.

Nervously, she glanced at her watch. It was almost five-thirty. What in the name of God was she doing? She still had dinner to make and a lot of work to do. Larry and the children would be waiting. She couldn't afford to waste any more time wondering about some silly old note. She grabbed hold of her cart and pushed it through the automatic swinging door, moving swiftly past the fruit and vegetable aisle.

She shot up the cookie lane and turned right into the dairy department where she grabbed a quart of Tuscan Low-fat Milk and a package of Diet-Delight, sodium-free yellow cheese. In the bread aisle she picked up a box of Thomas's English Muffins.

On her way to the checkout counter, she passed several shapely young women in high heels and business suits. One of them was standing in front of the condiment section eying a large jar of kosher dill pickles. Angela couldn't see her face, only the back of her head. She was slender with long flowing blonde hair that curled gently across her delicate shoulders.

For one brief moment--possibly two--a pair of marble-smooth burning white thighs flashed through Angela's brain. Startled, she jerked her cart forward, running smack up the heels of a fat hairy man in purple pants and a Mickey Mouse T-shirt.

"Hey, what the hell do you think you're doin'?" he shouted. "Why don't you watch where you're goin', lady?"

"I'm--I'm terrible sorry," Angela stuttered. "I--I didn't see you there."

"Didn't see me?" he shouted, lifting his foot and giving his heel a vigorous rub. "What are you, blind? Am I supposed to wear tail lights or somethin'? I was standing right in front of you. What do you mean you didn't see me?"

"I--I really am sorry," Angela said, her face reddening, as she caught a glimpse of the woman with the long blonde hair gliding past her.

"My mind must have been somewhere else."

"That's for sure," the man said. "Somewhere like Mars, maybe."

"Right on!" shouted a glassy-eyed teenager with pimples and a mohawk who zigzagged between them.

Angela's eyes were on the blonde woman as she came to a stop at the rear of the express lane a few feet away. A medium-sized bottle of pickles sat demurely at the bottom of her shopping basket.

Angela watched as the woman settled patiently into the long line, slipping her right foot out of her shoe and rubbing it lazily behind the back of her leg. She was wearing off-black pantyhose.

"Next time watch where you're goin', O.K.?" the man said, limping painfully away. "You women nowadays are a menace."

Over by the canned vegetables two middle-aged men in blue workmen's clothes were pointing and laughing. Angela steered her cart toward the check-out counter where the blonde woman was now absent-mindedly thumbing through a copy of Mademoiselle.

Angela inched up behind her, hoping to catch a whiff of her perfume, but all she could smell were oranges. Leaning over the woman's shoulder, Angela peered into her shopping basket. Sure enough, there were four oranges there, scattered among the jar of pickles, three bottles of Perrier, a wedge of Blue cheese, and a box of Tampax.

But there were no panties, no pantyhose, no lipstick, no mascara— Angela paused.

What on earth was she doing, snooping in some strange woman's shopping basket? Whatever had possessed her? Was she losing her mind? Her hands and underarms began to perspire. Quickly, she folded the note and stuck it into her purse. She was acting like a child. An utter fool. She had to get hold of herself.

She took another deep breath to steady herself. It was all so absurd. What had ever led her to believe that this woman was the one who had written the note? Was it only because she'd seen her pick up that bottle of pickles? Was it the off-black pantyhose? And why should she have cared whether the woman had written the note or not? What was it to her? Certainly it was none of her business if some person she had never seen before had chosen the Tunesboro Foodtown as the site for some illicit affair.

Angela was so embarrassed she could have kicked herself. In fact, she would have left the store right then and there if another customer hadn't come behind her, blocking her exit.

Slowly the line moved forward. She watched as the blonde woman bent over her cart, grabbing hold of each item. She wished she could at least see her face, but the woman's soft golden hair hung thickly in the way. She saw her fingers, though. They were long and thin, her nails sharp and blood-red. There was no ring, however. Not even an engagement ring.

If she were the woman, Angela thought, and she did have a female lover, she was certainly free enough to meet her some place other than the parking lot of a public supermarket. Why all the secrecy then? Why all the mystery? The answer shot like a bolt through Angela's body. More than likely the note that now rested in her purse had been intended for some woman like herself, who was married. A woman with some sweet, unsuspecting soul of a husband and a couple of nice, ordinary, wholesome kids. Angela could almost picture this woman: an older, fairly handsome lady with soft eyes and a gentle smile. The kind of person a younger, more attractive, but infinitely less experienced woman would feel comfortable with.

Curious, Angela turned and panned the store. The woman behind her was short and rather stubby. She was wearing a long gray dress and holding a thick loaf of Italian bread and a package of Boarshead salami. She seemed nice, but smelled heavily of garlic. Behind her was the mohawk with the pimples. Angela looked away. The only woman in the place who even faintly resembled a kindly, dignified person was the female butcher who was grinding chop meat. But if the note had been intended for her, why had it been left sitting outside in a shopping cart?

Frustrated, Angela turned back to the woman in front of her. Her slender hand was reaching out for the box of Tampax at the bottom of her cart. Angela's heart began to race madly, her thoughts flying and spinning like wild birds through an immense blue sky. She longed to lean over and talk to the woman, to find out who she was and what she was like. But she was afraid, fearful of what might happen. Of what the woman might think.

Perhaps she wasn't the person who had written the poem. Perhaps she had no lover, no one she lay awake for, longing for atop her bed while the pale moon raged and the world lay hushed. Perhaps the only thing that had ever come between her burning thighs was an innocent Tampax.

Angela grew dizzy. She didn't know what to do, what to think. And there was no way for her to find out, either. In fact, she really didn't know anything about this woman. Nothing at all. Not even the shape of her face or the color of her eyes. She watched as the blonde woman's cool, white hands slipped into her purse. Perhaps she would write out a check. Sign her name. Give her phone number and address. Instead, she handed the clerk two twenty-dollar bills, took the change, and disappeared out the door with her bag of groceries without once turning her head.

By the time Angela reached the parking lot, the woman was gone. Angela wandered up and down, in and out between the cars for some time, but there was no trace of her anywhere.

Was the woman gone forever?

***

That night, while Angela sat beside Larry in their living room, she thought about the woman. Every so often, when Larry wasn't looking, she took out the note and read it. All through the night she dreamed of the blonde woman, who was lying atop a narrow, white bed holding out her arms and softly calling Angela's name; outside her window a pale moon raged, and stars exploded in great, white bursts.

Early the following evening Angela found herself again at the supermarket, her eyes scanning all the shopping carts and the checkout lines, but there was no sign of any note, no trace of any secret rendezvous.

For weeks she returned every twilight. She diligently searched every scrap of paper, every crumpled note that she would find at the bottom of some cart. Once or twice she thought she saw the blonde woman disappear into a car and drive away, but she was always just a little too late to know for sure.

It was frustrating, and terribly depressing at times, especially when Larry began to complain that she didn't seem to be her old self anymore. But despite it all, Angela refused to give up.

Night after night she returned to the supermarket, hoping to find another poem, another trace of the blonde woman. She knew she was out there. Somewhere. She just had to be patient and wait until they would meet again. +++++

A MATTER OF PERSPECTIVE

One morning a young woman awoke in her bed with the sun streaming brightly into her room. As she sat up, yawning and stretching her arms high above her head, she felt a strange tug against her left foot, almost as if something hard and round had rolled against her ankle. She pulled down the warm, fluffy blanket that was wrapped so snugly about her body and lifted the hem of her pink and white silk nightgown.

There to her amazement, she discovered a huge ball and chain attached to her left foot. At first she couldn't believe her eyes. She imagined she must still be dreaming, or that her eyes were playing tricks on her, but when she tried to lie back down and lift her leg off the bed, she found she could not do so.

Baffled, she sat back up again and gazed at her ankle. The soft flesh of her skin around the tightly bolted lock looked slightly swollen and discolored as she might have expected from so rigid a confinement, but she felt no pain in her limb or foot, even though she suspected that the weight of the chain and the ball combined must have been over fifty pounds. In fact, the only time she felt any real discomfit was when she tried to move. When she remained perfectly still, it was as though the ball and chain didn't even exist, although she knew they were there.

But this woman, whose name was Shana, did not consider herself to be the kind of person who could remain perfectly still for very long without protesting or exerting some action on her own behalf. It infuriated her to think that she had no choice except to lie down passively in one spot in a position not her own with one of her legs bound and virtually useless beneath her. She considered herself a strong woman, one who could easily lift fifty pound in one hand and fling it over her shoulder without flinching. Yet when she attempted to bend over and grip the ball and chain firmly in her two hands, she found she could not budge them in the least. At the very most, she could only push the ball a bit to the side, shifting her leg a few inches along the sheet with immense effort.

"My God!" she thought, overwhelmed by her own helplessness. "How in the world did this happen to me? What am I going to do?"

She looked anxiously about her room. It was a perfectly ordinary room, comfortable, secure and absolutely dependable, and nothing in it seemed to have changed from the night before when she had arrived home from her date with Leo. On the table beside her were her purse, her hair brush, a half-filled glass of water, the telephone and her Lady Avon Cosmetic Kit. To her right, draped over the back of her reading chair, were her clothes, just as she had left them—her pretty satin white blouse with the ruffled puff sleeves and high-neck collar that Leo loved her to wear and liked so much to touch, and her long black skirt with the orange-red slash. At the foot of her bed wedged between the brass bedpost and the ball and chain were her panties, bra, and stockings.

It was true she hadn't remembered taking them off, but that in itself was not unusual. When she was sleepy and bored she never remembered very much.

Again, she thought of Leo.

He must have done this to me, she thought, tightening her fists and growing beet red. He probably came back in the middle of the night, undressed me, and hooked me up to this goddamn ball and chain. Probably it's his idea of a practical joke.

Furious, she reached over for her telephone, and felt her left leg wrench painfully beneath her. In a rage she shot up, lifting her buttocks off the bed and flung herself wildly to one side, but the ball and chain remained motionless, pinning her leg to the bed. Helplessly, she fell back down again against the thick mattress.

"Goddamn it," she cried, cursing herself for giving Leo a key to her apartment. "How could he have done such a thing after I had trusted him so?"

She lay back panting and desperate, wondering what she should do next. She glanced at the clock on the table and saw that it was already after nine. She had to be in her car and on the road in twenty minutes at the very latest or she would jeopardize her sales for the entire day. She loved being an Avon Lady and knocking on strange women's doors to sell them phosphorescent lipstick and iridescent eyeliner, while they went on and on about how awful their husbands were, or how much they hated their lives. It gave her a sense of peace to know how miserable other people were.

She had tried other jobs, but they never seemed to work out. Once she taught a philosophy course on Nihilism as an adjunct instructor to a class of female lifers at the local Women's Penitentiary, but the warden fired her when there was a sudden rash of suicides at the institution involving several of her best students. She thought that was really unfair of the warden, but there wasn't much she could do about it.

Another time she got a job teaching English as a Second Language to new immigrants in an adult night school, but when the chair of the department discovered she had assigned the class a book entitled "Go Back to Where You Came From: You're Not Welcome Here" written by someone calling himself Christopher Columbus Anonymous, Shana was dismissed immediately.

All these bad experiences left her feeling exhausted, exploited, and somewhat damaged, but when she became an Avon Lady life certainly improved.

The Avon job at least gave her the opportunity of moving around a bit, and if she found she didn't like a particular customer, well, it pleased her that she could always pack up her perfumes and go elsewhere.

But now with a ball and chain around her left leg, the likelihood of moving anywhere at all--even off her own bed-- seemed slim. The only thing she could think of doing was to somehow get to the phone, call Leo, demand that he come and free her at once, and then slap his face and refuse to ever see him again.

Taking a deep breath she raised herself slowly, and bent to grip the ball. With her eyes shut and her teeth clenched, she mustered all her strength and pushed it off the bed, toppling both it and herself onto the floor in one immense crash.

A searing pain shot through her left hip and her head wacked against a leg of the bedside table as she tumbled onto the floor, but all in all it was a rather smooth fall, and as she lay sprawled halfway beneath the bed with her nightgown clinging to her stomach and her bare legs pointing in two opposite directions, she was grateful nothing had broken and that she was miraculously in one piece. The ball and chain were still around her ankle naturally, but since she was no longer trapped in the bed she felt that she was at least making progress. She pulled down her nightgown, raised herself to a sitting position and then swung her right leg behind her. Using it as leverage, she knelt upright, gripping the bed for support. Slowly she crawled to the table and pulled the phone down.

She knew Leo would be at work, and so she dialed Information and got the number for the midtown Shop and Park where he worked as a butcher in the meat department. All the while she listened to the phone ring in the distance, she stared at the ball and chain and rehearsed what she would say, but when she finally did hear Leo's voice saying "Hello, hello" in her ear, she simply burst into tears and wept hysterically into the mouthpiece.

At first Leo did not know who was on the phone, but when he heard the short, quick rasps of breath and the sweet, prolonged sobbing, he recognized his little Shana. She always reminded him of a young lamb being slaughtered. It was what he loved best about her.

"What is it, darling?" he asked anxiously. Are you hurt? Has there been an accident?"

Shana could not speak at first, but as she calmed down she managed to say a few words.

"You. . . had no right . . . my leg . . .I trusted you."

Leo was baffled.

"Trusted me? Your leg? What's the matter with your leg? Have you fallen? Did you hurt yourself?"

"The ball . . . the chain. . . you. . . "

She was ashamed that all her anger had dissipated so easily into female hysteria. She longed to pick up the ugly black ball and slam it into Leo's ear.

"Ball? What chain?" Leo repeated. "What are you talking about?"

The tone of his voice frightened Shana into silence. She waited, suspended, for what would come next.

"Shana? Can you hear me? Tell me what you're talking about? What ball and chain?"

She drew a deep breath.

"Leo, did you or did you not come back to my apartment last night after I had fallen asleep, undress me, and attach a huge ball and chain to my left leg?"

There was a long silence on Leo's end.

"Shana," he said softly after a moment. "Are you kidding? What kind of creep do you take me for? Why, I would never do something like that in a million years."

Shana dropped the phone, staring blankly at her leg. If Leo did not do it--and Shana was convinced that he was telling the truth--then who did? Who could have entered her apartment while she slept and done such a thing?

She glanced at the room's one window. It was locked securely. No one could have entered there. Besides, she lived on the fifteenth floor and there was nothing between her window and the ground except sheer air. She turned her head and studied the front door. That too was locked and shut. Trembling, she pulled her nightgown tightly across her shoulders and gazed at the door of her bedroom closet.

If the person who had chained her was still inside the apartment, he would have to be hiding there in the closet? And if that were the case, what was he doing there? What was he waiting for? There was no way she could run away with a ball and chain around her leg, and she certainly couldn't put up a fight with only half of her body free to move. So what should she do?

She sat back quietly on her right leg, her left pulled out straight in front of her and thought about her options. Since the phone was in her lap, she could call the police, but if there were a man hiding inside her bedroom closet listening to her talk to the police, he would surely come out before they arrived and . . . and . . .do what? Strangle her? Throw her out the window? Attach another ball and chain to her body, this time around her neck. If that were his intention why was he waiting inside the closet all this time? He had had all night to do whatever he wanted? Why didn't he dash out when he first heard her calling Leo on the phone? What made him know she was calling a boyfriend and not the police?

Maybe he's a sadist, Shana thought, her eyes glued to the door. Maybe he will chop me up and send me in little plastic bags to Leo to sell as prime choice at the Shop and Park. Or then again maybe he just enjoys hiding behind my plastic clothes hangers and orange raincoat, listening to me go crazy? Maybe he's waiting for me to have a nervous breakdown, to fold up on the floor like some flimsy paper doll that he can simply blow away.

Shana paused.

But then again, maybe there was no one in her closet after all. Maybe she was having a nervous breakdown. A transient psychotic episode, as they called it on the Oprah Winfrey Show.

Maybe she had, in fact, imagined everything--her call to Leo, the ball and chain on the floor in front of her, her own humiliating helplessness.

Many women she knew had such breakdowns all the time. It was probably something deep within the female psyche, some sick, strange perversion that delighted in debasing its victims and transforming half the human race into whining, sniveling wretches. But no matter how hard she tried to convince herself that she was merely cracking up and not actually sitting on the floor with a ball and chain wrapped around her leg, she could not do so. Her whole left limb absolutely refused to move unless she wrenched against it violently and then a very real pain would shoot up from her ankle to her kneecap bringing tears to her eyes and a heavy dull thud and clink to her ears.

For over two hours she sat like that on the floor telling herself that soon she would be fine and completely free to come and go again at will, that the ball and chain would disappear the same way they had arrived--without her awareness or participation, but whenever she glanced down at her leg she saw the heavy black ball and ugly chain still there, bound to her flesh, holding her a prisoner within her own self.

After a while she started thinking of Leo again. She was hoping that he would soon appear at her front door, perhaps crash through it with his shoulder the way she saw good guys in the movies crash through doors to rescue women in distress. She longed to see Leo's porky blood-splattered face come sailing through the splinters of flying wood. He would smile down at her, stooping gently to pick her up, ball and all, in his arms, and carry her to safety. Certainly Leo, if no one else, could cut through and release her from her imprisonment, help her walk free again, upright and with dignity. She was ashamed that she had accused him of doing her harm. Leo was not like other men she had known. He was kind and gentle and loving toward her, despite being a professional butcher, and she was a fool for ever getting angry at his attentions and dirty fingernails.

Yet when he came near her she sometimes felt on the verge of suffocation. She wondered if it were the smell of dead meat and dried cow's blood that permeated his skin and never seemed to leave him, even when he was naked and in bed with her? Or was it merely his physical bigness which so dwarfed her own smaller self so much so that she sometimes felt diminished entirely by his very presence? One of his hands alone could cover and blot out her entire face. When he stood in front of her, she disappeared entirely behind his huge hairy shoulders and thick beefy torso, the very same parts of him she found so appealing when she first saw him slicing slabs of fat off a pig's hide.

As she sat on the floor thinking, she realized she had always been that way. Liking one moment what she came to fear or reject the next. She looked down at the ball and chain and smiled. Probably if Leo did suddenly come crashing into her room with some huge buzz saw to slice away her captors she would resent his interference and come to despise him.

The thought make her shiver, and she looked at her bedroom closet again. For a brief moment she almost wished there were someone there. Someone who would leap out and put an end to all her self-reflection. She was a tragic female Hamlet, of sorts. Always thinking. Forever in deep contemplation. Even when she was in the act of selling underarm deodorants and pubic hair removal cream to fat middle-aged women, her brain was a buzz saw.

It was maddening, being chained while her thoughts ran on so, plodding her with questions that went round and round and had no answers. Questions like why do good women get vagina warts, and why are certain ethnic groups prone to have big heads? And yet what did all her thinking amount to? Over the years, nothing at all. Now she didn't even have the imagination or sense to figure out how to get free from a goddamn ball and chain. Only a moment ago, she had looked to Leo to save her, as women have always looked to men to save them.

And for the first time in her life she began to wonder what it was women expected from men? What were men supposed to save them from exactly? Death? Darkness? Body Odor? Other men? Themselves?

She sat back and sighed. If she had any sense at all, she would stop asking such stupid questions and figure out how to help herself. She would come up with a practical solution on what to do with her ball and chain.

She closed her eyes and tried to think. She thought of calling her girlfriend Maureen who was something of an intellectual. She taught College Writing V and Advanced Guadalupian Women's Studies three days a week to recovering nymphomaniacs at a local community college, and she just might be available that afternoon. If she were free, she could come over and together they would think of something, some way to free Shana from her dilemma. Maybe she could bring a locksmith with her or maybe a blow torch, or maybe she could simply help Shana carry the ball and chain out of the apartment so they could, at the very least, get outside and go somewhere.

But where would they go?

To work?

Maybe they could go bowling? Bowling always lifted up one's spirits. Shana looked at her clock. It was only a little after eleven. She still had half a day left. If Maureen arrived by noon, Shana would have plenty of time to still do something useful with her day. Maybe she could make a sale or two as the friendly Avon Lady who comes calling with a smile and a bowling ball wrapped around her leg. That would surely be a first. Maybe she could even start a fashion trend in the cosmetic industry. Buy a lipstick and win a free bowling ball to wear with your favorite blouse and jeans.

Women across the country would take to chaining themselves instead of piercing their ears or painting their toe nails. She could make a fortune. Designer ball and chains to go. She could even sell them on eBay or in the local malls.

Shana began to feel a whole lot better about herself and the world. It was just a matter of perspective, she thought, gazing down at her leg which by this time had become as black and round as the bowling ball.

It was the way one looked at things: a simple matter of maintaining a positive attitude when life's path suddenly and inexplicitly took a dangerous turn to the left.

"When life hands you a lemon," Shana said aloud, making herself quite comfortable on the floor, "You've got to make yourself lemonade. And when life chains you to a big bowling ball, you've got to . . . ."

She would think of something. She always did. +++++

THANATOPSIS AND THE THOUSAND POINTS OF LIGHT

E die Edwards had one desire in life: to transcend her humanity and partake of the divine.

Day after day she engaged in a series of elaborate rituals designed to achieve this goal. From 6 to 8 every morning she sat mediating on the bare floor of her darkened bedroom, inhaling and exhaling in long, slow, deep breaths to the rise and fall of imaginary sea waves lapping lazily against a solitary shore.

From 8 to 9 she performed an intricate array of yoga exercises intended for the release of low vibrational energies and debilitating tensions, and from 9 to 10:30 she practiced opening up her mind's eye to the cosmic rays of the universe by lying naked in her bathtub and imagining the Universal Light of Life Consciousness descending into her belly button.

Her afternoon rituals, beginning precisely at high noon, were similarly arranged and carefully constructed. From 12 until 2 she lay on her bed listening to the deep, mournful wail of mating whales and dying geese drifting in ghostly waves from her stereo--authentic sounds from nature recorded onto $9.95 cassette-tapes, guaranteed or your money back, to raise internal frequency levels and to balance right-brain- left-brain hemispheres.

Even when she was having her lunch at 2--herbal tea and sprigs of organic parsley seasoned with rain water--Edie did not relax from her metaphysical labors. She continued her spiritual exercises, chanting her affirmations and creatively visualizing her all-too-solid-human flesh dissolving into a puddle of nothingness and resurrecting as a thin ray of white light arching skyward.

Why Edie desired such mystical transcendence, and why she undertook such extraordinary measures to achieve it was anybody's guess. From all appearances she looked like a fairly typical, normal, young woman. She was healthy, independent, and best of all, she was loved and cherished by someone who really cared: her dog, Thanatopsis, a handsome Golden Retriever who lay by her side from morning till night, gazing up at her with his large wet sleepy eyes.

What Thanatopsis thought of his mistress's strange rituals, God alone knew, but hour after hour he shared--by his faithful presence and the mysteries of osmosis—in their bizarre unfoldings. Daily from his vantage point on the floor he watched with half-opened eyes as Edie chanted her prayers for divine union and beat her breast in rhythmic harmony to the wailing whales and the dying geese who would lead her toward Cosmic Enlightenment.

In the evenings curled up at the foot of her bed he fell asleep to the monotonous dronings of her subliminal self-hypnotic, self-help tapes, designed for the express purpose of assaulting the subconscious with positive transformational messages ranging in content from such uplifting statements as, " Yes, I Have Been To the Astral Plane," and "Yes, my Third Eye is opening" to the more controversial "No, Evolution Did Not End in the Anal."

So powerful, in fact, were these messages and so convinced was Edie that they would help her achieve her goal of physical and psychic transcendence that she never failed to express surprise when she woke each morning and found herself sitting warmly in the flesh upon her bed instead of romping blithely across the universe.

"What do you suppose is wrong?" she would ask Thanatopsis, who inevitably would be either scratching himself or biting a flea. "Why is it I'm making no progress? Why do I have to be stuck here in this boring body on this boring old piece of earth with its crime and problems and pollutions and terrible old-fashioned ideas when I could be exploring the Fourth, Fifth and Sixth Dimensions like the incredibly beautiful Free-Spirit I really am inside this dumb old lump of womanly breast?"

Thanatopsis would merely look at her and wag his tail, his eyes glazed with sleep and doggy adoration, his subconscious etched like a tombstone with subliminal messages and the constant repetition of their mind-numbing programming.

"Do you think I'm being punished?" Edie would continue. "Do you think it's karma that I'm still a human woman, un-transformed and un-enlightened or do you think it's simply my destiny to live a long, stupid, unconscious, uninspiring life?"

Thanatopsis would flop down at her feet and sympathetically lay his enormous golden head on his mistress's bony knees, but Edie, too caught up in her own obsessions to notice his concern, would only sigh, push him aside, and then go off for more of her meditations and breast-beating lamentations.

One day, however, a rather peculiar thing happened.

While Edie was in the middle of listening to one of her progressive self-help tapes entitled How to Levitate while Channeling Your Higher Self, she heard a strange noise from across the room.

No sooner had her eyes and brain begun to refocus themselves, when she noticed a brilliant white light coming from behind her Lazy-Boy Recliner. As she sat on the floor peering across at it, it grew brighter and brighter, lifting itself slowly upward toward the ceiling as it whirled and churned in powerful waves of radiant energy, like the terrible eye of a mighty tornado.

"My God," she exclaimed, leaping excitedly to her feet. "It's here. It's finally come. After all these years—my Enlightenment has finally come."

Bursting with happiness, she dashed across the room, her arms open and outstretched in joyful expectation, but what she discovered when she finally reached the cloud of magnificent glowing light and stood gazing into it, took her completely by surprise. As perhaps all enlightenment should.

There, in the midst of all that whirling, churning, swirling energy, bouncing like a happy molecule among the glorious chaos, was Thanatopsis, her loving, all-faithful, constant friend and companion, channeling his higher self and levitating high above the floor in a joyful dance of highly evolved Canine Consciousness.+++++

HOW TO HYPNOTIZE
THE WOMAN OF YOUR DREAMS

Clyde Pepper Jr. sat behind the front counter of his father's pharmacy, Pepper's Apothecary, ogling the center- fold of a recent Playboy. Clyde Pepper Sr. lounged in the rear of the shop amidst the clutter of dusty pill bottles and tubes of boric acid ointment sipping a rum coke and listening to an old Benny Goodman record.

It was a warm day in early June and with the flu season long gone and most people out and enjoying the sun, business was slow. Only a few flies here and there and an occasional customer like old Mrs. Gooding, a nosy biddy who barged in several times a day to gossip and to buy hair pins, stamps, cotton balls or anything else she could think of that would cost practically nothing and take up a lot of time.

"Hey, Pa, what's with that woman? Clyde Jr. would ask, hiding his Playboy every time he saw her approaching. "Why does she like to come here so much?"

"Who knows?" Clyde Sr. would shrug. "Maybe she's got the hots for you, boy. You better be careful."

"Quit teasing, Pa," Clyde Jr. would say. "That ain't one bit funny and you know it."

But on this particular day in June even Mrs. Gooding didn't seem interested in hanging around the old shop. After buying a small box of Exlax, and promising to return it if it didn't do the trick, she said her good-byes and headed out the door.

Which was fine with Clyde Jr. It wasn't every day he got a chance to relax and catch up on his reading. Most of the time he was busy making a damn fool of himself, scooting all over town making deliveries in the little yellow Volkswagen with the idiotic blinking Mortar and Pestle atop the roof.

Talk about embarrassing! It was bad enough he was almost twenty and still working as a delivery boy for his father, let alone driving around in that silly car. It was downright humiliating. Especially when he had to go past a couple of guys he recognized from town or a crowd of girls that he knew from school.

"Hello, Clyde Jr.," they would cry out, grinning at one another. "Pushing any good drugs lately?"

It mightn't have been so bad if he were handsome or rich, or if he had something else going for him, but on top of everything he knew he was ugly.

He got up from his chair and stared at his reflection in the leaded glass window of the medicine cabinet opposite the front counter.

His face, round as the moon and pale as a baby's butt, belonged more on a turnip than on a human being. More than once, in fact, he thought he heard people say he looked demented.

Even his own father seemed ashamed of him.

"Clyde Jr.," the old man would say from time to time when he felt like philosophizing, "What the hell's wrong with you anyhow? How come you're so dull? Don't you know you've got to take the bull by the horns and wrestle him to the ground if you want to get anywhere in this world?"

"What bull?" Clyde would ask, blinking up from behind his greasy, thumb-smudged glasses. "I don't know what bull you'll talking about, Pa."

"It's just a figure of speech, boy," Clyde Sr. would sigh, trying his best to remain patient. "What I'm saying is that you got to learn to take charge. You got to learn how to wake up and get with it."

"But I'm doing my best, Pa, honest. I'm doing my best."

"Face it, son," Clyde Sr. would continue. "You ain't a kid any more. You're a man now. You got to live a little. Have fun, eat, drink, get yourself a woman. Some nice, hot- blooded female who can teach you a few things and introduce you to the finer pleasures in life."

Clyde Jr. would get so ashamed hearing his own father talk like that he wanted to die. To vanish like a cloud of smoke into the wide blue sky and never show his face again.

No wonder he had no esteem. No wonder his social life was rotten. No wonder he was still a virgin. What woman in her right mind would want to go out with a jerk like him--a nerd who drove around delivering aspirin and enema bags to old ladies with eczema and Parkinson's Disease? No woman worth her salt would be interested in him.

What he needed was a complete and total transformation. A change of image. A whole new personality. Something that would catch a girl's attention and make her drool with desire.

"But that would take a miracle," he sighed, wearily picking up the Playboy again and thumbing through it. "And, as everyone knows, miracles are pretty hard to come by these days."

Suddenly his eyes caught sight of a small boldface ad in the bottom left hand corner of the page he had been scanning.

Are you desperate? Are You in need of a miracle? Are You Fed up Being a Big Nobody? Send $17.95 plus $1.50 tax and change your life. Order today and receive your copy of How To Hypnotize the Woman of Your Dreams and Make Her Do Anything You Desire.

"Wow," Clyde exclaimed, his head beginning to swim with possibilities. "This sounds like what I'm looking for? It sounds great!"

Without another moment's hesitation, he dashed over to the cash register, hit the No Sale button, and quickly extracted a twenty dollar bill.

Two weeks later the book arrived in the mail.

***

Clyde Jr. never studied anything as hard in his life. All day long when he was driving around making his delivers in the little yellow Volkswagen he kept the book on the seat next to him, perusing it at red lights and stop signs and wherever else he had the chance.

He knew it backwards and forwards and could recite the Ten Most Important Steps to Hypnotizing a Beautiful Woman better than he could reel off the Ten Commandments. Now all he needed to do was to find that beautiful woman.

He seemed to be having little luck in that department, however, until one fine day, fate finally stepped in and delivered a beautiful woman right at his very doorstep. Clyde Jr. was minding the store for his father who had slipped out for his afternoon pick-me-up down at the local saloon, when the little bell above the front door pealed merrily. He had been reading his book for the nth time and when he glanced up, he saw the most enchanting, enticing woman he had ever seen walking straight toward him.

She was wearing a tight yellow sweater, a short blue skirt, and off-black stockings with purple little butterflies fluttering about the ankles.

Fascinated, he held his breath and watched. She seemed to float across the floor in waves of light like someone out of a dream, her face and head glowing with a essence he could only describe as unearthly.

"Jesus," he thought, "It's her. It's finally her. The woman of my dreams!"

"Are you the pharmacist?" she asked, coming closer and shyly smiling up at him.

Yes, there was simply no question about it. She was gorgeous. Absolutely stunning. The most gorgeous-stunning creature he had ever known. Every luscious curve of her beckoned to him, filling his head with infinite madness.

"Yee--yes," he lied. "I'm the pharmacist. What--what can I do for you, young lady?"

The woman blushed and lowered her eyes.

"I--I have a slight problem and I think I need some professional advice."

Clyde's heart was pounding so loudly he could barely see straight, but he forced himself to concentrate, staring the woman directly in the eye as he recalled Rule Number One.

"What--what kind of problem, Miss?"

"Well, I'm--I'm afraid I have a yeast infection," she said, blushing even more deeply. "I need something to take away the--the itch."

Clyde had no idea what the hell she was talking about, but he proceeded full speed ahead to Rule Number Two.

"I see," he said, his hand trembling as he pointed to a nearby chair. "Well, that's no problem. No problem at all. We can handle that. Please have a seat."

"A seat?" she exclaimed, looking a bit confused.

"Yes," he said, "It's--it's very important for you to relax. One must relax when one has a yeast infection."

"Really," the woman said, sitting down quietly. "I never knew that. I--I thought I just needed some kind of cream."

"Cream?" he said, speaking very softly now as he proceeded to Rule Number Three. "What kind of cream?"

"Va--vaginal cream. I--I was hoping you could recommend something?"

"Oh, of course," he said, pulling the closest cream he could find off a nearby shelf and waving it slowly back and forth in front of the woman's face. Rule Number Four. "I have just what you need."

"Shaving cream?" the woman exclaimed, her eyes rocking back and forth as they followed Clyde's hand. "You want me to use shaving cream? In--in my vagina?"

"Yes," he replied, lowing his voice an octave as Rule Number Five suggested. "It's the latest home remedy. Now in the meantime I want you to take a long slow deep breath and count backwards from eight to zero. Do you understand?"

"No, I--I--"

"It's very important," he insisted, giving his best shot at Rule Number Seven--taking control of the situation. "One must always breathe deeply and count backwards when one has a yeast infection."

"Well, O--O.K," she said, nodding her head. "If you say so."

She took a long slow deep breath and began to count backwards from eight to zero.

"Good," Clyde whispered, staring at her lovely breast as it rose and fell beneath her pretty yellow sweater. "You're getting more and more relaxed. Your eyes are growing heavier and heavier."

Slowly her eyes began to flutter.

"Your body is becoming sleepier and sleepier. You are going deeper and deeper into sleep. A long, peaceful, restful, beautiful sleep."

The woman's head began to sway, her delicate shoulders drooping more and more with each descending number.

"You are totally relaxed. Your body is in a complete state of calm. There is nothing for you to fear. Nothing for you to be afraid of."

He began moving in for the kill, his head spinning with the scent of rose petals from her irresistible perfume.

"Just follow the sound of my voice and do everything I tell you to do. Understand? Everything."

The woman sighed, falling back into the chair like a golden leaf dropping easily toward the waiting earth.

"In a moment you will rise from your chair and throw your arms around my neck. Then you will kiss me and together we will--"

The little bell in front of the shop pealed loudly.

"Hello?" a high pitched voice called out. "Anybody here?"

Clyde froze. The woman in the chair was getting up and walking toward him. Seconds later her lovely arms were around his neck and she was kissing him passionately.

"Yoo-hoo!" the lady out front continued to shout. "Mr. Pepper? It's me. Miss Gooding.

"Go away," Clyde cried, the woman hanging from his neck. "Go away. You hear me? We're--we're closed now."

"Closed?" Miss Gooding said. "Oh, it's you, Clyde, Jr. What in the world are you doing?

"I said go away. Go away. Do you hear me?"

Obediently, the woman began to remove her arms from around Clyde's neck.

"No," Clyde shouted, trying to stop her as she turned and began walking away. "Not you. I wasn't talking to you. I was talking to that old--"

But the woman continued on her way, calmly and quietly, as Clyde had ordered.

Miss Gooding watched her exit in amazement and then turned quickly to Clyde.

"Just wait till your father hears of this," she said, waving the half-empty bottle of Exlax in his face. "Just wait.+++++

LOVE'S A MYSTERY BUT FACTS ARE FACTS

Although Martha Foxwell considered herself a mature and worldly woman of many and varied experiences, she never expected that one morning she would wake up and find herself the center of controversy for sleeping between the beds of two men.

Not that there was anything illicit or even erotic about the arrangement. On the contrary, it was all perfectly innocent, and given the fact that both beds were in Room 423 of the Cardiac Care Unit of Oak Ridge Hospital and that one of the men was Martha's husband Paul, who was suffering from an acute case of heart arrhythmia brought on by the stresses of contemporary life, and the other man was Seymour Katz, a 61-year old gentleman with a pacemaker, it was even more than innocent. It was downright respectable, even admirable, as several, but not all, of the nurses insisted.

"Why, it's not every day you'd find a woman who loves her husband so much she'd sleep on the floor next to him when he was sick and in the hospital," Nurse Beckingwood remarked to her colleagues on the ward." That's what I call real devotion."

"Devotion" Gladys Cresthill, head of student nursing, replied. "I call it insanity. It sounds like something a deranged nun in the 15th century would do after whipping herself with her rosary beads."

"Gladys, that's a horrible thing to say," Miss Prill, the ward's supervisor, scolded. "You should be ashamed of yourself!"

"If you ask me I think the woman is masochistic."

"Well, I wouldn't know about that," Betty, the phlebotomist remarked, "but I have to admit she doesn't sound very liberated. I mean, just think about it. No self respecting woman in this day and age would go to such extremes. And especially for a husband.

"Oh, you two are terrible," Miss Prill said, shaking her head. "To me that lady looks very nice."

"Nice?" Cresthill scoffed. "Who cares if she's nice?" A lot of good that will do her. I've seen plenty of nice women in my time and they all wound up broke, lonely and divorced."

"Oh, you're just an old cynic, Gladys. That's your problem."

"Look," Gladys insisted, "I may be an old cynic, but I'm also a smart cookie, and when it comes to men I know what I'm talking about. And believe me, I wouldn't sleep on the floor for any man, not even Jesus Christ himself. No man is worth that kind of sacrifice."

Nurse Beckingwood closed her eyes and smiled, hugging a stack of patient charts to her bosom.

"Well, maybe that's because you've never been in love. When a woman's in love with a man, she'd do anything for him."

"Including damaging her spine on a cold hard floor?"

"Yes, for love, she would. I know because I was in love once."

"Oh, so that explains it then," Cresthill smirked. "I always wondered why you became a nurse. Now I know. You're attracted to sickness and pain."

"Gladys," Nurse Beckingwood said, shaking her head, "one of these days you'll regret this terrible attitude you have toward men."

"Don't hold your breath," Cresthill said.

"You'll wish you were young again so that you could fall in love and be swept away by your passions."

"What passions?" one of the younger nurses whispered. "I've seen hypodermic needles with more passion than old Cresthill."

"And what's more," Beckingwood went on, "you'll understand that any woman with half a brain would much rather sleep on a hospital floor than be apart from the man she loves."

"As far as I'm concerned," Cresthill replied, "any woman who sleeps on the floor for a man doesn't have a brain."

"Hey, wait a minute," Betty interrupted, eying the long row of heart monitors in the nurses' station that were registering the beats and rhythms of all the cardiac patients in the ward. "I just thought of something. What makes everyone so sure that lady is sleeping on the floor for love? We're only assuming that. For all we know she may have other reasons. Reasons we just don't know about."

"Betty!" Miss Prill exclaimed. "What on earth are you implying?"

Betty shrugged.

"I don't know. Maybe she's more liberated than we think. Maybe she's a very intelligent and powerful woman who knows the effects of bad vibrations. Maybe she figures if she sticks around and gets her husband excited, her matrimonial troubles will soon be over."

"Nah," Cresthill said, shaking her head. "She looks too dumb for that."

"My God," Miss Prill exclaimed. "What a horrible thing to say. What matrimonial troubles? You don't even know that woman!"

"Look, take my word for it," Betty insisted. "If she's married, she's got troubles."

"You two have to be sick to even think such a thing," Nurse Beckingwood said.

"That's what you think, " Betty replied. "As far as I'm concerned, I say it's better to be safe than sorry."

"She's right," Cresthill agreed. "I say we keep an eye on that woman."

"But have you no faith at all in love and marriage?" Beckingwood asked.

Betty and Nurse Cresthill thought for a moment.

"No," they replied in unison. "None whatsoever."

As word traveled around the hospital about the strange sleeping arrangements taking place on the men's cardiac ward, several wives visiting their sick husbands also began to discuss Martha's behavior.

"I think she is just showing off " Mrs. Mortimer, the wife of Mort Mortimer, a triple bypass survivor, complained. "She's just trying to make the rest of us wives look bad, if you ask me. What else could she be trying to prove?"

"Who knows?" said Mrs. Tyck, whose husband was resting comfortably in an oxygen tent in the intensive care. unit "But obviously she doesn't have any children."

"Yes," agreed, Mrs. Mortimer. "Or any other kind of responsibilities She wouldn't have time for that kind of nonsense, if she had .plenty of things to do like the rest of us."

"Oh, that's for sure," said Mrs. Tyck. "No woman with kids to look after, or with a decent job to attend to could spend that much time around a sick husband."

"It's so silly too, isn't it?" Mrs. Mortimer asked. "The way some women pamper grown men. I mean, what's a little heart attack considering what we women go through all our lives?"

"Yes, when the day comes that men have babies they'll know what real suffering is all about, believe me." Mrs. Tyck declared. "Until then a little heart attack is nothing."

"She should be ashamed of herself," said Mrs. Mortimer. "She gives women a bad name."

"You can say that again. Next thing you know, our husbands will be expecting us to sleep on the floor next to them. too!"

"It was bad enough we had to sleep with them in the first place, laughed Mrs. Mortimer. "But at least I got my little Louise and Richie in the process. They were worth it."

"If you ask me the hospital should never have given that woman permission to stay."

"Yes, at the very least if they don't get rid of her, they should keep an eye on her. Who knows what goes on in that room?"

As the days went by, that was the question that was being asked by most of the women connected in one way or another to the men's cardiac ward. However, despite the careful watch of Nurse Cresthill, Mrs. Mortimer and the entire hospital staff, no one could find anything amiss in the actions of Martha Foxwell toward her husband or, for that matter, toward Seymour Katz, who incidentally couldn't have cared less about Martha Foxwell's reasons for sleeping on the floor.

He was just glad she was there. In his wildest dreams he never imagined such a marvelous thing happening.

He had been in and out of the hospital ten times since his first heart attack fifteen years ago, and each stay had been more boring and depressing than the previous one. Most of his roommates had been sick old men who were either half-dead or semi-comatose with wires and tubes protruding from every part of their anatomy, and the few who were conscious sat up all night moaning, groaning, clearing their throats or ringing for the nurse. But now here he was at last in a big bright room with a young woman who was sleeping only inches away from his bed. It was almost too good to be true. Especially when he leaned over his bed in the middle of the night and took a peek.

Despite the cataracts in both his eyes, he liked what he saw--a long shapely body, sloping and curving sweetly beneath the thin white hospital blanket. And when she turned or rolled over on her back, he could see the smooth tops of her breast winking out at him from the open buttons of her pretty blouse They reminded him of two delicious scoops of vanilla ice cream. It was enough to make him weak, to set his head a-spinning. In fact, several times during the night his heart beat so fast, the emergency bell on his pace monitor went off causing a near panic in the Red Alert Station and sending nurses and staff flying.

But despite all the excitement--or perhaps because of it--Seymour, Martha and Paul seemed to be a remarkably happy threesome, chatting, joking, laughing and sometimes singing together for hours at a stretch.

"Come on, Gladys, admit it now," Nurse Beckingwood would tease every time she left Room 423. "You can see there's nothing wrong with that woman. I told you, she just loves her husband, that's all."

"Horseshit!" Cresthill would reply in spite of all the evidence. "No normal woman could be that happy around two men for that long. There's something really weird and unusual going on in there. I know it!"

And to Nurse Cresthill's credit something unusual was going on in Room 423. In spite of their both being in a hospital, Seymour and Paul were immensely enjoying themselves while making a quick recovery.

Paul's blood pressure had stabilized, and his heart had been beating normally and rhythmically since his wife had moved into his room and begun sleeping on the floor next to him. Seymour's vital signs had jumped from fair to excellent after Martha's arrival.

But even more surprising was the fact that all the patients in the rooms surrounding Room 423 were showing remarkable improvement. too Circulation problems were disappearing, high blood pressures were dropping, and liver and kidney functions were improving. Several patients were even becoming strong enough to get out of bed and take strolls down the hall to investigate where all the laughing and singing were coming from.

"What the hell do you suppose is going on?" Dr. Butler whispered to Dr. Mitchell one afternoon after making his rounds and seeing all the progress. "Do you think it's something in the air or what?"

"Who knows?" Dr. Mitchell replied. "But more than likely it's not something we have been doing."

Still, I hope we get the credit," said Dr. Butler. "We might get some discounts in our malpractice insurance."

"Do you think it has anything to do with that woman who sleeps on the floor? I heard some people say she's some kind of shaman or something. "

"You mean like a faith healer?"

"Yeah, Dr. Mitchell replied. Something like that."

"Ah come on, Larry, as a respected physician, you can't possibly believe in faith healers now, can you?

"Between you and me, Tony, as respected physicians who know the reality of contemporary medicine, how can we possibly not want to believe in faith healers?"

"Well," Dr. Butler replied, lowering his voice so no one but Dr. Mitchell could hear, "Personally, I think that Foxwell woman is just one hot chick. I don't know if she has magical powers, but I do know she's got one nice ass."

"I agree," said Dr. Mitchell. "She is hot. No wonder those two guys are doing better. Waking up with a woman like that every morning would make anyone feel better."

"Everyone except the wives," laughed Dr. Butler. "I heard they're fit to be tied that a woman is spending the night with two men in the men's ward, and that they were not going to tolerate it anymore."

"But one of the men is her husband, for God's sake."

"It makes no difference to those women. They just want everyone to follow the rules. They think women belong on the women's ward and men belong on the men's ward and never the twain shall meet."

"I gather then you're saying those ladies don't believe in the healing power of love?"

"Judging from the things they have been saying, I don't think those women believe in love."

"And how about you? Do you as a respected physician believe in the healing power of love?"

"It sure looks that way, doesn't it? laughed Dr. Mitchell. "But I suppose as good scientists we have to take more time to weigh all the evidence. We'll just have to wait and see. Only time will tell."

But time, unfortunately, was not on Seymour Katz's side.

"Do you mean to tell me that young woman stretches out on the floor and sleeps here all night besides your bed?" Mrs. Katz asked when she stopped by after her shopping spree to visit her husband.

"How would I know?" Seymour lied. "I'm always asleep."

"Well, you can rest assured I'm going to talk to the head administrator," Mrs. Katz said. "Imagine a thing like that being permitted in a respectable hospital. And in the men's heart ward no less!"

Before Seymour could protest, Mrs. Katz went to the head administrator and demanded that Martha Foxwell be asked to leave the hospital during the evening hours.

"But I want to stay with my husband," Martha protested when she was finally confronted by the burly hospital guard who came to throw her out. "I have a right to remain by his side. Especially now since he's doing so well."

"Look, I don't make the rules, Lady," the guard informed her. "I just do what I'm told."

"But I tell you, my husband needs me. And I need him. He loves me. And I love him."

"Not after visiting hours, Lady. Not in this hospital."

And so that night Martha Foxwell was forced to go home for the first time. To Mrs. Katz's, Nurse Cresthill's and the other cardiac wives' delight, the hospital went back to normal from that night on. Paul Foxwell and Seymour Katz slept alone and undisturbed in their room, the other patients in the ward ceased taking strolls down the hall and resumed watching television, and dutiful visits from wives and other acquaintances were properly monitored and permitted only during regular visiting hours.

The conditions of each patient responded dramatically. Over the next few days Paul Foxwell and Seymour Katz experienced sudden but unexplainable relapses. Mrs. Mortimer's husband, Ralph, fell out of bed and broke his arm. Mrs. Tyck's husband, George, lapsed into a coma. Mr. Burns in Room 420 had a stroke after being administered an enema by Nurse Cresthill, and Mr. Toole, Mr. Cahill, Mr. De Angelo and Mr. Thomas, whose conditions had been previously listed as excellent, went back on the critical list after suffering unexpected myocardial infarctions.

"What the devil is going on here now?" Dr. Butler asked after returning one morning from the side of a patient he had just pronounced D.O.A. "Are we in the middle of a medical mystery here or what? "

Dr. Mitchell shrugged his shoulders

"I guess that depends upon what you mean by a medical mystery. But I can tell you one thing, I would be willing to experiment. If I were in charge of this hospital I'd bring back that Foxwell woman again and let her sleep wherever she wanted. If things started to improve again, we'd have more evidence to go on."

"There's no question when she was here, we were on a roll. Everybody was getting better."

"Yes, that certainly seemed to be the case" Dr. Mitchell agreed. "Love's a mystery but facts are facts. Unfortunately she's not here now. So there doesn't seem much we can do for the moment except to rely on modern medicine and hope for the best."

"But if our patients in Cardiac Four continue to decline at the rate they are going," Dr. Butler cautioned, "I say we also look into getting more malpractice insurance just to be safe."

Dr. Butler's words were sadly prophetic. Over the next few days five more patients suffered setbacks and to make matters even worse new patients were being admitted to the cardiac ward at an alarming level. Rooms that normally held only two beds were now jammed with three and Nurses Crestwell, Beckingwood, and Prill, forced to work double shifts, were falling off their feet from utter exhaustion. So chaotic was the situation that no one, except the on-call physician, Dr. Mitchell, seem to notice that one of the new patients was Martha Foxwell, admitted to the women's cardiac ward via ambulance after suffering erratic heart rhythms late one night as she moped about her empty house, despondent that she could not be at her husband's bedside in the hospital.

"Have you heard the news?" Dr. Mitchell confided to Dr. Butler, as they encountered one another in the hallway outside of Room 423. "That Foxwell woman is back in the hospital, not as a visitor but as a patient."

"Really?" Dr. Butler replied. "What do you supposed happened?"

"Heart arrhythmia brought on my acute stress is my diagnosis. I think she got really upset because she was separated from her husband."

"Talk about weird. Most of the married people I know suffer acute stress when they're with their spouses."

"Well, as that French writer Albert Camus once said, every now and then —maybe three or four times in a century--people meet up with their soul mate and genuinely fall in love. This looks like one of those cases."

"Unfortunately, although they're both in the same hospital, they're still in separate wards and rooms."

"Yes, but. . .Hmmm," Dr. Mitchell said.

***

Neither Paul Foxwell or Seymour Katz were well enough to really notice when a tall, thin fellow in a St. Louis Cardinal baseball cap and cardinal red pajamas was wheeled into their room on a gurney by Dr. Mitchell. When he first caught a glimpse in his semi-drugged state, Paul, thought the man looked strangely familiar, like the brother of someone he once knew. Katz, on the other hand, first saw the fellow from a fog of sleep, and his first impression was that the newcomer was one of those gay guys that look more like women than men.

Dr. Mitchell gave strict orders to all the nurses on the floor that the new patient was not to have his baseball cap or red pajamas removed under any circumstances for reasons he would not discuss. Naturally all the nurses, especially Crestwell thought this rather odd but given the fact that they were nurses and had to follow the doctor's orders there was little they could do but comply. Besides they were too busy to really pursue the matter because so many patients were still so sick and needed round the clock care.

Fortunately, however, within a few days things began to slow down bit on Cardiac Four. There were fewer code blue alerts and fewer cases of ventricular fibrillation. Dr. Mitchell and Dr. Butler had fewer emergency resuscitations and angioplasty procedures to perform, and not as many patients were complaining at night of chest pains and fatigue. Even Paul Foxwell and Seymour Katz appeared to be getting stronger since both men now were able to get up from their beds and walk around their room for brief periods in the afternoon.

Marty, their new roommate, also began showing signs of improvement. "

"His heart has gone back to its normal rhythms," Crestwell said to Beckingwood as they conversed over their charts at the head nurses station. "But he never says anything when I'm in the room. Still, he's always laughing and smiling, and I can hear him talking really softly to Foxwell and Katz when I go by their room They seem to know one another."

"Do you think he's gay?" Beckingwood asked. "He looks gay to me."

"Yeah, he's got to be gay," Crestwell declared. "He gets really uncomfortable when I touch him. That alone tells me he's gay."

Two weeks after Marty arrived at the hospital, Paul Foxwell and Seymour Katz were well enough to go home. Marty, who had passed all the cardiac screening exams and performed well on the treadmill test, was also able to leave the hospital for home.

The entire staff on Cardiac Four was relieved and delighted that so many of the critical care patients like Mr. Mortimer and Mr. Tyck had stabilized and shown improvement over such a short period of time for reasons no one could really explain.

Only Dr. Mitchell and Dr. Butler felt absolutely confident to discuss the turnaround with one another.

"Well, I guess, I have to give you credit," Dr. Butler said to Dr. Mitchell as they sat chatting over coffee one morning in the hospital cafeteria. "Your little experiment proved to be very useful and successful."

"Thank you," Dr. Mitchell said, taking a sip of hot coffee. "I'm rather happy with the fortunate results."

"I got a kick out of Nurse Cresthill visiting the Foxwell-Katz room with you and saying 'I'm glad there isn't a woman sleeping in here any more.'

"Right," Dr. Mitchell laughed, "and she hadn't the faintest idea what I was talking about when I said, 'You may not see her, but she's there.'"

"But how you managed to outwit and fool so many people in the process was really a stroke of genius."

"Oh, it wasn't that difficult," Dr. Mitchell said modestly. "Besides, I had a lot of help from Martha. As some wise old man once said, 'Love's a mystery, but facts are facts.' No good doctor can deny that."+++++

WHAT GOD HATH JOINED TOGETHER, LET NO ROOF PUT ASUNDER

July 14—This morning Carol came over for coffee. She asked where Jimmy was.

"He's in the cellar," I said

"What's he doing down there?" she demanded.

When I told her, she looked at me rather strangely. Doesn't her husband ever go down to the cellar?

July 21—Tonight we were supposed to go to Ceil and Tom's to celebrate their fifth wedding anniversary. When I told Ceil we couldn't make it, she looked hurt. I was about to explain it wasn't anything personal but decided against it. It would be much too complicated. Some people have a hard time understanding these things.

July 28—While shopping in the Pathmark today, I ran smack into Edith Williams and her little boy, Todd. He whined all through our conversation. Edith seemed awfully depressed. Her face was yellow, and her eyes had big puffy bags under them. I started to ask if there were anything wrong, when suddenly right there in the middle of the fruit and vegetable aisle she started crying. Told me Dave asked for a divorce. That was a shock to me. She and Dave always seemed so happy. But who knows? Appearances can be deceiving, as they say.

August 2—The dumbwaiter broke today. When I opened the door around nine o'clock to see what Jimmy had written, I saw the carriage dangling by one rope. I guess the other rope snapped while Jimmy was sending up his morning messages. I called the repair service but couldn't get through to them. The line was busy until ten. When I finally did speak to a serviceman—he didn't sound too bright—he told me to forget about it." "No way, lady, we're too booked up. Try us again in about a month." I told him I couldn't wait that long. "Ah come on," he said. "You're trying to tell me your life depends upon a dumbwaiter?"

"No," I said, "but my marriage does."

He was quiet for a while, but eventually he agreed to send someone over by three o'clock.

Poor Jimmy was starved by then. All the while the repairman was there he kept asking what Jimmy did in the cellar all day—as if it were his business. When he left, I sent Jimmy down a roast beef sandwich and a pickle. He sent back this poem.

Let me not to the marriage of true minds
Admit impediments. Love is not love
Which alters when it alteration finds,
Or bends with the remover to remove.
O no! it is an ever-fixed mark
That looks on tempests and is never shaken.

Now who would have ever thought of writing something like that except my Jimmy. What a sweetheart! There aren't many men like him who give their wives credit for having good minds and smart brains. Jimmy knows me like a book. He knows once I get my heart set on something there's no stopping me. Come hell or high water, I'll be true blue. Jimmy knows that.

August 20—I think Jimmy is getting a bad cold. I heard him sneezing and coughing all morning, and in his afternoon letter, he asked for some big white handkerchiefs. I sent those down with some vitamins and a box of aspergum.

Tomorrow I must remember to ask him if he thinks the dampness is making him ill.

August 22—Jimmy was still coughing all day. I wonder if he has the flu. His morning note didn't sound at all like him. "The cellar is getting on my nerves,' he wrote. "I couldn't get any sleep with all the clacking of your damn high heels."

This certainly doesn't sound like my Jimmy. It must be his cold. He never complained about things before.

August 25—It was one of those days. Jimmy's notes kept coming non-stop. I couldn't get a thing done. First he complained about the strange smell in the cellar. "Like Limburger cheese," he said. Then he bitched that he hadn't seen the sun in ages. "I might as well be dead and buried." Finally he said that he was beginning to forget what I looked like.

Well that did it. I wrote back: O.K. Jimmy. I guess it's time for a change. Tomorrow we'll begin all over again."

August 31—Long letters back and forth all day. Six of them, in fact. Something of a crisis. Time will tell.

September 3—I cleaned the house most of the day. Straightening out the medicine cabinet alone took me over an hour. I could hear Jimmy moving through the other rooms carrying his things up the backstairs and then walking across the roof. It was so distracting, all that racket overhead, but I didn't let on to Jimmy. He hates it when I nag.

September 5—Jimmy is at last settled in his new home. I hope this change does him the world of good. His first note sounded pretty cheerful. He said his cold was almost gone and that he felt like a new man. If only I could feel like a new woman. What does a new woman feel like, I wonder?

Sometimes I think my Jimmy is a poet. The last few lines of his note sounded like something right out of a book.

"I love to see the sun dying in the West as day
Fades into night and people drift so very far
Away like ghosts in lost dreams."

How he ever came up with that, I'll never know, but I always said there was more to my Jimmy that what meets the eye.

September 8—Some major changes for me now that Jimmy is in his new home. I can no longer use the dumbwaiter for our messages, and so communication is a bit of a problem. I never know when Jimmy feels like eating or talking or whatever. Naturally it is much harder for me to walk up the stairs with a heavy food tray than it was for me to simply haul it up on the dumbwaiter, but then again I guess every marriage has its sacrifices. No sense complaining, as they say. The real problem is letting Jimmy know that the food is outside once I get it up to the roof. If I knock, there's a chance I'll be still there when he opens the door. However, if I just leave it, everything will get cold, and there's a chance the cat will get it. I suppose if things got really out of hand we could set up a telephone on the roof, but I think that's really asking for trouble.

We'll find a solution, I'm sure. I always said while there's a will, there's a way.

September 9—I think we solved the food problem. We decided that I should knock three longs and two shorts when it's time to eat. Jimmy will wait five minutes before opening the door. This will give me plenty of leeway to get back downstairs and into the kitchen.

September 24—For the last two weeks I've had trouble sleeping at night. Just when I am about to drop off, I hear Jimmy moving around up there. Last night he was singing! This has got to end. When he was in the cellar, he was so quiet I forgot he was even there. Now there's no escaping him. I don't want to tell him he's beginning to annoy the hell out of me because I know how sensitive he is, but goddamn it, that constant racket up there is driving me bananas. I don't know how my husband could be that inconsiderate. Besides, he didn't write once today!

September 25—Still no note from Jimmy. What the hell is wrong? If I didn't know better, I'd think he had a woman up there. I wouldn't put anything past the lying bastard.

September 27—I was at the end of my rope so I wrote to Jimmy and complained about all the noise he was making. I really laid it to him. Told him he had some nerve and all that. He was very understanding and asked what he should do. Since I was still angry, I told him to figure it out for himself. If you ask me, women pamper men too much nowadays. Anyway, Jimmy was all apologies. He even agreed to buy a thick rug for the roof and a pair of soft felt slippers to wear at night.

When that end of it was all settled, I asked him why he wasn't writing.

"Hey, Jimmy," I said, "why the cold shoulder? What did I ever do to you? Shit, I mean women need affection too, you know. No one wants a stranger for a husband."

Jimmy replied that he had been too busy to write. Doing what? I asked.

"Thinking," he said.

Imagine that—thinking? What the hell is there to think about when you're up on a roof?

October 4—Today Jimmy sent this letter:
Dear Maria,
I've lost all notion of time up here. The world seen from my roof is so very, very beautiful, and I'm so happy that it's hard to come back to reality and write to you.
You should see it up here when the sun breaks at dawn and the whole sky is flooded with red and gold. At night sleeping under the stars in the immense darkness is almost as wonderful.
I guess I have to be honest: I've fallen head over heels, not off the roof but for it. You were right, darling. This is the best thing that ever happened to me, besides you.
> *Keep in touch,*
> *Your Jimmy*
P.S. When you get the chance, could you send me my old army blanket? It should be getting a little chilly up here in a week or so.

Frankly, I don't know what to make of it, Sometimes Jimmy is a total mystery to me.

October 26—It's Jimmy's birthday. I baked him a strawberry short cake, his favorite. Although he is 36, I put one candle in the center and wrote, *"Jimmy, you're Number 1."*

I also cooked his favorite cheese casserole. Anything for the man of my dreams. The man I adore. My Jimmy!

October 27—When I brought Jimmy a late breakfast this morning, I noticed that the birthday cake and cheese casserole were still outside the door. He hadn't even touched them. I began to wonder if he had heard our secret knock yesterday. Not knowing what to do, I took a broom and pounded it against his door as loudly as I could. Then I brought the casserole back downstairs and waited. I didn't hear a peep from Jimmy all day. I hope nothing is up. Except Jimmy, of course.

October 30—Jimmy hasn't touched his food or written for three days now. I'm starting to get worried. When Carol stops by tomorrow I think I'll ask her to take a look.

October 31—Carol just left. She was supposed to show me the pattern for her red and white calico curtains, but since she seemed in a big hurry to leave, I didn't press her.

She wasn't much help with Jimmy either. I showed her the way to the roof and left her at the door which she insisted on keeping unlocked. Apparently she was afraid of being trapped up there alone with my husband. I don't know what the hell she was afraid of. You'd think Jimmy was a murderer or something. I mean, my god, I told her he was harmless. Still, she looked kind of funny and pleaded with me to wait outside the door.

When she came out I asked her how Jimmy looked. She said Jimmy wasn't there. Then she bolted down the stairs like I was contagious or something.

I tell you, people are strange.

I've got to go now.

There's someone at the door. +++++

1940803